making him
want it

making him want it

renee luke

APHRODISIA

APHRODISIA
KENSINGTON BOOKS
http://www.kensingtonbooks.com

APHRODISIA BOOKS are published by

Kensington Publishing Corp.
850 Third Avenue
New York, NY 10022

All Kensington Titles, Imprints, and Distributed Lines are available at special quantity discounts for bulk purchases for sales promotions, premiums, fund-raising, and educational or institutional use.

Special book excerpts or customized printings can also be created to fit specific needs. For details, write or phone the office of the Kensington special sales manager: Kensington Publishing Corp., 850 Third Avenue, New York, NY 10022, attn: Special Sales Department, Phone: 1-800-221-2647.

Aphrodisia and the A logo are trademarks of Kensington Publishing Corp.
Kensington and the K logo Reg. U.S. Pat. & TM Off

ISBN: 0-7582-1446-4

First Kensington Trade Paperback Printing: May 2006

10 9 8 7 6 5 4 3 2 1

Printed in the United States of America

making him
want it

Chapter 1

Jamal James sank back into his leather office chair, smoothed both palms over his clean–shaven head, then laced his fingers behind his neck. Staring at the strategic placement of the photos spread across his desk, he tried to decide if he wanted to accept the model as a client.

While his primary focus was as a literary agent, a few years back he'd started taking on models to go along with the sexy stories his headliner wrote.

The models and other authors offered him chump change compared to what his super–star brought in. Kat Mason and her skilled way with words had him living in luxury. But it wasn't only the hefty contracts with five of the largest men's magazines in the world that made him value Kat as a client.

Her humble, almost innocent demeanor over their extensive email relationship had left him baffled. Part sexy talker. Part girl–next–door. While never having met in person, thanks to her plentitude of ready excuses, their author–agent bond had progressed to a point where he felt comfortable telling her about the hard–ons he'd get reading her work.

By the twentieth of each month, he found himself checking his email hourly, so rocked–up to read what she'd sent him. Forgetting the pictures of the man posing nude on his desk, he turned toward his computer, right clicking twice on his internet connection.

Damn!

His email was filled with nothing but unsolicited submissions. Nothing from Kat. Sliding a hand from behind his head, he moved to the aroused flesh held in check beneath his expensive trousers. He adjusted himself, making room for the expanded length, and released a low and hungry groan. He'd long since imagined a body and face to go with Kat's submissions and emails, a fantasy that left him breathing hard and downright horny.

"You about ready, JJ?" Kent asked, strolling into Jamal's office. He glanced at his watch, his eyes widening when he caught sight of the sprawled male model photos gracing the surface of the mahogany desk.

Knowing where this was going, Jamal willed away his erection but the blood didn't vacate as quickly as it took residence. Following Kent's eyes, he saw when his colleague dipped his gaze from the desk to his lap, where Jamal's flagpole was standing.

Kent roared with laughter.

Great! *Just what I need.* Some loudmouth over–sexed player thinking a man's photos turns me on.

"You swinging that way now, JJ? No wonder you take on men when no one else in the office does, besides Rebecca." Kent laughed harder, his mouth opening wide enough that one of his gold fillings reflected the overhead light. "Do you eat Fruit Loops and keep lube in the shower?"

"Screw you, Kent."

"You wish."

Jamal tightened his fists. Sometimes the only way to shut up punks like Kent was to smash them in the mouth, giving him a reason for gold caps on his teeth. Kent was a pompous ass who wore three–thousand dollar designer suits daily and went to the barber three times a week to keep his fade lined up. Certainly not worth losing his temper over, despite being irritated.

Sliding his chair forward, concealing his lap beneath the shadow of the desk, Jamal swept the pictures into a stack and set them aside, ignoring Kent's continued laughter and barbs.

"Come on, JJ, you get hard looking at a guy? You sure you're a man?"

"More man than you," Jamal replied, keeping his tone light despite the growing anger.

Kent lifted his arms to the side and bucked his hips suggestively. "Yeah, I got women beggin' for *this*. A different woman every night if I want. Sometimes two."

Every man's fantasy.

Every man but him. He longed for a woman he'd never seen. Forbidden flesh—his client—Kat Mason. But her passionate words on the computer screen were about as tangible as smoke. *You can feel its effects on your body, but you can't hold it, sink into it, or relieve your aching flesh when you're gasping for breath.*

"When was the last time you fucked?"

Kent's question tugged Jamal from his thoughts. It'd been a while, but there was no way in hell he was admitting it. Not to this fool.

"I get it when I want it." Jamal shrugged his shoulders. Sure, pulling in hot women had never been a problem for him, thanks to the gene pool that had made him an image duplicate of his father, "Player of the Century," as far as Jamal was concerned. His father's apartment had been like a revolving door, more women going through than turnstiles at Grand Central Station.

He'd dipped into his fair share of chicks when he was younger, but sex for sex had grown boring and despite what others might think, predictable. He just wasn't into wham–bam don't–call–again nights. He'd matured out of it.

"Come on. This club has the finest female flesh you'll ever see." Kent blew air between his teeth. "I mean hot."

Not like this punk. Jamal snickered at Kent. Some leopards can't change their spots. Getting to his feet, he tossed the stack of pictures into the reject bin. The model didn't have the goods needed to make it in the sex industry, when looks and size were everything.

"Yeah. Let's get out of here. It's hours past shut down time." Glancing once more at his computer screen, hoping to see a new incoming message from Kat, he rolled his shoulders to ease the mounting tension. Nothing. Hopefully by Monday, she'd give him exactly what he needed.

He flicked the switch, shutting it down for the weekend. Moving toward the door, he tossed his jacket over his forearm and turned off the overhead fluorescent lighting. Kent tagged along at his heels.

"What's the club called?"

"Night Kitty. You'll soon see why," Kent said, rubbing a hand over his chin. "You can get more pussy there than an alley cat."

"I'm just going for a couple of beers. I'm not into picking up strangers at bars." They walked down the dimly lit deserted hallways of the office building. This late on a Friday they'd be lucky to see a janitor still about.

"You sure you're not a little fluffy? What kind of man turns down getting some when it's offered?"

"I have women I *know* where I can make a booty–call. And, I'm man enough to snatch your girl if I wanted." All these comments about his manhood were grating his last nerve. So what if it'd been a good while since he'd had sex? That didn't mean anything.

So what if he relied on emails for pleasure? It didn't make him any less of a man because he had a fantasy woman who made him jerk off his own wad after he read her work.

"What'd you say this place is called, again?" he asked, tension coiling in his gut. They walked across the parking lot now, but not even the cooler night air offered relief to his irritation.

"Night Kitty."

They entered Jamal's SUV in silence.

"Good. Let's go." He slid his Escalade into drive, anxious to get there. Last month's issues of Kat's magazines wouldn't be enough for long.

A blank screen.

For a writer this spells disaster. The screen was bare, and all Kat Mason could do was sit there staring. Chomping down on the inside of her cheek, she gulped down a deep breath as she attempted to focus her mind on past projects. Not like anything else she'd done could save her butt now.

Feeling the rise of nervous tension, she twisted her fingers, wondering what others in her profession would think of her, leader of the pack, in this frantic position. To most people a blank screen may not seem like a big deal, open and ready for whatever comes to mind, but for her it was ruin.

Prostitutes don't get paid when they don't turn tricks, just like she didn't get compensated if she didn't put out stories.

With slumping shoulders, dread pressed upon her. The tiny cursor on the top of the page flashed like a big *loser* beacon. Clamping her lids shut, she fought off a surge of frustration. Deadline loomed and at this rate she'd have to email her agent and tell him she wasn't going to make it.

Taking a squeeze of baby lotion, she rubbed it into her tired hands. *What do I know about sex?* She thought back over her disastrous past relationships. There weren't many, but they'd all sucked. She was a wallflower and good men kept their distance.

"Three years, nine months, and almost two weeks, and I'm fresh out of material." She smirked at the irony. As a favor to her momma, who'd written headlines for a men's trash magazine, Kat had taken over when arthritis ended her momma's career. She wasn't sure how she pulled it off with her limited amount of sexual experience. But somehow she did.

Articles for the single erotica magazine had blossomed into many. Now she had an agent who pimped her pieces to the mass market. Before she knew what hit her, her persona was the hottest name in the genre, garnering national attention, top sales, and more than a thousand hits a day to her website.

Her most prominent column, *Glory's Stories*, was published in five different monthly magazines that released the hottest, sexiest stuff she could imagine. Masturbation, fornication, threesomes and orgies—yeah, she'd written about those and then some. But right now, on a Friday evening, the article due Monday morning, she had a blank page.

Not even word one.

Glancing around her upstairs bedroom, Kat saw all of the toys of the trade—things she'd gathered over the years—for what she called research. Reaching across the desk, she lifted a translucent pink dildo; its weight heavier than it appeared. *Batteries.* How could she write about a vibrating dildo if she'd never felt one in her hand? She stroked down the smooth length of the plastic cock.

Bringing the shiny head to her mouth, she glided it along her lower lip, using her tongue to smooth it. It tasted faintly like her pussy, held the subtle hint of sex and caused a moistening in her cotton panties. Feeling heat lick across her skin, she tossed the dildo to the bed.

This wasn't time for self–gratification. She'd tried that too many times, written about it nearly as often. "Good brothas aren't easy to come by," Kat mumbled to herself, to justify her need for the synthetic flesh, rather than enjoying the feel of a real man. "Or *cum* by." She laughed at the oh–so–sorry truth. "Call me desperate."

With her eyes closed, she slanted her face toward the ceiling, silently willing some wondrous idea to strike her. She needed something—a spark to make her next story fresh and exciting. To make it something she'd never attempted before.

She needed brilliance that would make her agent, Jamal, eager to pursue the money she sought for hours of writing, not to mention the added bonus of knowing about the erection he got when he read her work. She only wished she had a face to match to the hours of email conversations they'd shared. Knowing what his eyes looked like when he got aroused would have been the icing on the cake.

Spinning her office chair, Kat's gaze landed on her stuffed and overflowing extra closet. Repressing the turn of her lips into a smile, she studied all she'd acquired. She had it all—none used, but all there—for when she needed to describe an outfit or get into the mood of a character. There were whips and handcuffs, some fur–lined, some cold–hard steel. Black leather boots that reached mid thigh and tipped with four–inch silver spikes as heels.

She had sexy lingerie, lacy blacks with g–string panties. Red one–piece suits open to the nipples and crotchless. She even had a few baby–doll type sets, complete with pink lace, rose–shaped ribbons and petite satin bows. None seemed to offer the inspiration she desperately required. She needed something new. Different. *Thrilling.*

Flipping the button on her computer, she sent it into sleep mode and hit the switch of the light. Kat stalked to the mirror and studied her lackluster outfit. Her usual writing garb: sweatpants, t–shirt, floppy–eared bunny slippers. Her black perm–straightened hair was secured into a loose ponytail, in need of a root touch–up.

Pressing her full lips together, she thought of adding a touch of gloss, but feeling drab, decided what she needed was a splash of color to match the caramel tone of her skin. Glancing back at her computer, Kat released a pent–up breath and decided to escape her self–imposed dungeon. She needed

time away from work, to freshen up and go out. Out any-
where, where there'd be people to watch and where she'd be
able to draw new material.

A crushing blow of realization hit Kat square in the chest,
knocking the breath from her. She knew what she needed to
do. Not just go out and watch but to participate in a night of
spontaneous carnal pleasure.

Gasping for air and keeping her wobbly knees from collapsing, she stripped out of her clothes and stepped into the
shower. Then, she lathered the shea butter Olay bar across
her skin.

Fear momentarily tightened her gut. In thirty–one years
she'd never experienced a one–night stand, but that's exactly
what she was planning. Her roommate in college had gone
from one to the next like Kleenex, but she'd had youth and
alcohol to attribute such behavior. Kat could only blame
being horny and behind deadline.

"I have nothin' to lose, and plenty to gain." With the decision made, arousal poured through her blood like a shot of
whiskey. The overhead spray of tepid water tightened her
dusky–colored nipples into beads, the wash of moisture like a
damp mouth, hungry with need.

Stepping from the shower a while later, clean and more excited than she'd been in a while, Kat went to the closet to select the right costume to go out on the prowl. She settled on
a combination of several styles, the spiked high leather boots,
a suede black mini, and a black lacy bra, only slightly hidden
beneath a sheer rosy shirt.

A satisfying combo of sweet and sexy.

She applied a covering of make–up, including deep red lip-
stick, and touched the hot tip of a curling iron to areas af-
fected by the moisture of the shower. She skipped securing
her hair back, allowing the dark locks to hang loose around
her face. She thought it erotic to have her hair grabbed during sex.

Sex and ideas was what she was after.

Grabbing her purse and heading out the door, Kat decided to take a cab to the closest meat–market since in all likelihood, she'd need a couple of drinks to follow through with what she'd planned.

Chapter 2

Twenty minutes too soon, the cab pulled up in front of the bar. Kat sat in the dim sanctuary of the car's interior, her forehead pressed against the cool glass, her cheeks on fire. It'd been easy to choose a super thigh–high skirt and a bra–exposing shirt when she'd been in her bedroom, but now, presented with mingling with the public, she wanted to run.

"You getting out?" the cabbie asked.

Kat didn't answer, afraid she'd order him to turn around and retrace their path. But back at home she'd be faced with the same problem, an article due and no material to write it. Drawing a deep breath, she fished inside her tiny purse, then shoved a twenty toward the driver. Getting into character, she slid from the car and steadied herself upon four–inch spiky heels on the sidewalk.

Above her, the pink neon sign read The Night Kitty, though in reality all men knew that kitty meant pussy and pussy meant sex. *Come here*, the sign called, *and you'll be assured pleasure.* Kat squared her shoulders, lifted her chin, and sashayed to the door mustering false confidence. She slipped into the dark smoky interior.

The scent of cigarettes, alcohol, sweat, and endorphins all tuned and primed for fucking crashed around her like a sensual wave. Bass throbbed a heavy beat that blared from the surrounding speakers. A nervous slither crept down Kat's spine as she kept herself from finding the nearest exit. She hadn't been to a place like this since her early years of college, but even then she'd had girlfriends to accompany her.

She was alone now, playing a role. Creating a façade. She stepped forward, determined to see her plan unfold.

Fine–ass men littered the room. A most beautiful specimen of male flesh stood alone across the dance floor from her. Yummy enough to be a cover model. LL Cool J–fine. Sex appeal of Wesley Snipes. She'd be happy with a piece of him.

Turning away, the crush of bodies hindered her slow advance to the bar.

"Give me a shot," Kat said to a young man standing behind the counter who looked too young to drink, let alone serve the stuff.

"A shot of what?" he asked.

"It doesn't matter. Just get me tipsy and fast."

"Not a prob," he replied, reaching beneath the smooth surface of the bar and withdrawing a shot glass, which he then filled with a blue liquid, fuller than the standard two fingers. "Enjoy." He slid the glass in her direction.

"What is it?" *Please be strong!*

"Does it matter?" he asked, a lopsided grin spreading over his lips.

"Nope." She grabbed the glass and downed the contents in one smooth motion, not even gasping as the fiery liquid slid down her throat.

"Can I get you anything else?"

"Yeah, another," she replied, lifting her empty glass.

It was quickly refilled.

"Thanks." She downed the second serving, left the empty glass on the bar along with another twenty, and walked toward the flashing lights and couples crowded on the dance floor. Stud though he may be, the bartender was on duty and with the blue fluid already making her feel more at ease, she needed material now.

Kat inched her way around the room, watching the couples bumping and grinding on the floor, a planned seduction—foreplay—in view of everyone. Good stuff she filed away in her memory for future articles.

With groping hands, men held women to their groins, hiding the swell that undoubtedly pulsated there. With bodies rubbing, palms were tightly held to feminine hips. In the center of the dance floor the couples took it one step further, backs arched, the women allowed the men access to their necks and breasts, the steady rhythm of their dancing a mimic to fucking.

"What was in that drink?" she mumbled, suddenly aware of how her black thong rubbed against her clit as she walked. She shifted her hips, completing the tantalizing contact. Her pussy became damp, moisture pooled at her crotch and she could feel the telltale evidence of her arousal slick on her inner thighs.

Glancing back at the bar, Kat had to wonder if something had been slipped into her drink. Booze alone had never made her this horny. But she'd watched the entire time as the drink was poured into the glass right before she'd emptied it. Nothing had been added.

The blue liquid she'd swallowed quickly shed the last of her inhibitions. It was unlike anything she'd ever tasted, a heady combination mixed with her resolve to get laid that made her almost desperate for the right man to come along.

Her made–up persona offered her a newly found freedom. She shrugged off the euphoria of her sexual charge and she focused on her mission. It was made easier by the slight alcohol induced lulling of her fear.

She studied the dimly lit room, searching for a man not already coupled. For the hunk she'd seen at the beginning of the Too Short song.

"You here alone?" a husky voice asked her from behind.

Warmth spread across Kat's skin as the height and breadth of his body closed in behind her, more solid than the wall had been.

She need not bother to turn around, for she'd watched the advance of the man as he'd made his way from across the room, working the border as if he could remain unnoticed. Like hell—every available female in the joint had to be primed for a piece of ass from this guy.

How'd I get so lucky? She'd wanted him from the moment she'd seen him.

Through the pump of music their words were barely audible. "Not anymore," she answered, hoping he didn't hear the tiny hitch on her voice as she struggled to keep the real Kat hidden.

He stood a good six inches taller than her, his masculine presence as heady as the drink she'd consumed. Taking a deep breath, she leaned her back toward him and was surprised to feel an impressive length of aroused cock nudge against the small of her back. She shifted her hips against the erection eliciting a grumble from the man behind her, though most definitely not a complaint.

"What's your name?"

Biting her bottom lip, Kat thought about her reply. This wasn't her. *She* was a wallflower. A self–made recluse who made a habit of avoiding the public. This was a woman she'd created, and as ballsy as she was feeling, delving into real names meant revealing a part of her she didn't want to face tomorrow. "I don't want you to call me in the morning."

For a moment only the incredible hum of drums could be heard above the steady breathing of the man. His warm breath on the back of her neck sent her nipples aching. He knew what she wanted. They both wanted the same thing. *Was he going to walk away?* Did the fact she'd turned the table on men's usual tactics make him think twice before taking their experimental material forward?

In answer to her silent questions, one of his large palms snaked across her lower stomach. With a slight tug, he brought her back flush against his chest, his seeking fingers caressing the hem of her suede ultra–miniskirt.

"Do you want to dance?" he whispered in her ear.

"No." Breathing was now difficult. The dance floor, though a good place for foreplay, was not nearly private enough for what Kat had in mind.

"What do you want then?"

"I want your cock inside of me, now."

Jamal felt like laughing. He didn't go to bars to pick up on women, but here he was now, with this little hottie tucked against his chest telling him she wanted a good bang. He'd seen her the moment she'd entered the bar, a Fly–Girl with a J–Lo booty.

He smoothed his fingers along the hem of her skirt, barely touching the silken brown skin covering thick, juicy thighs. Her legs jetted a mile to the floor. Her calves and feet were encased in tall, black leather boots, tipped with heels high enough to make any man with testosterone beg for mercy.

Dressed as she was, she could have stepped off the set of any Puff Daddy video, though none of those models were as luscious as this babe. The details of her face were obscured by the low lighting and haze of smoke enshrouding the place, but he could tell enough to know her beauty matched her exquisite body.

Jamal moved his hand lower, until he felt her tremble before him, her knees becoming jelly as he eased her legs apart with a subtle hint of pressure between her thighs. The honey whimpered slightly, lolling her head back against his chest, allowing him the pleasure of her fragrance.

She smelled sweetly exotic. Definitely enticing. It wasn't a scent procured in any store or produced by any brand name perfume. Her lingering aroma was purely her own, feminine and inviting.

Glancing around the packed dance floor, Jamal's gaze came to rest upon Kent as he gyrated his hips against some skinny broad in the center of the room. Outkast was pumping through the speakers now.

Jamal dipped his hand beneath the material of the woman's skirt, his fingers encouraged further with each of her breathy moans. Easing aside the narrow strip of cloth covering her treasure, he parted her lips and dipped two knuckles deep into her oh–so–tight pussy.

Womanizing Kent, who had poked fun of his manhood, hadn't managed to score the way he had, still bothered by being caught with a hard–on earlier. But it wasn't merely the drive to prove himself a studly man that spurred the slow rhythm of his fingers as he moved in and out of the woman in his arms.

There was something about her that had drawn him from across the room. Maybe it was the wide–eyed stare she'd had when she'd first entered the bar, or the I'd–like–to–eat–you–for–dessert look she'd tossed him during that brief moment when she'd glanced his way. A siren call for sure; he'd been helpless against it.

In the dark room no one noticed how he pressed his fingers into her wet, accepting flesh. Using his thumb, Jamal found the bead of her clit and rubbed against it. The hottie went limp in his arms, sagging against him. He wrapped his other arm around her, holding her curvy body against his, and took the weight of a firm breast into his palm, tweaking the hard crest with his fingers.

"You want it now, huh?" he whispered, bending his head so he could nibble upon the tender skin just below her ear. She shuddered, then slanted her head for him to further explore her skin with his tongue. Nuzzling his face into her straightened locks of hair, he slowed the in and out of his fingers to long sensual movements.

His effort at seduction was rewarded.

"Please . . . Please . . . Please . . ." Her begging whimpered chant was driving him crazy. A little more of this and he'd cum in his pants. Jamal shook his head, finding his behavior hard to believe. Foolish. He'd never done this before, but something about her had him press on.

"In the club?" He moved his thumb to her clit and circled twice. "Reach behind you and undo my pants."

Kat couldn't have stopped her hands if she tried. They moved behind her, like steel to a magnet, finding the large bulge straining his pants. She cupped him in her palms, the damn fabric preventing her from feeling what she wanted so badly to touch.

She flicked her fingernail against the rough teeth of his zipper, the jagged edge abrasive against her skin. In the momentary sting of pain, reason penetrated Kat's lust miasma, his suggestion ringing loud and clear in her ears. Her blood roared through her veins.

She wanted sex and pretty badly, but she'd never been one for public displays of affection. She certainly wasn't brash enough to actually have sex while everyone there could watch, had they the mind to.

She stalled her hands' progress, though not an easy feat. Where was the shy girl, she wondered briefly, taking on her new role so completely?

"Perhaps we ought to take this to . . ." Her voice trailed off. To where? She hadn't thought her plan through. Once decided, she'd rushed to the bar afraid if given too much thought she'd change her mind. Now she realized the error, too late, and too horny. She should've secured a hotel room nearby to ensure once she'd lured a man to her lair, she could enjoy him thoroughly. Her mind searched for answers. His car? The bathroom? The back alley?

The back alley. Surely there would be some boxes or something to offer a bit of privacy from the street front. Besides, the thought of a cold brick wall against her back and the heat of his body before her sounded like an exciting turn–on.

"Come with me," she demanded, wiggling his hand free from her sex, moisture following his slow withdraw, knowing too, that given too much time to think she'd dart for the door. Alone. Shifting her hips to lower the skirt back into place, she grabbed his hand, slick with her juices, and pulled him after her.

He willingly fell into step beside her.

The bartender gave a knowing smile as she darted past, a man in tow, then shifted his head to the door that read EXIT like he knew exactly what she'd been looking for. Kat tried to ignore the burning heat on her cheeks as she used the door.

Once shut from the thumping of the speakers, a bass vibration worked its way through the walls and filtered into her.

Mr. Gorgeous moved his hands to her back, turning her toward the wall, and urging her forward. But she stepped from his grasp. This was her game and she meant to play it as *she* chose. She set the rules. The pace.

"Not so fast, Bad Boy," she said, hitching her hip to the side and acting like she'd often written her heroines. Trying not to be Kat but the character she'd created, she smoothed her palm up his abdomen feeling each rippling contour beneath the silk of his button–up shirt. He sucked a breath between his teeth that further incited her desire.

Staring at the man's handsome face, purely masculine but definitely beautiful, she saw dark eyes the color of midnight. They gleamed like a queen bed draped in black satin sheets, beneath a pair of thick, but well trimmed, brows. His dark brown skin reflected against the distant streetlight, showing how recently he'd shaved his head.

"Back up," she urged, using a slight push on his chest.

He complied.

"Put your hands above your head." She smoothed her hands up each of his arms, pulling his muscular biceps with her until she had his arms pushed up. His elbows bent, he intertwined his fingers behind his head, groaning as she shimmied up his body.

She leaned in close, inhaling the lingering scent of the club and the freshness of Ivory—splashed with the subtle hint of cologne. Needing to stand on tiptoes despite the extra four inches, she placed her elbows on his shoulder and framed his face with her forearms. She stroked her curious hands over his sleek head, enjoying his smooth and warm skin beneath her fingertips.

"I like your head," she commented when he pressed his full lips to the curve of her outstretched neck.

"Oh yeah? Which one?"

She laughed. This guy was in a hurry and that suited her just fine. No time to chicken out. She eased away from him, allowing her hands to slide effortlessly down his well–defined chest. Her fingers came to rest on the buckle of the black leather belt holding his slacks in place. Releasing the spike from the hole, she then found the single button at the top of his fly. Bulging and straining beneath the fine twill of his pants, she could feel his erection, solid and pulsing, eager for lack of restraint.

A smooth swish of jagged zipper teeth and he was left confined only by a pair of thin cotton boxers with an easy elastic waist. Kat touched his flat stomach and felt him quiver, heard him suck in a breath. Her nails scraped over his skin, swirling through the silken dark pubic hairs that plunged from his belly button to the base of his cock.

"So which head do I like? Well, I don't know yet do I; I haven't felt them both." Finding previously untapped courage, she slid her fingers beneath the band of elastic and bent her knees, drawing down his boxers as she crouched before him. The spikes on her heels clicked against the cement.

There, in the fake shades of neon signs and the soft glow of the distant streets' overhead lighting, his dark cock sprung free. A bubbling of excitement swept through Kat's body as she slid her hand down the rigid shaft, measuring all ten rock–hard inches.

"Impressive," she mumbled, because there was nothing else she could say when a dick as glorious and large as his was inches from her face and making her pussy hungry. Damn, she couldn't wait for him to ease open her lips and fuck her brains out.

"You know what they say," he replied, his voice sounding a little strained.

She laughed. Yeah, she knew black men had big cocks, but while the limited amount she'd known in the past had been well endowed enough to please her, none had been hung like his. "No. What do they say?"

"That it's not the size of the boat but the motion of the ocean."

She laughed again. He's funny *and* fine. Yummy! His answer was not what she'd been expecting. Winding her fingers around him, she wasn't surprised they didn't meet. Hell no, he was too damn thick for that. Famous for writing about it, she knew just what to do. Twisting in a languid pace, she slid her hand to his base, feeling the size of his balls brush against the heel of her hand. *Oh, yeah, those will feel great slapping against me.*

"Really? Is that what they say?" She didn't wait for an answer. She licked the satin tip of his plum–shaped head, tasting the ball of moisture that had formed there. His natural lubricant. She didn't need it. She was wet.

Chapter 3

Jamal shut his eyes and slanted his face toward the sky, fighting damn hard to maintain control. The fine–ass hottie swirled her tongue around the swollen ridge of his head. He couldn't breathe. He gasped, air hissing between his teeth.

Opening his eyes, he lowered his gaze to the top of her head, bent level with his crotch. Her expressive brandy eyes glanced up at him, a smile faltered on her lips just before she went to work. A talent for sure, she held up his dick and licked down the underside until she reached his balls.

She licked there, too. Jamal felt his knees tremble as her tongue traveled across his sac, her gift with her mouth almost unbearable. Then, she retraced her damp path to his head and nibbled, all the while her soft hands rested on each of his thighs.

"Mmhmm, that's what they say," Jamal muttered. He could hardly form a rational thought, but knew he wanted to be inside her. He tilted his hips toward her. "Can . . . you . . . take it?"

Tempting fate. Much more of this and he'd be shooting his load down her throat before he even got to encase himself fully in her. He wanted to sex her, but with her mouth titillating his flesh like a champ, he'd take it any way he could get it. Right now between her lips.

"Can you?" she asked. Again she didn't wait for his response. She opened wide and closed around him, taking him so deep into her mouth he could feel his cock press against her tonsils. A wickedly slow tempo she set, in and out.

With his fingers tightening into her silken hair, Jamal glared at her tiny purse praying it was big enough to hold at least one damn condom. He hadn't packed one around in his wallet for years, since events like this weren't an everyday occurrence. Had hell frozen over? He planned booty–calls, not back alley screws with strangers. *She's not a stranger anymore*, he thought, watching her head bob up and down, taking him deeper with each of her strokes. Pulling him along until he felt the building climax.

She tightened her cheeks and sucked. A hand slipped from his thigh to his sac. Her palm gave a tender massage as she gave him the blow of a lifetime. She took him deeper, still, until he felt his shaft pressing against the roof of her mouth.

"Damn, girl," he groaned out.

The honey paused, releasing him from her mouth slightly. Before he could complain, she'd taken him in again, finding a rhythm equal to the dance music pulsating through the brick walls of The Night Kitty.

It wasn't more than a few minutes before he felt the telltale buck of his impending orgasm. He pushed it away. No way in hell he was going to get his nut off before he'd made her scream with pleasure.

Jamal let out a long, low moan as he placed his hands on her shoulders and eased her mouth off his erection. She whimpered slightly, releasing him completely. He heard her gulp for air, then she rose.

She kept perfect balance in her spiky heels, a satisfied smirk marring her pouty lush lips as she stood before him. She knew she'd been about to get him off, and he could tell by the sparkling passion in her eyes she was damn proud of it.

His hands had fallen limply to his sides. They both just stood there, looking at each other. Sizing one another up. There was a hint of vulnerability in her sexy stance. Jamal balled his hands into fists to keep from reaching for her.

He wanted to touch her. To feel the weight of her tits in his palm. To rub the hard tips of her russet nipples that strained against the black lace of her bra. To use his tongue and return the favor of the blowjob.

In bad shape, his erection ached and pulsed with unreleased desire. But she'd demanded control before, and he intended to honor her request. He'd wait for her to make the next move despite feeling as desperate as if it were his first time.

"Touch me," she demanded, licking her bottom lip. She moaned and Jamal knew she could taste him.

Not needing to be told twice, with one hand he grabbed her by the waist and dragged her forward until his solid cock pressed between them. Using a free hand, he framed her face, his palm upon her jaw, his long fingers extending into her soft hair. With his thumb, he traced her bottom lip where seconds before her tongue had been. The gleam in her eyes told him she wanted to be kissed, but the look vanished and he halted before his lips made contact.

"No, kissing is intimate. Kissing is for lovemaking, we're just going to fuck. A plain old, hardcore, don't ask my name, don't call me in the morning, a one-night stand—fuck!" Her tone was so seductive.

He could handle that. He wanted to be inside her. *Oh, yeah*, his cock affirmed.

No, no, no. Kat shook her head, trying to forget the tender stroke of his thumb on her mouth and the sensual way his lips curved when he'd been about to kiss her. Kat wanted to kiss, to love, but Kat was retired for the night. The *new her* had taken the lead. She moved her head from side to side and smiled. "None of that. Just do me."

He didn't need much urging. His hold around her waist slipped down to the backs to her thighs, to the thin line of exposed flesh above the tops of her leather boots and the bottom of her suede mini. He lifted her, spreading her legs until he wrapped them around his hips so her ankles crossed atop the curve of his finely shaped butt. Her silver spiked heels tapped together.

"You just want to fuck." It wasn't a question. He wasted no time turning her so her back was against the cold, hard wall of bricks. Just like Kat had wanted. She repressed a laugh and settled for a smile. Laughing would have destroyed the intense mood and she liked this guy brooding. Yeah, ten thick, dark, hard, inches of aggressive cock was just what this sex–starved kitten wanted.

Meow. "Can you take it?" she asked, tossing his earlier tease back at him.

"You got a condom?" His voice was gruff.

Kat smiled as she reached for the small purse that hung from a narrow strap on one shoulder. She'd brought what they needed. Pulling a foil square from her purse, she ripped it open, yanking the latex free.

"Yeah," she whispered, "let me put it on for you." His muscles bunched as he held her weight, leaning away from the wall just enough so she could work the condom down the rigid length of him that rose like a statue between them.

With unsteady fingers, she extended the latex around him, his hips grinding into her. His dick, stiff between them, rubbed vigorously against her clit. She trembled. The old Kat tried to create a mental picture of what they must look like against the wall. This was research after all and if she got so carried away that she couldn't remember, what good would it have done her? Besides pleasure, of course, she thought with a grin. Using her mind's eye, she saw his wide shoulders draped with silk. His bare tight ass and pants pooled around his ankles.

Like an out–of–body experience, she could see her high–heeled shoes. Her suede skirt bunched around her waist and her sopping wet t–back, black lacy panties. Wet enough to get her juices on his cock that was tucked against her. Yep, she'd better be able to write this. It was the new material she'd been searching for.

With the bashful Kat making an appearance, doubt started to form. What was she doing? Her heartbeat quickened. Shaking off her unease, she pulled the new Kat out, full of confidence and—hiss—sassy cat. Relaxing into his embrace, she urged him on.

Mr. Gorgeous ground his hips again, wedging his erection between Kat's lips but not yet entering. Damn panties. She should have gone without. What had she been thinking? Apparently she hadn't been, because with the cloth in the way, how was she going to get him inside her? Now!

He solved the problem easily enough, reinforcing what she already knew. She was out of her mind with lust. He slid one hand beneath her butt, found the line of cloth, and yanked it to the side. Far enough to the side so the panties moved sufficiently for him to get inside her.

Kat couldn't help the little whimper she made when he eased away from her. Far enough to put ten inches between them. Ten inches that disappeared when he slammed into her.

"Yeeessss!" she cried out. Her body stretched to make room for him. But he didn't stay—damn him. He slid out, taking the hard length of his dick in his hand and rubbing his silken head around her vagina, first easing the lips open, then finding the button of her clit. He pushed against it several times. What the hell? Was he trying to make her cum before she'd even had a good hard fucking?

"Inside me."

He didn't answer, just kept up his slow torment to her clit

until she knew she was going to cum. There was heat everywhere; her body felt like bursting, her fiery skin was so tight. And then his swollen head probed her clit one more time and a bolt of hot light caused her to shatter. The convulsions of climax made her pussy quiver, then her entire body succumbed to the tremors, leaving Kat out of breath and dizzy. No one had ever brought about such a quick orgasm.

He must have known a woman's body pretty damn well because he waited a few moments—for her to enjoy it—before he plunged in. He was inside of her so deep his mat of pubic hair ground into her manicured triangle. Kat was surprised she could take a cock as big as his. She could feel him everywhere. The tips of her toes rejoiced. Her nipples became so tight they hurt and only a warm damp tongue could help them. Poor things. Not this time, maybe the next, she mused, already thinking she was going to have to do *this* again.

Once he got started he didn't quit. Oh, yeah, baby, he was hitting his stride. His strokes lengthened, each time slipping out a little farther, then driving hard into her again. The new sexy Kat was enjoying the ride.

Jamal pushed inside her again, hardly able to think while he was buried in heaven. What the hell was he doing again? In the alley with a stranger? But with passion pushing all the right buttons, he couldn't have walked away had he wanted to. Her pussy gripped him, unwilling to let him go. He surged in. Retreated. Surged in. Ground his hips. Retreated. Again and again and again and again, until a dusting of sweat arose across his brow.

Trying to get a grip on his out of control restraint, he tried to back off. To slow down. A rush of heat started where he was joined with her. He fought for breath in the sultry night air. A liquid current stole over him like a wildfire to dry grass, causing ripples of flame to cover every spot on his body.

He hadn't noticed the biting sting of her nails when they dug into the flesh of his shoulder; not until the hottie withdrew her claws. She moved her seductive fingertips up his neck, then higher so she could glide her palms over his shaved head. "Yeah, I like them both," she whispered.

Her bedroom voice built the tension in his body. His muscles bunched, straining, working as he pumped into her. And when the tension reached crescendo, he knew he was about to cum. He wanted this honey to join him.

Slipping a hand between them, Jamal found her clit with his fingers. She was wet for him, his thumb swirling in her cropped, black hair. To hell with holding back. He needed it all now. Grinding into her wasn't enough. Not nearly enough.

Orgasm hit fast and intense. She trembled around him, whimpering sweetly. On his final surge, her lush lips opened, letting out a husky cry. His body shook and he grunted a primal sound from the back of his throat. He climaxed. Biting back his holler of victory in fear of discovery, he buried his face in the curve of her neck. The feminine scent of her smooth skin mixed with the heady odor of sex and latex. Each of her little pants and moans sent a shimmering of warm air across his sweat–dampened skin.

It took Kat awhile to catch her breath and to keep the blush of shame from crossing her cheeks. She didn't urge him away but took comfort in his half–hard cock inside her. In his nearness. Her body sated, conservative Kat was returning. But it wasn't regret she was feeling, more like confusion.

What happened to her? Was it the dirty dancing in the club? The sensual hum of the bass? Having the power of freedom to take a man of her choosing? And, she'd wanted this stud all right. She could feel him getting hard again; the longer they remained locked together. She could do him some more, all right. But run the risk of forgetting the details she needed to write her next piece? *Not!* Her deadline was looming and that, after all, was what this escapade was about.

Putting her hands on his chest, she gave a little shove. He backed away, his dick sliding from her sex. The creamy liquid droplets lingered white against his dark brown skin and black pubic hair. Evidence of her arousal and climax. Unable to resist, she swirled one finger into it, then in a light glide, slid down his semi–hard cock.

She hitched her hip to the side. "Thanks, I needed that," Kat said, shaking off her insecurities and calling upon the façade she'd created for the evening.

The gleam of his white teeth cut through the darkness. She liked his smile. Her heart skittered. She pretended his grin had no effect on her.

Liar.

"You all right?" he asked, bending to gather his pants and drag them up over his hips.

Oh, yeah, men's macho crap that they can fuck anything that walks and has a pussy but women are too soft–hearted. Too bad in this case, it was hitting the nail on the head. It could take her weeks to recover, to get her emotions in check. Kat gulped, then forced what she hoped was a sexy smile. "I'm fine. Why wouldn't I be?"

He shrugged but remained silent as he zipped, buttoned, then buckled up. "Women just tend to feel a little funny . . . after."

She laughed. She couldn't help it. If his skin hadn't been so rich and dark she would've sworn he blushed.

"Don't worry about me. I got just what I wanted." Kat's eyes studied his handsome features.

Unexpectedly, he reached out and tweaked her nipple between his thumb and forefinger. "You're made for sex."

Thinking of her job and all the research, she silently agreed. Most people thought that if you sold sex for money you were a prostitute. She laughed at the idea. Don't they know better? Don't they know their spouses were reading what she wrote to get their ideas? They ought to. She bit her bottom lip to suppress a grin.

"I know," she said, thinking of all the men who'd be getting off on reading her fictional account of tonight.

"Can I buy you a drink?"

"Thanks, but no. I've got to go." She didn't wait around. She couldn't or she might take him up on his offer, just to get to know him better.

Gathering her deflated pluck, she decided walking away was the best thing to do. She didn't want to think about good–bye kisses or other awkward bullshit. Shifting her hips so the fall of the mini would look natural, she sauntered down the alley toward the front street, her spiked heels clicking a beat to each step.

"What's your name?" he called after her.

She paused. A moment passed. She'd gotten just what she'd come for, but something about him made her want to answer. Like saying nothing would have cheapened the wonder of what had just happened. "Not this time, Baby," Kat tossed over her shoulder. It was no lie. Not this time, but if she were ever lucky enough to meet up with this fine piece of chocolate again, she'd do more than share her name.

Shy Kat regained control while her newer persona scratched her way into a hole. She couldn't give him her real name, despite the arrival of compunction, the nudging of shame. Kat Mason writes relationship columns for the Sunday paper, she doesn't do strangers, she doesn't write porn.

Keep telling yourself that, sistah. Pausing mid stride, she looked back at the gorgeous man, the inspiration for the sexing–him–good article she was about to write.

She kept walking. With his scent on her skin, the taste of him on her lips, Kat swiped a tear from her cheek. She couldn't believe she'd done this.

"How will I find you again?" he shouted, his voice echoing off the brick walls. There was a note of sincerity in his tone that panged in her heart.

She didn't stop, but turned the corner and walked out of sight, pretending she hadn't heard him. A few more lingered moments and he'd have seen her knees wobble and more liquid fall from her eyes. Part of her wanted nothing more than to see this stranger again, to know him.

But getting to know him would only reveal her as the shy, quiet, sit–in–her–sweats all day writer. Not the brazen woman she'd been tonight. He'd be disappointed. Better to leave him with the memory of the hot chick than to learn the fantasy wasn't real.

Chapter 4

Kat stared at the email to her agent—her finger hovering over the send button—narrowing her eyes at the five attached files. Grit blurred her vision; her butt was numb from sitting so long in her office chair. The five completed articles were the result of her thirty–six hour, uninterrupted writing spree. Well, broken only by her T&P, her code for brewing hot tea and trips to the potty.

Five? Wow, she couldn't believe she'd done it. Drawing bits and pieces from her night out on the prowl at The Night Kitty, she'd managed separate and unique works, each purely inspired by Mr. Gorgeous and her own shocking behavior.

It wasn't the speed of her typing that had stunned her the most—but the incident. How irresponsible. How careless. How dangerous. *How stupid*.

And the best damn orgasm she'd ever had—no batteries required.

Taking a deep breath, Kat was hit by the lingering scent of sex, of sweat, of *him*, that not even her scented soap had been able to vanquish.

Him? She knew nothing about him. The hunk could be married, a father of two. Guilt sliced through her. This wasn't what she was about, not her style, not her moral code, and yet she'd been so caught up in lust, she'd not used her head. She shouldn't have done this. Shouldn't have cheaply offered her body to an unknown man just for pleasure, just to assure a writing deadline to a career she wasn't all that proud of.

No matter how fine. No matter how horny.

Biting back a moan of dismay, Kat closed her tired eyes, the sting of shame burning at the back of her throat. The sassy–meow Kat knew deep down, if she crossed paths with that chocolate–skinned lover again, she'd melt right into his arms. A shiver shimmied down her spine.

Focusing her eyes on the pale computer screen, she read over her brief note to her agent, assuring all the needed info was included, then refusing to acknowledge her attachments as anything but pure fiction, she jammed her finger into the send key. She watched as the confirmation page slid slowly into place.

Spinning away from the desk, she slumped in her chair, feeling a weight settle onto her shoulders. No turning back now. Through the curtains covering her bedroom windows, sunshine filtered across the room. Dust fairies danced and floated in the air. From some place outside, Kat heard distant children playing, the joyful yells, followed by mumbled laughter.

Sunday, midday, and she was tired. Barely able to push herself from her seat, Kat moved across her room, headed for the shower. Intent on scrubbing clean the scent of her escapade, she stripped off her clothing, tossing it toward the hamper. She was no Jordan, most landed on the floor.

The cold spray shocked her body, sending a frisson across her skin, but the water soon warmed, soothing away the strain. Steam arose, swirling about her feet. As the heated water slid over her naked flesh, memories flooded her senses. Remembering dark eyes flared with passion, exploring fingertips, the hard length of cock, the soul–deep ache of wanting him. Of desiring a stranger, a man in all likelihood, she'd never see again.

Warm droplets of water landed on her cheeks, more salty than the shower. Kat swiped them away. What good did tears do her now, she wondered as sobs broke free. Overtired, focus lingered on his full lips and the brief moment he'd been about to kiss her. "You ho, why'd you stop him?" she berated herself, wondering what his kiss would have been like. How his breath would have tasted.

But kisses were dangerous. They opened up hearts, revealed old hurts, threatened her self–imposed exile of existence. A back alley fuck was not a relationship, and solid relationships didn't begin with her back against the bricks.

Leaning back into plush leather, Jamal tapped his fingertips against the curve of his steering wheel in beat with the bounce pumping from his stereo. The sun crept up over the horizon too damned early as far as he was concerned, and Monday morning traffic had been worse than usual, thanks to a four car pile–up on the freeway.

Putting his SUV into park, he closed eyes against the brightness of the mid–August morning, too exhausted to be at work. Should've called in sick, but it was too late for shoulda, woulda, coulda's he thought, opening his eyes to glance up at his office building.

Lack of sleep made him irritable. It's not that he hadn't had the chance to rest. Hell, he'd spent all day Saturday lounging around his apartment, but his mind kept returning to the little honey he'd met Friday night and the way they'd screwed in the back alley.

He'd thought his bow–wow days were behind him, but just like a dog with a bone, he'd buried it home without pausing to think of the repercussions.

And who the hell was she?

Even in the wild days of fraternities and college parties, he'd never met another woman quite like her, with looks enough to stir any warm–blooded creature, and an oh–so–hot body. Even now, an erection wouldn't be out of the question with a little more thought of how she'd knelt before him. How her tongue had worked his flesh.

Refusing to get caught back into the web of desire that had tormented him all weekend, he slid from his Escalade, pulling out his briefcase with him. Taking a deep breath, he headed inside. At least he had something to look forward to, his hopeful submission from Kat Mason. It should have arrived by now. Perhaps the return of his fantasy lover would ease his mind from memories of the real one–night–back–alley–fling thing.

And just like that he was hard.

Kent was the first to greet him. The ass came charging over as soon as Jamal had slipped in the building.

"Hey man, what happened to you?" he asked, taking a swig of OJ from a small plastic bottle.

"You take a cab home?" Jamal asked, ignoring Kent's question. He kept walking to his office, having no wish to disclose the true facts of his Night Kitty trip.

"Yeah. Well, you should have let me know you were ready." Kent didn't slow even though Jamal was trying to give him the brush–off.

"You looked busy."

A wide grin spread across Kent's face. "Oh, yeah, and did I ever get busy. That pigeon let me go home with her. Now, don't be such a prude, JJ, sexing don't hurt no one."

"As long as she knows nothing's coming out of it, Kent. That's your problem."

"What you mean by that?" Kent asked. A brow arched and a forced innocent smirk marred his face.

"I mean, it's why you end up with crazy–chick stalkers

thinking you're their man. You've had more than your share of 'em, too. If you're just hittin' it for the night, the girl should know ahead of time, not after." Jamal opened his office door, glancing at his computer. He couldn't wait to check his email and see if Kat had sent him anything.

"Like you know anything about getting lucky. Ha, how long has it been?" With the barbs renewed and laughter filtering down the hall, Kent sauntered away.

A good thing too, because Jamal had no desire to enlighten him. Flicking on the computer, he slipped into his chair and waited for it to warm up, his mind returning to the advice he'd just given. Damn, he felt like a fool, getting lured into sex by a fine chick who refused to give her name. What was she hiding?

At least they'd both known what they were after and there was no need for guilt when there'd been no follow–up phone call. Shit, the truth was, had she given him her name and number, he'd have used it by now. Her little cries of delight were pure torture on his memory, and though her scent had been washed away, he could swear her fragrance lingered just to play tricks on him.

Opening his email, Jamal scanned through more than six dozen incoming before his gaze settled on the one he was looking for. A double click and it was open, just a short hello note, and five attached files.

"Damn. You've been busy," he muttered to the screen. He was grinning like a boy looking at a lollipop. He opened the first, and quickly read through it.

"What the hell?" His smile fell. His brows plunged forward. He read it a second time; flashes of a weekend memory scattered the page. Brick walls, neon signs, cries of passion.

"Get a grip, Jamal," he said, opening the second and third file. His eyes scanned the stories, his pulse drumming in his ears. Tall leather boots, throbbing music, desire.

His hands were shaking as he clicked open the last two files, and read them over quickly. A stranger, a shot of booze, a kiss that didn't happen.

"Holy shit!"

Jamal could hardly breathe as he leaned away from the computer and shut his eyes, bringing to life the Fly–Girl from The Night Kitty. She was a perfect woman, a perfect fuck. And then there was Kat, his perfect fantasy, his perfect wet dream.

The similarities between the submissions on his screen and the tell–all memories of lust were a bit too real, or was he imagining things? Maybe Kat just knew how to tap into the wanna–screw market. He'd always known she was great at creating fiction.

The other possibility freaked him the fuck out! Could he have just banged his best client? *His super–star.* Sucking breaths between his teeth, Jamal stared at the ceiling. Oh, yeah, bow–wow was right. He was a dog that deserved to be neutered. Good time, no string, public fucks had definite consequences.

He could only hope now that things didn't get screwed!

Chapter 5

Pussy-whooped had never been a name he'd have called himself. Never a category he'd fallen into. Especially not after one dip of his stick. Until maybe now. Unnamed pussy at that.

Smoothing a hand over his shaven head, Jamal let out an exasperated breath. What the hell was wrong with him? He'd had one-night stands aplenty, years ago, and had never been so drawn into this shit before. He'd hit it and forget it. With no regrets.

Closing his eyes, Jamal rubbed the bridge of his nose between his thumb and forefinger, trying not to be sucked into the unrelenting guilt. It grew daily, even though he'd spent the week trying to forget how his bow-wow lust had gotten the best of him. He opened his eyes and stared accusingly at his computer, the black shut-off screen mocking him with the knowledge of what'd been in Kat's files.

What he feared had to be more than a coincidence.

Tossing a stack of papers on his desk, he rose from his leather chair and glanced at the green digital clock displaying quitting time. Well after.

At least he'd been able to make it to Friday without rereading Kat's submissions again. The first half-dozen reads had been enough. Enough to know that Kat had an undeniable talent to arouse and that his fantasy of her had been usurped by some get–down–and–phunky chick that had rocked his world.

It'd been pretty much the only thing he'd accomplished on Monday. Reading and remembering. Remembering the sweet honey and how closely her actions resembled the fictional characters of his client.

Somehow, on Wednesday he'd managed to print and package up her articles, sending them off to their appropriate publishers. He'd even done the entire task, only skimming the material, to make sure each was going to the proper house, and not giving it a thorough view. But that hadn't stopped him from thinking about it. From remembering word–for–word how she'd described just how *he'd* fucked last Friday night.

One week ago. One week of hard–on misery.

"Was it Kat?" he mumbled, clicking his briefcase closed, then adjusting his rocked–up dick behind his slacks. Maybe it *was* the three–year erection from desiring the fantasy image of her that had him trippin'. Lack of blood flow in his brain. His body reacted like a well–trained hound after a scent, only he'd caught the scent of her articles and the chase of wanting her was on. Of getting between her thighs.

If there was a chance it'd been his super–star he'd given a good, hard bang between bricks and his dick, he wanted to know.

But it was more complicated than just casual sex. Sometime during the last three years, he'd developed an affection for Kat, the perfect cocktail of sweet innocence and enough aphrodisiac to make—and keep—a man hard. That's what she was paid to do. Only he was her agent and not supposed to be getting–off on her work as much as he did. He was supposed to have maintained some level of professional distance.

That line had been crossed already—they'd become friends. They talked about personal matters and only Kat's insistence had kept them from meeting in person. But it was more like skipping–rope than line–crossing if he'd fucked her. More like taking a lighter to the business–relationship card and burning the shit out of it.

Leaving his things in his office, Jamal headed down the hall. Even though it was late Friday afternoon, he hoped to catch Rebecca before she cut out for the weekend. He needed another perspective on this, though he had no intention of telling her he'd acted like an under–sexed irresponsible ass.

Rebecca was gathering her things when he looked in her office. He tapped his knuckles against the open door. "Hey, Bec."

She glanced up from her bag, smiling as she greeted him. "Hi, JJ. You're here late."

She was blue–eyed, blond. Tall and thin, a professional beach–volleyball player before she'd become a literary agent, and every bit hot enough to be the sort of cover–model he'd represent. *If* he was a brother who was into the white chick thing.

Jamal shrugged. Working late every day, including Fridays, wasn't unusual for him. "So are you."

She laughed. "True. But I'm on my way out of here. What's up with you?"

"You in a hurry?"

She turned toward him, leaning a slender hip against the edge of her desk, and flipped a few long curls over her shoulder. "Why?"

She might not be his type, but she was easy to talk to. "Nothing serious." He sat down in a chair, spreading his legs, he leaned forward to rest his forearms on his knees.

Rebecca laughed again. "Oh, not serious? Right." Setting her things aside, she took a seat opposite him. "You're full of shit. So spit. What's going on?"

"You ever had a fling at work?"

"Are you hitting on me?" She winked at him. "Get in line behind Kent. He's got first dibs on working–my–nerve if I ever leave my man."

Chuckling, he glanced toward her. "He bothering you?"

"Nothing I can't handle. You didn't come in here to talk about me. What's up?"

"Have you ever been fuzzy on what's appropriate with a client?"

"Do you mean commission splits? Contract clauses? What exactly are we talking about here?"

"You blonde or something?" he teased. "Hell no, I'm not talking business here. I'm talking being attracted to. Messed with."

She bit her bottom lip, but Jamal knew she was trying hard not to laugh in his face. "Oooh, JJ, whatcha do?"

Bending his head, Jamal interlocked his fingers behind his neck and exhaled slowly, the air whistling between his teeth. *Hell if he knew*. Banged a stranger? Screwed his client? Let the dawg in him out? Ruff!

"Nothing," he lied. He shook his head. Not like he could exactly make a full confession to Rebecca without looking like a sucker. He'd been played. He'd already figured that out. Innocence his ass, the little hottie from the bar was a sex–pot, made to please a man. He'd been at her mercy. Still was.

Damned cock of his thickened.

He rolled his head on his shoulders. "I'm just wondering if you've ever been tempted to cross the professional line?"

A moment of silence passed. "Who is she?" Rebecca finally asked.

His gaze shot to her, the look in the clear–blue eyes was so knowing, explaining last Friday night's events nearly rolled from his lips.

"Hypothetically."

"Wanna know a little secret?" She grinned, then continued after he nodded his head. "At the Christmas party two years ago I had a few too many glasses of champagne and made out with Kent."

"Just made out?" he asked, arching a questioning brow. "You didn't sleep with him?"

"Some kissing and heavy petting. That's as far as it went. But that fifteen minutes sure made life at work hell for months."

"Was he pissed he didn't get more?"

"Not so much. He took a different girl home. And a different one the following week. But our working relationship was uncomfortable. Strained. As I see it, JJ, unless you're thinking of marrying her and living happily–ever–after, it can only end two ways. Both badly."

Rebecca didn't speak for a moment, then added, "JJ, mess with a chick you work with and she could sue your ass for sexual harassment. Mess with a client and it could end your career. Just make sure the shot–of–leg is worth it."

"Humph." He hadn't been thinking about marriage. He waited for the usual shudder of distaste, when thinking about being tied down by a ring round his finger. His typical reaction, but it didn't come. What the hell? Sure he was getting older, but was he really contemplating settling down?

Nah . . .

But when the time came, it'd be the cherry–on–top to have a fly girl with a tight pussy that clung to his dick, and cried out mewing sounds as he thrust her toward climax.

But what if she lived as sassy as she'd walked away?

What if it *had been* Kat, would that mean every single article she'd written had a different man she'd fucked? Was this her MO? The way she'd inspired horniness from the men who read her articles and jerked–off?

Disgusted even thinking about it, Jamal stood. "I'm feeling

you. No mixing business and pleasure." He forced down the bile that'd risen in his throat. Couldn't be the way his client worked. Not his Kat.

"Like oil and vinegar."

"But oil and vinegar work well on salads."

Rebecca laughed, then asked with a wink, "You planning on tossing salad?"

Heat spread across his face and a pulse ticked through his cock with a vivid image of smooth caramel skin covering a nice round ass. He cleared his throat and moved toward the door. "Naa, I'm planning on getting out of here. It's late."

Rebecca glanced at the golden and silver watch circling her wrist. "You still meeting my friend, Tonya, for dinner?"

Damn! Jamal had been so preoccupied with Kat and his dick–sprung fling, he'd forgotten about the blind date that Rebecca had set up for him. Again. Calling him a good catch, she was always fixing him with one of her friends. So far nothing worth mentioning relationship wise, though several had been worth the price of dinner. They provided dessert.

"Yeah." Too late to cancel. "I'd better go. And, Bec, thanks for listening."

"No problem, JJ. Let me know how it goes with Tonya. You're going to thank me." She smiled wide at him, added a little finger wave before turning her attention back to gathering her things.

Walking down the hall, Jamal attempted to clear his mind from the lingering thoughts of juicy thighs and shoulda–kissed lips. Attempting to get rid of his erection before Tonya mistook it for her. Trying to muster a little excitement about his date, he headed to fetch his briefcase and keys.

The room was dark, a haze of lust mingled and swayed with the pounding rhythm thumping from the surrounding speakers. "What the hell am I doing here?" Jamal asked himself, standing just a few strides in the front door of The Night

Kitty. His dick needed pussy—that's what, he realized, adjusting the half–hard flesh that'd been flaccid all night.

Until he'd gotten close enough to this bar that he could actually taste need. Could almost imagine the scent of sex. Of her.

And if there was a chance *she*'d be there, where–the–hell–else would he be?

Shoving away minor fragments of guilt for skipping out of his date with Tonya early, Jamal narrowed his eyes and focused on the wild thrusting movements of the dancing and grinding couples, half praying he wouldn't find her there tangled up and simulating fucking with another man.

The other half praying she would be and interested in getting freaky with him again—anything to ease the blue–balls of wanting her for the last seven days. Seven cold shower mornings.

A Snoop Dogg remake of Slick Rick smoothly took over the pulse of the music just as cleverly as his Fly–Girl honey had taken over his fantasies. Oh, yeah, he was pussy–whooped after all and didn't even know the hottie's name.

He might well as be a tongue–wagging puppy. Where his pussy was, he'd follow.

Hell, he'd given up the sure bet of hitting it tonight with Tonya. She'd been a give–it–up–girl. She'd been attractive enough. Into him. But he hadn't been interested in her not–so–subtle suggestions of all the sweetness she could give. He hadn't been into it.

Instead all through their casual conversations, Jamal's thoughts drifted away from his date and back to the bar where he'd hooked–up with the woman he'd much rather be with.

Though he'd intended on heading home after dropping Tonya off, he'd steered his Escalade down the streets, taking the route that would lead him to the nightclub. Here. He'd even driven by twice before he'd parked and come inside.

The lure of her strong. Oh, yeah, baby. Strong enough to entice him here on the memory of passion. Ecstasy.

Pushing his way through the rotating hips and swinging arms, Jamal worked his way to the long, dark wooden bar, backlit with small lights that illuminated a few dozen top–shelf bottles of liquor.

All the stools taken, he found a narrow section and eased in, holding up a hand to get a bartender's attention. A light–skinned brotha glanced his way, a wide, knowing grin spreading across his face. He moved closer, lifting his chin and arching a brow. "What can I get you?" he asked, speaking loudly enough to be heard over the bass boom and the buzz of sexual energy.

"Beer. What do you have on draft?"

"You're not drinking alone are you? You're not having what she had?" he asked, his I–know–what–and–who–you–came–here–looking–for grin now reaching his hazel eyes.

Jamal knew the *she*—the sex–pot—the bartender was referring to, but he couldn't help the question from slipping from his lips. "She?"

He laughed, slanting his head toward the back exit sign. The back door leading to the alley. "Yeah. *She.*"

Jamal turned away from the bar, again his gaze fixing on the crowd. "Is she here tonight?"

"I haven't seen her."

"You ever seen her before?"

"Can't say that I have. Have you?" The light–hearted taunt was soothed by sliding Jamal a frozen glass mug filled with a dark beer.

Taking a long pull of the beer, he allowed the cool liquid to ease the dryness of his throat. He was a fool, getting suckered into a one–night stand the way he had, but he didn't doubt it wasn't the first time the bartender had seen over–boozed chumps getting played the same way. Or playing.

The bartender moved farther down the bar, serving a couple a pair of shot glasses filled with a blue liquor that looked to be the *it–drink*, Hpnotiq. Mesmerized by the intense color, he watched as they took the shots quickly, then asked for more.

When the light–skinned brotha moved back in his direction, Jamal stuck out his hand. "Jamal James."

"Lloyd Hall," he replied, giving him a firm shake. "You new around here?"

Jamal shook his head. "Just too old for the pick–up scene, ya know."

Lloyd laughed. "Right. Aren't we all."

"So, Lloyd, you going to give me what you gave the honey?"

"Hpnotiq, bro."

"What's in it?"

Lloyd shrugged. "I gave it to her straight. She snatched the glass and shot it before I added anything to it. Usually it's a mix. Alone it's potent."

"Just one shot enough to mess her up?" Jamal asked, wondering why she would have gulped it down and if that was the reason his Fly–Girl had been so wild that night. What wasn't a good idea was going home with a rocked–up cock with no pussy to ease it.

"Depends. It'd make her feel good. What she drank wouldn't get most people shit–faced drunk, though. All about tolerance." He grabbed the liquor bottle and sloshed it around. "Been told this junk makes you feel Missy Elliot."

"Missy Elliot?"

"Getcha–Getcha–Getcha freak on. Like finding a chick to go home with. It makes you hot, and cold showers and self–inflicted hand–jobs won't cut it. You'll need to get–up–in–it, or suffer. Not something you drink then go home alone."

"You ever tried it?"

"I serve it. Don't drink it."

Jamal glanced away from the bar, scanning the dance floor

again, desire making him desperate to find his mind–blowing fuck from last week. His gut knowing she wasn't there.

"Just fill up my beer."

The music changed again. The sultry voice of Mariah Carey seduced Jamal away from the bar, leaving his drink behind. Hottie wasn't here. He was going home alone and didn't need an aphrodisiac to give him a painful hard–on. *She*'d already done that.

Chapter 6

Kat shifted the basket off her lap and stretched out her knees, her legs tired from the hours they were folded beneath her. Searching through the letters neatly stacked within the circular weave didn't ordinarily take so long. She relaxed against the cushions of the backyard lounge chair and allowed her mind to float away from the pages of couples' cries for help. Her lids drifted closed as she breathed in the morning air, still crisp enough to offer a measure of solace, but quickly warming in the lift of the summer sunshine.

It was going to be a hot day, she realized, opening her eyes and reaching for a tall glass of iced tea, the beads of condensation wetting her fingertips. An answering droplet of sweat slid between her breasts.

Is that how his tongue would feel? Hot and wet and slick. Arousing.

Repressing a shallow pant, Kat opted for a long drink of tea to chase away the memories. The need of wanting a nameless man she'd never see again.

Mr. Gorgeous may have been hot to trot for one night, but he didn't belong to her and she'd had no right to sample the finger–licking goods he'd offered. But that didn't stop her from fantasizing. From dreaming of his touch. His cock. How good he'd felt inside her. From wanting him inside her again.

She wedged the ice cold glass into her cleavage, chasing the heat from her body. Her nipples puckered from the cold. With want. With a hungry need to be on the receiving end of the moisture's attention. A cold line of liquid slid from the glass along her body, puddling in her shallow belly button.

"Get over it, girl," she whispered, setting her glass aside and using her t–shirt to mop up her damp skin. She chose to ignore the wetness in her panties as if it didn't exist. Better to pretend it didn't than to dwell on the fact that she was single. And horny. And not getting any. Not any time soon.

Kat reached for the basket. She had a second deadline looming and couldn't lament continuously that her job for the weekend had already been met. Yeah, it'd been a wham–bam, mind–blowing flash of writing, inspired by an equally mind–blowing screw, but she had another task to deal with now. Best she focus on that. Reliving the way Mr. Gorgeous fucked did no good but leave her body on fire, drenched with want, and aching. Unsatisfied.

Better to focus on her more respectable job. The one she put her name on and took credit for.

Balancing the basket on her lap, she sifted through the letters lined up in order of receipt and tried to decide which of them she was going to answer.

Easing one from the envelope, she unfolded the pages and read over the carefully written words of the well–crafted, but desperately–needy plea. These weren't words of sex, but of love. Of a wife who needed reassurance that her man was true. Begging for advice on her relationship and how to save her marriage.

A pang of regret radiated through Kat's heart. How was she supposed to comfort this woman? What could she possibly say to ease the writer's concern about her man's fidelity— or lack thereof? For all Kat knew, she'd been on the receiving end of this man's dick just the past Friday night. Oh, yeah, baby and what a glorious dick it'd been.

She shook her head. Mr. Gorgeous. Fine–ass brotha with ten inches of sex therapy had been the man she'd been with. Not this woman's husband. Not anyone's husband, Kat assured herself. The flesh that had been all–up–in–her had been unnamed and unclaimed as far as she was concerned. She had to keep reminding herself not to think of all the horrible consequences of what could have been.

Damn! Writing a relationship column had been a whole hell of a lot easier last week.

But this week was well underway and what was she supposed to tell her editor down at the paper? "Sorry, I didn't make deadline. I got fucked hard and fast against a brick wall and now I can't think. *Apparently, I got my brains fucked out!*"

Lifting the small silver cell phone resting against the cushion beside her, she thought about calling Jamal. Maybe she should just tell her agent she didn't want to write these fix–it relationship columns anymore. She didn't have a clue about what real relationships were or how they worked. She'd never actually been in one.

But she could hear Jamal's rich tone gently reminding her of her contract. Kat sucked a deep breath, holding it in her lungs until it burned, then allowed it to slowly slide from her lips as she bucked–up and faced the truth.

If she was going to give up any writing, it'd be the prostitution work she did—selling sex, albeit stories of sex, but it was sex just the same. It was a rhythm of words rather than hips, but still for one purpose. To get a man off.

"How's my favorite little hooker?"

Kat dropped the phone back to the cushion. Closing her eyes, she tried to calm the nails skidding across a chalkboard when reminded of the inside joke that went along with her mother's nickname for her.

"Speak of the devil," Kat responded, turning her attention

to her momma as she made her way across the stone patio toward her.

"Shouldn't that be Madam and not devil, baby?" her momma said with a grin and a wink.

"Is there a difference?"

"Depends who you're asking." Leaning over, her momma affectionately kissed her cheek, then sat down in a patio chair across from Kat.

Thinking she'd been asking her momma, Kat mumbled under her breath, "Guess not, then."

Her mother's laughter rolled across the morning air, so rich and sincere that Kat couldn't help but join in. It'd been her mother after all who had gotten her into this business. By accident actually. Kat had only meant to help her momma make deadline when the arthritis in her fingers had made typing too difficult. She'd never intended for this to end up her career. For her to be world famous as the greatest–of–the–great when it came to getting men to masturbate.

"What are you doing here, Momma?"

"Checking to see how my favorite girl is doing."

Kat smiled. She had two sisters and didn't doubt for a second that Momma said the same to each. Not that it mattered. It was nice to hear. She let out a slow breath. "I'm doing okay."

"Don't look okay to me," her momma replied, slanting her head toward the spiral notebook resting by Kat's feet, by an unused sharpener and a dull pencil. "Don't you normally make notes before you sit down to write?"

Kat glanced down at the paper, knowing it'd be empty. She hadn't jotted down a single word, as blocked as she'd been the last time she'd needed inspiration. Only getting cocked was a whole lot easier than getting hitched. Quicker too. There were no easy fixes when it came to finding the right words for her relationship column. No local bar where she get boozed up, serviced well, and come home ready to repair marriages.

"No biggie, Momma, I'm just having a hard time with this deadline."

"Finding creative ways to use dick, cock, penis always stumped me up, too. Your daddy—"

Kat put up her palm. "Momma, don't." The last thing she wanted to think on was her parents messing in any sort a way she wrote about.

"You're such a prude, Kat. It's what men and women do. You should try it out sometime. Get a little inspired."

Or a lot inspired. Long, thick, hard inspired. *Oh, yeah, that's worked out real fine.* Five articles fine.

Kat shook her head. She wasn't supposed to be dwelling. Besides, writing the sex had worked itself out. It was writing love that was giving her trouble. "Do you always got to be so suggestive?"

"Can't imagine, baby, that you'd be surprised by anything I say. Sex sells, and you're walking the streets real well. Selling sex isn't a crime. Not the way you're working it."

There it was again, her mother's teasing about being a prostitute and her agent being her pimp. It didn't used to bother her. In fact, most of the time she thought of her pseudonym, Glory Cockin, as the perfect excuse to think slutty. It was liberating to escape the more reserved Kat, to allow her tigress to show through her writing.

But deep down something nagged at her. A too–long–hushed voice that told her sex could be more powerful than just an orgasm. An orgasm could be more powerful during sex with a man who gave a damn.

And that was the problem. She'd never had one.

Trying to lighten the glum settling around her mood, Kat smiled at her momma, offering her a sassy–Kat wink. "I already got my pimp and make–a–man–beg articles. Now I'm struggling with my make–a–man–stay deadline."

"If it's such a struggle, what you ought to be doing is telling that agent of yours that you quit. Life's got enough struggle, baby, no sense adding to it."

"Quit selling my wares on the street corners?"

"No. Quit writing about relationships when your heart's not into it."

But that's exactly where her heart was at. She was missing something in her life and it wasn't getting off. She had molded plastic for that. Extra packs of AA batteries. What she needed, what she missed in the still of the night was a flesh–and–blood body to cuddle up next to. The heat of a man.

Swallowing down the lump in her throat, Kat forced a smile and reached for the notebook and pencil. "What I write helps people. I enjoy that."

"Writing sex helps people, too."

"Not the same."

"Maybe not, but it's nothing to be ashamed of."

"Nothing to be proud of either."

"You're wrong, baby." Momma folded her arms over her chest and let out a heavy sigh. "You've been gifted with a talent to make others feel good, but if it's not making you feel good then don't do it anymore."

How many times over the last three years had Kat told herself that each article was the last? Countless. But proud of it or not, when she was Glory she was allowed to be wild and free. To be as nasty as she wanted to be. To be a freak. And more articles would come. She'd commit to another contract.

Looking into her mother's eyes, she dropped her voice to a whisper, "Stop writing?"

"If it makes you happy. Or write what you love."

She tapped the eraser against the paper several times. Thump. Thump. Thump. "I guess, Momma," she mumbled, feeling the beat of her heart match the tapping of the pencil end. The words *happy* and *love* doing funny things to her gut. Creating a hole that she didn't know how to fill.

Kat reached for her iced tea. A chill scurried down her spine, the glass now just leaving her feeling cold and empty.

"Think about what I said, baby," her momma said, getting to her feet.

"You're leaving?"

"You've got a deadline. I've got some Jimmy Choos on hold." Like she was going to miss the next best thing to sliced bread, her momma jetted from the yard with hardly a quick wave goodbye.

Alone again, Kat reclined against the cushions and shut her eyes. She needed to shrug off the melancholy stirred up by her momma's visit. She didn't want to think about the pain of being alone. But the pleasure of being with Mr. Gorgeous.

Pleasure of having him buried so deep within her, she finally felt whole.

Warmth moved across her skin. Shifting her hips against the lounge chair, heat dampened her lips. Tingled her clit. Tightened her nipples.

If that chocolate–skinned lover was her man, what would she do to satisfy him? What would she do to keep him?

What would it take to keep a man with as much raw hunger and sexual prowess from sniffing up every skirt? To keep the dog interested in only her pussy? In her?

Opening her eyes, Kat grabbed up the sharpener and put a fine point to her lead, then started writing.

She didn't know the first thing about going to bars and picking up strangers. Hell, she'd done alright. She may not know about relationships. But, she could fake it.

Chapter 7

"You make your deadline?"

Flashes of memory burned Kat's cheeks as she slid into the booth opposite her friend, Sasha. "You bet." There was no way Sasha, or anyone else besides her agent and momma, knew about the sort of deadlines she was keeping. As far as the world was concerned, Kat wrote about sweet relationships for couples in trouble.

Like she knew one danged thing about either. Sex. Love. What business did she have writing about those things?

Pasting a smile across her lips, she leaned back against the vinyl seat covering, the cool, slick material chilling the bare skin above her summer tube top. Helped ease a bit of the heat created by a three–week old vision of cold bricks and a man hot enough to do damage.

"So how many break–ups did you fix this time?" Sasha asked, tapping a tapered nail against the pizzeria menu. "Did you tell those bad boys to be good to their wives?"

Kat laughed. "Like you know anything about being good."

"Hell no. Who'd want to be like you?"

Kat knew she was teasing, still shame developed restlessly in her blood. That was a once–upon–a–time scenario, one that no longer applied. Wild Kat had made an appearance.

Kat winked at her. "That's right, sistah, I'm nothing but *pure sweetness*." What Sasha didn't know wouldn't hurt her. In this case however, her friend would be ecstatic that she'd managed a hell of a memorable one–night stand.

"You really have to get out more or—" Sasha's words were cut off by the arrival of the waiter.

"What can I get you ladies?"

"You. Hot, melting, sliced up and ready to devour." Did Sasha have no shame?

Warmth covering her cheeks, Kat dipped her face, placing a hand over her mouth as she held back the burst of laughter. Hell yes, the waiter was hot, but could her friend not refrain from propositioning every guy worth doing a double–take?

Poor man was blushing like a school boy. "Maybe later." He grinned. "For now, can I get you something to drink?"

"A couple of beers. We're busy talking sex, if you want to join us."

"We're not talking sex," Kat croaked. *Can the floor just open up and swallow me? Please*. She should be used to Sasha. They'd been friends for years.

"No. But we're about to."

Lifting her eyes, Kat stared at the waiter, pretending Sasha wasn't there and that her words weren't making Kat long for Mr. Gorgeous just one more luscious time. She'd talk sex with him, all right. Right now. Tonight. If only she knew where to find him. The Night Kitty, maybe?

She cleared her throat and repressed the all too real memories. "We'll take a couple of Coronas, and a large pepperoni."

"Make it double pepperoni. I like lots of hot, spicy meat," Sasha directed at the waiter.

"I'll keep that in mind," he said, smiling from ear to ear as he eased the menu from Sasha's fingers. He moved away with a confident stride, but Kat didn't miss the moisture on his brow or the way he walked like he had a stiffy stuffed be-

tween his thighs. Poor guy. Sasha had made him both embarrassed and *horny*.

"So . . . let's talk about sex."

Kat nearly groaned. "Do we have to?" She wasn't prepared for the same old lecture about how she really needed to
get *some*. They'd skipped down this path before. Sasha insisted that a good lay would free up her creativity. Get her in
touch with her artistic side.

Did she have to be right?

A month ago Kat had argued. She could write erotic Glory's
Stories and her relationship columns without getting fucked.
A month ago she hadn't known any better. A good screw was
exactly what she'd needed. Still, it hadn't been right to do it
with a stranger. Wrong. Very wrong, Kat reminded herself
for the billionth time. That didn't make it any easier for her
to forget him.

Kat gave herself a mental shaking, and refocused on what
her friend was saying. It was foolish to wonder about him, to
miss his heat.

"You know, Kat, you've really got to loosen up. With your
talent, you could be writing something far more interesting
than how to keep your man from straying. Hell, Pure Sweetness, you should write how to keep him sat–isss–fied."

If she only knew.

"I'll think about it," Kat agreed, knowing it was the only
way to keep the conversation from stalling on her lack of
sexual activity. "Now, tell me what's new with you."

As planned, their talk changed directions, and even when
the beers and pizza arrived, her friend somehow managed to
hold her tongue from licking the waiter all over.

Kat ate and talked, but deep in the recesses of her mind,
Wild Kat started scratching. It'd been three long weeks of
need aching between the legs. One week before her September
deadline. Would she be able to make it, or would she need
another night of exploration?

*   *   *

Was there no other possibility? Somehow, for more than three years she'd managed to come up with fictional material, now she was reduced to participation.

"Not tonight. Tonight I'm only watching," Kat whispered reassuringly to herself.

Liar!

She didn't plan on watching. She didn't dress for standing-by. She didn't need to watch. She needed sex. Shifting her hips, Kat rubbed the thin strip of thong panties against her clit. A low, husky moan escaped her lips. Oh, yeah, she needed cock. Badly.

The strength of her desire and unfiltered boldness shocked her. When had this happened? she wondered, pulling her white tube top up, just slightly, as she adjusted a couple of twenties tucked into her cleavage. When had she realized the lure of sex was as powerful as a drug habit? Had it been ten inches of hard, dark enlightenment?

Shoving away all the tormenting uncertainties, developed through years of single-life confinement, Kat took a deep breath and held it. She was going through with this—again. She needed masses of muscle on the other end of her joy-stick, not on an on/off switch.

Slowly releasing the burning breath, she stared at the door of the dumpy looking bar. *Dan's.* The door was plain and unassuming. Faded, half-lit neon beer signs hung in the long, narrow front window.

Daylight persisted late into the evening, but now the moon was rich and aglow. Finally. Kat glanced up and down the dark street, gathering her courage. Sasha would be so proud of her, recalling her friend's words as they'd dined earlier that evening. She did need a good fucking. That's why she was here.

Teetering on the narrow heels of her strappy sandals before she found her balance, Kat stood on the sidewalk, which rippled with the lingering heat of the hot August sunshine. Indecision clung to the thick and sultry night air.

The thumping music seeping through the walls didn't beckon to her, but instead acted like a verbal warning. Run little cat, there's dogs out to get you. With her pulse making waves, Kat contemplated finding a different place. Something less intimidating. Something more familiar.

She swallowed hard. This was the bar. She was horny. Now, not later. Besides, this place was close enough to her house that material would be fresh on her mind when she got home in order to write it.

Close to The Night Kitty, too.

But she wasn't going there. No way was she going to be seen as a *regular*. The bartender would surely recognize her after he'd tossed her that oh–so–knowing look when she'd tugged a stranger out the back door. Despite not looking nearly as nice, this place would have to do.

Lifting her chin, squaring her shoulders, and allowing her new, wilder side to guide her, Kat sauntered through the door. The room was warm, the air stale and sweat pungent. The back–lit bar stood on the far wall, each counter stool occupied. The hum of the occupants a roar, blended with the heavy bass pounding out of the speakers.

Taking a deep breath, she moved further into the bar, hugging the perimeter. She scanned the faces. There had to be a man here as fine and as appealing as her one–time lover. A man equal in size and ability, she thought with a grin.

But smiling didn't mean she wanted to be accosted by players who thought to make her their next piece of ass. She was a little more choosy.

"You want something, Sugar?" a twentyish looking guy asked her, rubbing one hand over her bare shoulder. "You want some of this?" He grabbed his crotch, the gesture vulgar.

Kat shivered, and ducked away from him. "I'm meeting someone," she whispered the first lie that came to mind.

"You're missing out."

"I'm sure." Kat didn't wait for a reply, but moved away from him quickly, scanning the bar for someone more respectable. Maybe a little older.

Not that she frequented clubs all that often—like never— but, she could tell right away the vibe here was different. Less welcoming. It was filled with a younger set, more thuggish with their oversized baggy attire.

More about one–night stands and less about finding that special someone. Ha! Kat laughed. Exactly what she wanted. A special someone—for one night only.

Finding an empty table, Kat slipped into the seat. She was only there for a moment before the waitress arrived and she ordered a drink, wishing she knew what she'd been served at The Night Kitty. Whatever it'd been had made her feel good. Good, meaning hot and ready. With her hands trembling nervously, mild, shy Kat looked for excuses. Any reason to high-tail it out of here for the security of home.

But she couldn't get laid at home. There was no order–in cock service like dialing–up for food delivery. Too damned bad, too, considering that would have been a hell of a lot easier than braving nightclubs like a panther on the prowl.

Sipping the blended fruit drink that had been placed before her, Kat studied the men assembled, looking for just the right mouse to get caught in her trap. She'd be careful not to hurt him. Not too badly, anyway.

She just wanted a wild screw 'em good game. One that would make her cum like she did for that fine piece of dark chocolate. The memory of him tingled vividly between her thighs and beaded her nipples shamelessly beneath the thin cotton of her braless top.

She may not be able to get her fill of Mr. Gorgeous here, but there had to be a good alternative. One less addictive. But equally satisfying.

And there were plenty of lookers—hot looking guys with nicely toned bodies. One of them would surely do. But most of the men with sex–appeal were already claimed by bitches in way less clothing. They had their claws sunk in, and weren't letting go without tangling.

With her stomach fluttering nervously, she looked out at the dance floor where couples were grooving, the beat of their hips thrusting like a well–practiced fuck. She filed it away to recall later. If it were only a little more interesting.

Kat's gaze moved over the boy toys, wondering which one she should select for pleasuring. Which one would get her off. There was a group of men gathered a few yards from her, one giving her the I'd–like–to–do–you eye. He was fine. A light–skinned brotha with a muscular body.

Drawing in a jagged breath, Kat tried to stand up. She would approach him and tell him exactly what she wanted. But her knees were weak and her legs refused to cooperate. Inside, a battle raged. Wallflower Kat hissed to stay seated.

If she was going to get the serving of hard cock she was after, she was going to have to seduce a guy into joining her. The man she'd been eyeing, maybe? But he didn't live up to the memory of her three weeks ago lover. The man who'd made the last nights unbearable to sleep. The reason she woke up hungry. Starving.

Covering her face with her hands, she realized she wasn't as brave as she needed to be. Not nearly as bold as she thought. Despite the back alley screw, she didn't have the balls for this.

It was one thing to do a stranger, another completely to pretend any of them would do when only one had gotten in-side her.

Kat stood so quickly her drink tilted and nearly tipped. Not looking back, she had to get the hell out of here. She fled out the front exit.

Taking a deep breath of the humid night air, Kat turned on her heels with a click down the pavement. She needed cock. Desperately. She needed tall, dark, and gorgeous. If there was a chance he'd be there, she knew just what to do.

She turned toward The Night Kitty.

Chapter 8

He was one pathetic puppy, Jamal realized, taking a swig of his beer. The third beer he'd nursed at a rate of about one per hour and the third damned Friday night he'd returned to The Night Kitty in hopes that *she* would too. He was a fool, completely sprung off of his one night back alley screw.

Taking another long drag from the tepid brew, he finished the bottle and closed his eyes, letting an exasperated breath whoosh from his lips. He was tired of this shit. Tired of needing to see her again. Tired of being tormented by reading Kat Mason's submissions over and over. Damn tired of getting rocked–up every time the words brought back memories of the honey's moans and tight flesh. A pussy he couldn't forget.

Too many nights he'd gone to bed, hard, aching, and restlessly alone. Burning with lust to see her again. To drive into her again.

But as the days had ticked away, confusion held on. He replayed the brick wall scene in his head, the neon lights, the pants dropped around his ankles and he wondered a million times who he'd fucked, and if it was going to leave him fucked in the end.

Dog school didn't offer advice on how to keep the player from getting played.

Opening his eyes, Jamal scanned the dimly lit bar, the crowd thick around the dance floor, a deep bass rhythmically thumping from the speakers. The entryway. Again.

Sliding a palm back over his cleanly shaven head, he realized they made words designed for men like him.

Pussy–Whooped. A pussy–whooped fool said it better.

She wasn't coming.

But hell, what did he expect? She hadn't been here the last two Fridays either. And over those long weeks he'd pretty much shaken the idea of his client being his sex–thing. Her words and his actions were pure coincidence. That's it. Kat Mason knew what a man desired sexually, and delivered.

On paper.

But her email demeanor had remained the same. Each time they'd chatted online after his one–night stand, he had a hard time believing that his down–home super–star author and his hard–core bang were one and the same. Nope. No way. One chick was his fantasy, the other was never happening again.

Damn!

Rolling his shoulders, Jamal figured it was past time to leave, to put this ridiculous fuck–lust behind him. Time to accept it. He was pathetic, and going home alone to a magazine.

"You leavin' so soon?" Kent asked, sliding up next to him, his silk shirt sticking to his skin from so much bumping and grinding. "You need to find a hit–it, stick–it, quit–it chick to pleasure you tonight?"

"Not what I'm looking for," Jamal replied, his gaze swinging away from the entry he'd been eyeing with a near a desperate beg, back to the pompous–ass standing beside him.

"Like hell you're not. Can't fool me, Dawg. I know what you're here for." Kent bucked his hips, spreading his hand out in a sweeping motion across the room. "Pick a hottie and get on with it, man."

"I'm out." Jamal stood, turning to leave a tip on the counter for the bartender, Lloyd.

"Hot damn! Would you take a look at that?" Kent whistled a breath between his teeth, rubbing his chin in appreciation. "Mmm . . . mmm . . . mmm!"

Feeling the stir of aggravation, Jamal glanced in the direction Kent was looking. His heart stopped cold. His mouth fell open, and hell if breathing didn't come to a halt. Blood rushed to his cock with dizzying speed.

His Fly–Girl. She was here tonight.

Thank God.

She looked different than she had before, but he couldn't mistake this fine–looking sister for anyone else. She was just a few feet farther down the bar and hadn't seen him yet. Chances were, she wasn't even here for him. Please, baby, he wanted to sing. *Baby, baby, please.*

"Check her out," Kent continued, grabbing his crotch. "I'm getting me some of that." He stepped forward.

Jamal put his hand on Kent's shoulder. Not with a firm grip or hard–edged bite, but the movement was menacing enough that it stopped Kent's advance.

Jamal didn't say shit. His heart thundered, but his mouth had gone dry. His eyes clung as the sweet thing leaned on the bar ordering a drink.

Dressed all in white, her light–brown skin glistened like it'd been frosted with glitter, a thin band of white cloth embraced her ripe, full breasts. Only slightly wider than the tube top, a white skirt draped from her hips, barely covering her luscious thighs, and leaving her midriff open for his appreciative eyes. All that smooth, light brown sugar skin.

Mile–long legs dripped like honey to the floor, sassy white leather strapping four–inch heels to her pedicured toes. Legs he'd do just about anything to wrap around his waist once more.

Peeking over one hip where her skirt drooped low, a string of her thong panties could be seen, encrusted with rhinestones.

A sparkling tease of *come–and–get–me*.

The bartender filled a glass on the counter in front of her.

"Put it on my tab, Lloyd," Jamal said, his voice huskier than intended.

Uncertainty plunged her brows forward as she turned toward him. Then her gaze settled on his face. Her eyes widened, the amber tone twinkling as she smiled. Not a tentative, unsure sort of grin. The whole nine yards. An I'm–happy–to–see–you, melt–chocolate smile.

"Thank you," she mouthed, her lush, glossy lips beckoning him with a siren song. Lips that had once been wrapped around his dick.

Had any blood been left in his body, it found its way to his throbbing erection. Her hair was changed tonight, pressed straight and smoothly pulled back so he could fully see the fine structure of her face. Model material. She could be gracing every magazine cover. She should be. *Was she agented?* briefly crossed his mind.

Whereas last time she'd looked wildly sexual, tonight she was purely stunning. Sexy as hell, yet elegant.

He wanted her. Any way he could have her. Mostly one way. Jamal wanted—no needed as badly as he needed his next breath—to be inside of her again. Now. He needed to sex this hottie or face disgrace of cumming in his jeans when she smiled.

Not sure how she balanced in the spiky–heeled sandals, she had no trouble stepping in his direction, every movement of her body sensual and alluring. "I'm glad you're here tonight. I was hoping you would be," she whispered as she drew close.

Would he look like a fool if he dropped to his knees and kissed her feet?

Shaking off his stupor, Jamal reached for her. Lightly grazing his fingertips over silken skin, he touched her shoulder, moved across her collarbone, then settled his palm against her drumming pulse, his fingers curving around the back of her neck.

"I've been waiting for you."

Her brilliant gaze settled on his. She stepped closer. A mere foot separated their bodies. The jostling crowd shifted around them. Dressed in white, her beauty was spotlighted against the dimness of the bar.

She licked her bottom lip. Oh, this honey knew how to hurt a man. His hard–on pled for mercy. She didn't grant him a single measure of relief, stepping closer even, the entrancing fragrance of her enveloping him.

"Thank you," she whispered, that damn smile of hers threatening his composure—again.

"You know her?" Kent asked, brushing his shoulder against Jamal's.

Hell no. But he wanted to. And, he'd fucked her. Jamal ignored the question. Kent wasn't worth the breath to explain. Besides, he could only focus on a repeat performance of the brick wall escapade.

He smoothed his thumb across her jaw line. "Let's get out of here."

She nodded, her intoxicating eyes flashing toward the back exit. The one they'd taken before. Hard–core was cool, but he had something else in mind. Something that would continue a little longer than the wham–bam of last time.

Sliding his hand down her arm, he took her delicate hand, her fingers instantly intertwining with his. "Come on." Easing away from her, he led her toward the front door, through the shuffling couples. The thrusting hips. The over–boozed, lust–crazed crowd.

"You leaving, just like that?" Kent hollered behind them.

Saying nothing, Jamal knew he must be grinning ear–to–

ear as the honey dropped into step beside him. The door couldn't arrive soon enough. Together they stepped out onto the sidewalk, the pink neon of The Night Kitty sign reflecting against her outfit. The tap of her heels on cement drowned out the bass rippling through the brick walls of the nightclub.

Thank God their first encounter wouldn't be their last.

Still holding hands, Jamal turned and looked at the eager Fly–Girl who'd already rocked his world. Despite the throb of his cock, there was the nagging worry that wouldn't vanish no matter how he tried. She had one hell of a pussy, but was she his Kat?

"Let's go someplace where we can talk," he said, his voice thick with need.

"I don't want to talk." Her voice was pure sex, just as his dreams recalled.

"What *do* you want?"

She hitched a hip to the side, the jewels on her panties sparkling under the street lighting. "Same as last time," she purred.

Shit. Groaning, Jamal held back the buck of impending orgasm. Ruff! Bad dog. Settle down.

Kat witnessed his body's reaction. The shudder that vibrated across his muscular frame spurred her confidence when wallflower Kat tried to make an escape from where wild Kat had locked her away.

They stood a moment, the hum of the bar seeping into the night air, electric energy infusing Kat with desire so strong her knees felt weak. Or was that fear? No. She wanted him. Badly. Her nipples tightened beneath the thin material of her braless top, straining further when Mr. Gorgeous's gaze settled there.

His thumb smoothed circles across her palm, causing an answering slickness to dampen her pussy. Her inner thighs. Oh, meow, this wasn't fear. This was bang–me–now, deep–down, soul–aching need. She needed to fuck, and soon.

"Where should we go?" she asked, moving up to stand before him, enjoying the way the hard length of his erection lurched against the skin of her stomach. Though he was encased in jeans, she could feel him well. She wanted the bad boy naked.

He cleared his throat. "I have an Escalade. Let's go." A sincere smile spread across his handsome face, his dark eyes warmed her core.

Kat followed Oh–So–Fine down the street for a block, her gaze swaying back the other direction several times. Toward home. Could she do this again? Should she? Indecision bloomed in her blood. What about all her moral dilemmas? As much as she lusted for him, as hot as he was, he was still a stranger she knew nothing about.

Mr. Gorgeous turned down a small alley where cars and trucks were parked along the narrow, dark street. She hesitated and nearly tripped, but his strong arm was there to support her.

She chewed her bottom lip between her teeth, the timid shy Kat coming on strong now, clawing the sexually needy Kat out of the way.

His voice was low and soft and understanding. "You're uncertain."

"Yes," Kat whispered. How did he know? "How do I know you're not dangerous?"

"Did I hurt you last time?"

She shook her head.

"But . . . ?"

"Are you married?"

He smiled, lifting his left hand, he showed no ring. "No."

"Have you ever been?"

"No." He tweaked her nipple between his thumb and forefinger, then circled lightly.

Her breath was jagged, with a little hint of a tiger–pant. "You're not involved?"

His smile broadened. A wicked gleam glistened in his eyes,

but his hand worked magic against the pert flesh being tamed by even the slightest of his touches.

"Only with my fantasies . . . of you."

Oh, yeah. She was going to give it to him good. "How far to where you're parked?"

Chapter 9

Beep–beep, and the automatic door locks popped open. With her palm warm where her skin touched his, Kat stood by his side as Mr. Gorgeous opened the SUV door for her. His tender touch and sexy–as–all–hell smile did wonders easing the fear that seemed to linger just beneath the surface of her aggressive kitty façade.

Fear? Yeah, right. The only thing Kat's body was afraid of was not getting served his ten–inch cock quickly enough.

There was no backing out now. Not while her body hummed with need, while her inner thighs ached with lust, while arousal poured through her more thoroughly than any alcohol ever had. Not while another deadline approached and her agent would be expecting new material again. She needed this. She needed him. *Meow!*

Shaking off the last twinge of trepidation, she glanced up at the tall, dark lover–man holding her hand, his midnight eyes sparkling with equally eager anticipation.

"Nice wheels, Bad Boy."

With his free hand, he smacked her firmly on her backside. "Nice ass, Fly–Girl."

Kat laughed. Oh, he knew how to play her game, and judging by the ridge of rock–hard flesh pressing on the front of his jeans, he was about as needy and ready as she was. Just the way she wanted him. And though fast and hard had been nice the last time, she sure hoped to take it a bit slower now. To appreciate his cock fully. Every thick inch.

Time to get on with it. *Or on it*. She'd waited hours for this. Hell, she'd waited three long, painful weeks. Two seconds felt like two seconds too long. Stepping up, Kat slid onto the leather seat, the new–car odor mingled with the masculine scent of the man who drove the truck. The man who rounded the vehicle in a hurry and climbed into the captain's chair beside her, closing the door with a finalizing thud.

The keys jingled in his hand as he tapped the steering wheel with his fingers. "Where do you want to go?"

The sound of his rich voice made her pussy tingle. *Wet.* "For a ride."

"Yeah?"

"Mmhmm, a nice, long ride," Kat whispered, smiling at him through the dark interior of the cab, her gaze dropping to his lap.

"Alright," he replied, reaching the keys toward the ignition.

"I'm driving." Kat moved from her seat across the open space. Spreading her legs, forcing her skirt to creep higher up her thighs, she straddled his lap.

"Yeah, drive me." The keys clunked to the floor.

With a groan, his hands moved up her legs, smoothed over her hips, then he hooked his thumbs beneath the rhinestones decorating the side–strings of her thong, while his fingers danced in circular motions across her skin in the most provocative way.

Supporting herself with her forearms against his chest, Kat rocked into him, feeling his cock buck hard against her cunt, the cloth from her panties rubbing against her clit. Need shot fast to her core. She stroked a palm over his cleanly shaven head, then downward, her fingers grazing his skin, touching the lobe of his ear. His dimpled cheek. His lush lips. ·

He kissed the pad of her fingertips. Kat sucked in a breath at his intimate gesture. She badly longed for his kiss despite knowing the pain that contact could cause her after this escapade. But she wanted to feel his mouth on hers, to taste his breath, to stroke against his tongue. To ignite a fire. Indecisive, her body wavered, leaning slightly toward him. Before she could act on it, he shifted her, pulling her hips down on his as he thrust in a fucking motion against her.

"You're *driving* me crazy." His tone was husky, his hands smoothing upward now, over her skin, pausing at her belly button, then moving toward the small tube top doing a poor job disguising the hard tips of her tits.

Jamal had died and gone to hell. Surely no angel would torture him this way, rubbing her fine little ass against his lap in a seductive dance of foreplay. Even with the lack of light, he could see her dark areolas and puckered nipples beneath the skimpy see–through cloth.

"Are you going to tell me your name?" he asked. Not waiting for an answer, he grabbed her top and yanked it down.

He wanted those luscious tits where he could see them. Feel them. Taste them. Leaning forward, he closed his mouth over one dark pebbled nipple, nibbled with his teeth, then sucked.

The hottie arched her back, pressing her flesh further against his lips, her ripe body draping over his steering wheel as her head lolled to the side. But her damn fingers didn't stay still.

Her soft hands and erotic touch moved over his body, inciting a rage of lust that hammered at his gut and throbbed in his dick. She stroked down his body, to his abdomen, then dipped beneath his shirt, swirling her fingers in the dark hair that plunged beneath his jeans and shorts.

She flicked the top button of his jeans open, then rather than finishing the job, squeezed the hard aching length of him through the material. Rubbing against him, he could feel the penetrating damp heat of her pussy and he'd never wanted his damn pants off more in his life.

Much more of this touching and he may just blow his nut and this would be over with. Just another wham–bam, don't-call screw. Exactly what he didn't want it to be. Jamal fought for control, breathing heavy as he feasted on tits made for sucking. Hell, everything about this honey screamed sex. *Fuck me*. And he planned to.

It may be wicked, doing a stranger like this, but this honey was pure heaven in the form of a body. The alluring fragrance of her arousal, the fine texture of her skin, the way she wiggled and moaned. Holy shit. Ruff! He was in deep trouble. And sinking.

He eased her nipple from his mouth. "Tell me your name," he demanded. His tongue lapped and swirled over the tight peak, across her perfect brown–sugar skin.

She answered with a moan that sounded more like a purr. "I want you."

"Your name?"

She squirmed against him, one of her hands returning to his button fly and working the next hole free. The next. "Does it matter?" she asked, gliding her other hand behind his head and dragging his mouth back to her begging breasts. He couldn't answer with his lips busy working against her flesh.

He mumbled a reply. "No." *Yes!* He needed to know who she was. He wanted to be able to see her again.

She freed his dick from his boxer shorts, her silken skin working him, stroking down to his balls, then ever–so–slowly up again. Like he could think straight now. Yeah. Bow–wow, he could only think of getting inside her. At least this time he was prepared. He'd shoved a few condoms into his wallet after the last time. They'd been there for three weeks.

Kat closed her eyes and tried to think. Tried to recall her emotions after their first encounter, but found her mind hazed with a fevered lust. He sure knew how to use his tongue. He moved it against her nipple with so much care she wondered how well he'd work her clit. Oh, kitty needed some of it.

She trembled. Finding a rhythm, she fondled his cock, pulling a dewy bead of moisture to his plum–shaped head, swirling it with her thumb. "Do you want me?"

He chuckled, causing a vibration to ripple through her body. "Can't you tell?" He pumped his hips.

Wild Kat knew. The old shy Kat needed a boost of confidence. "Say it. Tell me you want me."

"I want you." He sat back, leaning against the black leather seats, leaving her breast naked, wet, and feeling abandoned. A gloss of sweat lingered on his brow and shaven head, his dark skin shimmered in the minimal amount of street lighting filtering through the shaded windows. His intense eyes captured hers and he repeated himself, sounding deadly serious. "I want you, Sweetness."

Kat paused. *Sweetness?* She liked it. Pure sweetness. Smiling, she bent her head and broke her own rule. She kissed his mouth. Oh, those LL Cool J luscious lips. But she didn't stay. She just wanted a tiny sip so she could relive his taste and texture. When he tried to open his mouth, to capture her more fully, Kat moved away, pressing another slow kiss to the corner of his mouth, then his cheek.

Mr. Gorgeous brought his hands up to frame her face, bringing her lips back to his. He kissed her again, with that sort of half–opened mouth that caressed rather than claimed. And weakened her knees.

He suckled her bottom lip, then tried to deepen the kiss, sweeping his tongue across the line of her lips. Kat trembled. Shaking her head, she sat up. "No kissing."

"Why?"

Yeah, why, you ho? The timid Kat clawed at an answer to know why a little tenderness couldn't be included in this night of reckless play. Because of heart consequences later, hissed her reply. Recluse Kat wanted to be loved. Sexually needy Kat wanted a good bang. And it was the tigress in charge. "We're here to fuck."

"I brought something," lover–boy said, reaching for his wallet.

Kat wiggled her butt, pulling her short mini higher so it bunched around her waist. "So did I." She tilted her hips so he could fully check out her little white thong panties, complete with a small pocket in the front to hold a condom.

Tall, dark, yum laughed out loud. His hands went to the rhinestones resting along her hips. Sliding his hands forward, he caressed her through the cloth, then with his fingers traced the circular outline of the rubber she was packing in the front of her panties.

"I like. I've never seen anything like these."

"They're a novelty item. I've go–" Kat stopped and gave herself a mental warning. Author Kat had it all. For research. The man on the other end of her joy–stick wasn't supposed to know about that life. Her heart racing, she cleared her throat. "I've seen all kinds."

Jamal's eyes snapped to her face as he read the emotions play across her beautiful features. Her amber eyes glowed like a fire burned from within. There was something she'd almost said, but didn't. Fine. She didn't want to tell him about it. He'd do her good anyway.

Rubbing against her clit through those sexy–as–hell thongs, he turned the tint of worry on her face back into passion. She moaned, rocking her ass along the ridge of his dick as he stroked her. The cloth was wet.

Pushing the panties aside, he smoothed over the short, black manicured hair. He petted her velvety fur. *Nice little pussy.* Damn, he wanted in.

Easing open her labia with his fingers, he thrust two knuckles deep into the welcoming slickness of her cunt. She whimpered, rolling her hips against his hand, arching as she leaned back over his steering wheel while her stacked chest called for his attention, her dark pebbled nipples a candy offering.

Jamal could feel her inner thighs tense and ease as she rode his buried fingers, his thumb working at her clit. He could feel the tightening in her body as she fucked him. Just not his dick. His damn dick was about to explode, orgasm lingering at the end of each of her long breathy thrusts onto his lap. Holy shit! His poor nuts were going to be blue if he didn't get in her. Quick.

Putting a hand on her hip, he slowed her motion to a stop, her eyes finding his in the dark. "I need that condom," he said, working the foil packet out of the small pocket above her crotch.

"I'll do it." She took the packet from him and tore it open eagerly, though he caught the slight tremor as her fingers worked the latex from the packaging. "Push your pants down a little bit."

Jamal complied, shoving the cloth out of the way as she grabbed hold of his cock and touched his head with the cold lubricated plastic. He trembled. With delicate care, she eased it over his head, her breathing short and uneven as she rolled it down the length of him.

When he was fully encased, she eased up on her knees and brought his sheathed head to the opening of heaven. It took every bit of strength he had not to just buck his hips and enter her tight little pussy. The one she teased him with by shoving him in just an inch when what he wanted was to stick all ten in.

He was so hard he ached.

The seductress gave him another penance, sliding farther onto him, the tight hot walls of her welcoming his intrusion.

"Do you like this?" she whispered, leaning toward his ear as she held him half buried in the sweetest cunt he'd ever fucked.

Her tongue touched his earlobe, licking along the edge, then brought the fleshy part between her teeth and nibbled.

Aw, hell. That did it! Jamal put his hands on her hips and thrust upward. Powerfully.

She cried out, rocking her hips against his. Then the honey laughed, her breath sugared against his damp skin. "Oh, you feel *so* good."

"You like that, do you?" he teased, rhythmically stroking the hugging wet flesh of her pussy.

It didn't take much to convince her to play this game. She took control easily, riding his cock with long measured thrusts. Resting his hand against her round booty to urge her on, he leaned her back and sought her titty, suckling the beaded nipple in his mouth as they moved.

Jamal knew his SUV was rocking on the dark side street and that anybody going past would know exactly what was going on. They were fucking. Hard. He didn't give a shit. This honey knew how to give pleasure and he was damn well enjoying it. They may know what was up, but no one could see, thanks to the high–quality factory tint.

He held her hips firmly, plunging in wet pussy until her little purring moans grew louder, then her meowing turned to a scream.

Kat giggled between pants as she leaned back. This is what she'd wanted. A good hard screw, no bricks included. No batteries. Tall, dark muscle giving it to her just as she wanted him to. She'd tried to take it slow, to ease onto him, to make this moment last. To be able to remember it. She liked this.

Scaredy Kat didn't want to do this. Didn't want to like this so much. Didn't want to like *him* at all. But she did. A lot. Clutching her claws against his shoulders, all sorts of warning bells rang around her heart. But those alarms were silenced by desire, and the incredible feeling of fullness.

Those warnings were inside her, she could only hope damn hard that the vigorous movements of this mating didn't push the horn on the steering wheel that her back was pressed up against. A loud beep could bring their action to light to anyone passing by.

Untamed Kat laughed again. She was going to write this. The essence of erotic. She kissed his forehead, his brow, his closed eyelids. The soft skin below his ear, smiling against him. Moans mingling with his dark chocolate skin.

"Do you . . . need . . . harder?" Mr. Gorgeous asked, slamming into her.

"No." This was perfect. Ten thick inches of pleasure. Moving her hips back and forth, she was able to rub her clit against the pulsing cock inside her, bringing climax so close she could nearly taste it.

Inside her, she could feel the pulsing of his cock and knew he was about to lose it. That's all her body needed. Her muscles tightened, trembled, then she cried out. "Oh . . ." One last thrust and she was soaked in hot sticky orgasm, her body responding with a shuddering climax.

"Oh, Sweetness," the man beneath her ground out between clenched teeth, burying his face into the curve of her neck, his harsh breaths washing over her damp skin.

He came hard inside her. The pulsing of his cock told her just how violently. Long and raspy, his groan seeped across her, his pleasure settling in her heart. She liked that she'd brought him so much satisfaction.

He hugged her tightly to him, his t–shirt wet with sweat. Their breathing jagged.

When her skin began to cool, Kat eased off of his half–hard flesh. "I should go."

He framed her face with his hands. "Please, tell me your name."

"I can't tell you."

He kissed her collarbone. "Please." His voice was hoarse.

She swallowed hard. "Sweetness," Kat whispered, but it was breaking her heart. Secrets were like lies. He deserved better. She was afraid. She choked back a sob and tried to ease off his lap, but he held her.

"Are *you* married?"

"No."

"Then can I see you again?" He touched his forehead to hers, slanting his full lips over her mouth. He brushed a tender kiss against her, but didn't try to deepen it. "Please."

What could she tell him? That he was research, and she had no intent to get involved? She didn't take boyfriends. She had toys for the regular pleasurings. For the nightly needs. He was a diversion, but to remain anonymous.

Kat wanted to see him again. Hell, she wanted to take him home with her now and enjoy him again. Slowly. Devour him completely.

Taking a deep breath she cleared her throat. There was a way to continue this. If he played by her rules.

"Every other Sunday morning, I go to River Café for coffee and a muffin." She kissed his lips softly. A mere peck but it spoke volumes. "At 9:00 am."

Sitting back, Kat straightened her tube top so it covered her breasts, then reached for the door handle. "I've got to go."

"I'll drive you," he replied, his hands smoothing the skin around her waist.

"No. I've got a car." A taxi, but he didn't need to know that.

Besides, remaining anonymous meant he couldn't know where she lived.

She slid from the SUV, her heels striking the pavement. Shifting her hips, she allowed her skirt to fall back down her thighs, then turned away and walked down the sidewalk, not looking back. Reaching into her top, she looked for the cash she'd shoved there, but it was missing. It must have fallen someplace in his truck when he'd claimed her skin with his mouth. She kept walking. Forget the taxi, she'd walk all the way home.

She couldn't look at him again without wanting to go back into his arms. He knew where he could find her. If he cared about seeing her again—and shy and wild Kat hoped that he did—he'd be there. She'd see him again.

Chapter 10

In heels. She thought it'd be a good idea to walk home—all the way home—in four-inch heels. Admittedly, Kat reminded herself with a sigh, she hadn't intended to walk. Hadn't planned on dumping the cash out of her cleavage someplace in the dim interior of lover-boy's truck. More like he'd been the cause with his eagerness to get to her tits. Not that she'd minded. The memory of his LL Cool J lips nipping and sucking at her nipples was well worth the cost of the loss of three twenties. She'd be happy to pay double that to have him there now, keeping her mind off of the pain in her feet and smack-down on some tongue action. Meow!

"Oh, well. That's what I get for not carrying a purse," she mumbled, regretting the decision with each step. Sixty bucks would have been more than enough to catch a taxi. Including tip. And then some.

Little good the wad of money did her now, she surmised, trying to ignore the aching arches of her feet, or the way she cringed with each painful stride. Better to keep her mind focused back on finger-licking-good sex thing and all the yummy things she wanted to do to him.

With her inner thighs slick with cum—hers—it wasn't difficult to recall the way she'd left bad-boy fifteen minutes and one mile back. With his half–hard cock still sheathed in latex that glimmered in the overhead street lighting with her juices, and a brooding look of lust shining from his midnight eyes.

"Oh, baby," Kat whispered, her nipples puckering and fresh cream wetting her panties. The evidence of just how hot he made her feel. How sexy. How desirable. So far from the shy wallflower she believed herself to be. "How do you do this to me?"

She knew how. Chocolate–skinned lover had ten inches of glorious dick, and better yet, he knew how to work it. But there was more. Lifting her chin, she continued walking toward home, listening to the vibrating rhythm of her heels striking the pavement, pretending that these encounters were all about sex.

Pretending her emotions weren't involved after their first back alley fling—telling a bold face lie if she tried to deny it now.

Hell, if it was about ten inches of well–worked cock any man would do. Any dildo would give the same pleasure. But she didn't want man–made synthetic dick. She didn't want just any man.

She wanted two–time, no–name, fucks.

She wanted Mr. Gorgeous.

Even after just having him, she wanted him again. And again. Wanted the tenderness of his touch as his hands smoothed across her skin. Wanted the urgency of his mouth as he moved those luscious lips over her. Wanted the thickness of him shoved all–up–in–her.

Wanted to take him home and do him right.

But remaining anonymous meant not letting him know where she lived. Meant that she couldn't count on getting served his yummy body again, and could only hope that he'd use the info about where to find her every other Sunday.

She didn't want to see him again.

She needed to.

* * *

Kat was biting her bottom lip in agony by the time she let herself into the back door of her place. Not bothering with the lights, she sank into a chair and worked the straps of her sandals free. With a thud, one then the other dropped to the hardwood floor. Sucking a painful breath between her teeth, she rubbed her thumb against her arch. A searing burn shot up her leg.

A little over four miles was nothing. Nothing in sneakers and shorts. Four miles was way too long in four-inch spiked heels, a tiny mini, and a braless tube top.

The walk had taken more than an hour. She'd been forced to take longer routes several times to avoid areas she'd rather not cross through. Alone. Dressed like a hooker. In the middle of the night.

Her entire body ached.

A mewing whimper worked its way past her lips as she relaxed against the cushioned chair, her lids fluttering closed. Exhaustion mingled in her blood.

Sex lingered on her skin. The scent of cum. Of sweat. Of latex. Of him. Though her body was sated and her eyes tired, Kat had no doubt that it'd take very little to make her body respond to fine-brother-with-a-body-to-please.

Rather than fall asleep where she sat, Kat gingerly got to her feet, each movement stiff and arduous. Moving to the kitchen, she removed a bottle of wine from the rack near the fridge, a corkscrew, and a glass. Though the early evidence of dawn had begun to stretch across the neighborhood outside, and creep through her half-closed blinds and window coverings, Kat was strangely wound.

The rush of orgasm still burned in her blood. The headiness of climax still sang in her gut. Her heart still raced at the memory of his touch.

Emptying the first glass of wine, Kat refilled, then carried her drink upstairs to her master bathroom. A few minutes later she stripped naked and eased her body into a frothy jasmine scented bath. The hot water was a welcoming reprieve to the aches of her walk.

"Like this, Bad–Boy," Kat whispered. Pretending he was there, she grabbed a bar of soap, guided it across her flesh. An image of dark–chocolate skin rippling over muscle flashed behind her eyes as the cool bar made contact with her nipples, each straining desperately for attention. Pulling into tight peaks.

"Oh, baby, right here." She moved her hand downward, touching her belly. Lower. Caressing the wet folds of her pussy, pressing her thumb against her sensitive clit. Small tremors of pleasure shimmied through her body.

She imagined glorious brown skin and his gentle touch as she eased two fingers into herself, thrusting in as slow a rhythm as Mr. Gorgeous would if he were taking his time fucking her.

There was something sensuous about the lapping sounds of her flower–scented bath. Something alluring about the warmth and gentle way she stroked her flesh. Something exciting about imagining that those fingers making her feel oh–so–good were not hers. But his.

Reaching for her glass, Kat downed the burgundy liquid, trying to calm the rapid pace of her heart. A cadence more implicit with a good, hard bang than lounging in the tub. Than bringing about passion with her own fingertips. Her own strokes against her clit.

Masturbation wasn't new to Kat. She'd been single a long time. So what was different about tonight, she wondered, the thrust fuller now. Water sloshing to the floor. Moans breaking the silence of a new day.

What was different now? What caused the urgency as she worked her fingers deeply within her, thinking, imagining that lover–boy's cock was buried there instead?

A low, steady moan rent from Kat's lips, building in volume and pitch. Breaking in a scream as heat sped through her veins and the tiny tremors of her pussy clamped down hard on her hand.

Her entire body trembling, Kat sucked a breath deeply into her lungs, and leaned back against the chilled porcelain tub. The water was tepid, the scent of jasmine faded. The soapy bubbles gone.

Easing her cum slickened fingers from her body, Kat scooped up the bar of soap from the bottom of the tub and summoned enough strength to cleanse her skin, to wash away the odor of the bars she'd been in earlier that evening.

As the pink rays of sunshine claimed the eastern sky, she rose from the chilled water and wrapped herself in a fluffy white towel, her empty glass left bath–side and forgotten. Sliding into smooth, cool sheets, too exhausted to dry completely or bother looking for a t–shirt to sleep in, she thought about the intensity of her self–delivered orgasm.

What was different about it wasn't her.

It was *him*.

Chapter 11

Jamal's heartbeat pulsed hard beneath his blue silk shirt. It's not like it was unexpected. Hell, no. He'd known, if not with his cock, at least with his head. He'd been fucking his super-star. He'd suspected it.

Closing his eyes, he sucked a sharp breath between his teeth and held it until it burned. Slowly, like he didn't want to see the damn message poking fun of him on the computer screen, he forced his eyes to open and looked at Kat Mason's incoming email.

She was early for the deadline. Not surprising considering all the hot inspiration he'd given her over the last weekend. Aw, hell yeah, he'd seen this coming.

It was the condom–pocket panties. That had sealed the deal in his mind. Their agent–author relationship was unusual. He understood that, but Kat told him everything. Online, via their extensive email chats. Including about the assortment of novelty undies she'd picked up for research. So while he was filling her tight, wet pussy with his throbbing dick, he'd known who he was screwing. At least he'd been pretty sure about it.

Her submission had confirmed it. Sweetness. Fly–Girl. His hard–core fuck against the wall, the honey rocking his SUV. All his client.

Kat Mason. At least now he knew her name.

"Fuck!" Jamal stood, dropped his laptop onto the couch behind him, then paced across the hardwood floor. Hands balled into fists, breathing jagged. He'd waited all week to get it, all day to open her file. All day at the office it had tormented him, tortured him, but he'd held back his hard–on and waited. Waited for the privacy of home because he knew damn well this shit would be good.

It was.

Everything about her haunted him. The scent of her arousal, mixed subtly with perfume. The taste of her candied nipples on his tongue. The slight yet not nearly enough kiss. The sweetness of her lips.

Stalking back to the sofa, he glared down at the laptop, the Word file open and every detail of his Saturday night sex–me–good fling was outlined perfectly. Right down to the color of his Escalade. Screw that. The color of his boxer shorts. Every single one of her supposed–to–be–fiction words were from his few days old memory.

All except what she was feeling. Oh, he knew he'd made her cum, but judging by her submission, she'd loved every fucking minute of it. And wanted more.

"What am I supposed to do now?" he murmured to his empty living room. Flopping back against the pillows, he scrubbed a sweat dampened palm over his face. Kat was so quiet. Shy. Reclusive. In more than three years, he'd never talked her into meeting face–to–face. She'd always had her excuses. After a while, he'd just quit asking and accepted that she'd rather keep things from getting personal, or at least physically personal.

Her submissions were pure fantasy–fire, made to make a man hot. Every single one succeeded. But in her emails he'd been able to see feminine vulnerability. Sensitivity. For years he'd visualized an image to go with their relationship. The real Kat had by–far surpassed his wildest dreams. Even the wet ones.

There were moments when he and sex–pot were together, that he'd seen the doubts, worries, and insecurities he'd imagined from his client—in his lover's eyes. The same innocence.

Getting to his feet, Jamal walked to the kitchen, tossed a frozen burrito in the microwave and grabbed a beer from the fridge. He leaned forward, bracing himself with his forearms against the cool marble countertop, questions plaguing him. His head drooped in defeat.

"What am I going to do about this? I'm trippin'. What am I going to do?"

But that's not where the questions stopped. Hell no. Those were the easy ones. If he got the chance again, just like a dog, he'd fuck her. Whenever she wanted it.

No. The questions that lingered and jeered, they were far more serious.

Did she know who he was?

Had she been playing him? Faking it?

For some reason he doubted it. She thought he'd been a stranger, when all the while he'd been her friend. His daydream. His deepest nighttime desire.

The truth was, she did want to see him again. She'd told him exactly where and what time to find her. Jamal downed his beer, knowing he intended to use her info. So now the only thing left to do was figure out how to break it to her where their first encounter had led them. And wait and dream and suffer a half–hard erection until she was able to ease it for him again.

After a second read and a third beer, Jamal couldn't take the throb of lust wound into a ball of hunger burning hot in his gut.

Restlessly pacing his apartment didn't help. Fucking might be the only thing that could. A tight pussy to ease the bark of the dawg. Setting aside the empty, tinted beer bottle, he reached for the phone. Never being one to sit back and not be proactive, his fingers hovered over the keypad. Kat's number seared into his memory.

He'd call her. Talk to her. Maybe the purr of her voice would ease his desire. Or make it worse.

"To hell with it," he stated, jamming the pads of his fingers onto the well oiled memory of her digits. Maybe he'd be able to say something that would prompt her to tell him that she'd been fucking a stranger, which would lead to the opportunity for him to tell her "no stranger." Him.

It rang four times. About to pound down on the off button, a voice on the other end halted the action.

"Hello?" Her voice was rough, tainted with sleep. Husky. Sexy. And shot right to his dick.

"Hey, Kat. It's Jamal. You awake?"

Silence.

Had she hung up the phone? "Kat?"

Silence.

Fallen back to sleep? "Kat?" he repeated again, this time a little louder.

"I'm here," she purred through the raspiness of being awaken from what sounded like a deep sleep.

"You're quiet. Everything alright?"

She yawned. He could hear the rustling of blankets. Of her moving in her bed. "I was listening."

"To what?"

She sighed. "Your voice."

Damn. He about came in his pants. Jamal held his breath, fighting a losing battle for control of his libido. He wanted to be in her bed with her. Naked against her caramel skin. Kicking her blankets to the floor and getting her sheets wet with sweat. With the essence of their sex.

"Were you?" Jamal asked, adjusting the bulge straining behind his pants, then running his palm over his smooth-shaven head and gripping the back of his neck. "Why?"

"I don't know, Jamal. There was something about it." He could hear her moving in her bed again, the smooth swishing sound of sheets against her body. Her voice dropped to just above a whisper. "You sound different to me tonight."

Hell, why did her whispered words remind him of the tone a woman would take when she told her darkest desires in a man's ear after lovemaking, during the moments before they fell asleep. In each other's arms. He cleared his throat. "It's just me."

He could hear the smile in her voice. "Yeah . . ."

Massaging the building tension in his neck, Jamal struggled to think of an excuse for calling her. His gaze roamed across the room, falling upon his laptop resting on the coffee table. "I read your submissions tonight."

Did he hear a slight intake of breath from Kat on the other end of the line? Silence lingered again. When she answered, the words were airy, yet husky. "Did you like 'em?"

"They're good. Real good." You were better Friday night. *Better naked and riding me*, he thought. "You put those novelty panties to good use."

She stifled a yawn, the sound like she muffled it into a pillow. "I'm glad." Another yawn. "I worked on them late last night. Couldn't sleep until I'd hit send."

"Thanks."

"Jamal . . ." the sound of her voice trailed off.

She'd been about to say something he wanted to hear, he was damned sure of it.

"Yeah, Kat?"

"I was just . . . Nothing. You're welcome."

"Night. Sleep well."

"Oh, I am. Night."

Oh, yeah, she was his Fly-Girl, able to bring a man to his

knees with a husky bedroom voice and a choice of words that left him painfully, throbbingly hard.

He clicked off the phone, gripping it tightly in his fist. Groaning with urgency, he tossed it to the couch, then flicked open his button fly, tugging his heavy cock from behind the thin walls of his boxers. One strong stroke. Two. On the third, he came. Hard. The silence of his apartment shattered violently by the roar of his release.

Pearls of his cum littered the dark denim of his jeans. Their beauty mocking. He'd done this alone, aroused merely by the sound of her voice and the memory of how her pussy felt melting around him.

Hell. It was either jerk–off his nut or go to bed too damned aroused. And wake up blue. Walk like a bow–legged cowboy. Blowing his wad over Kat was the only thing he could do. His gaze skittered across the living room as he pulled in a jagged breath, his eyes settling on the shelf housing the stacks of Kat's magazines.

The truth was, she'd been doing this to him for years.

After a tepid shower and dressing in clean clothes, Jamal found he was still too wound–up to turn in. Instead he did something that would make his co–worker, Rebecca, happy. He called her friend, Tonya, for a second date.

Despite it being after nine, she willingly agreed to meet him at the small hole–in–the–wall bar at the end of his block. Within walking distance. Good thing. He'd about polished off a six–pack by the time he went out the door to meet her.

He arrived before Tonya and found a small corner table. He wasn't surprised that he had to wait close to thirty minutes alone before she arrived. During that time, he questioned why the hell he'd called her. He hadn't been interested last time they'd gone out on a date. Nothing had stirred between them. Nothing had jived, and despite being an attractive woman, she didn't make him hard. Didn't make him want it.

But if he'd just wanted to be aroused, to hit–it and quit–it for a single night, he had plenty of booty–call numbers programmed into his Blackberry. He hadn't used them. Instead, he'd called a down–home girl. The type of woman he could take home to Momma without creating a fuss.

Ordering a drink, he tried to ignore his motives. But they fought with him. Made him think. Why was he here waiting for a woman he really wasn't interested in?

Was it because deep–down he *did* want something more serious than booty–calls in the middle of the night? Than wham–bam don't–call–again encounters? Than fucks that were leading nowhere? That left him alone when she was through?

And he knew just who *she* was. She was the reason he was here. He needed distraction from his need. To forget that pulsing drive to see her. To claim her. To piss on every fire hydrant on her street like every respectable possessive dog staking out their claim.

"Hi, Jamal," Tonya said, making her way through the crowd to the table he'd chosen.

Jamal got to his feet. She looked nice, like she'd dressed to impress. Him. A low–cut blouse spilled out her breasts. Tight black pants hugged her curves.

"I'm glad you could make it," he said, leaning toward her to give her a quick hug.

Tonya didn't settle for an embrace, but planted her lips over his when he would have merely kissed her cheek. She opened slightly, her tongue darting out to run the length of his closed mouth. She was testing him, he knew. Testing to see if she was going home with him tonight. She wasn't. Kat was already there. Her file still open on his computer screen.

"I'm glad you asked," she said as she stepped back, her tone purposeful and overly seductive.

Jamal shrugged, feeling like an ass. Poor Tonya was being used. As a distraction. He needed to keep his mind clear until Sunday when he'd be able to see Kat again. If she showed this week at the café she'd told him.

Right. He needed a distraction and tonight Tonya was it. So he wouldn't be stuck at home wanting the woman who'd been his fantasy lover for three years. The real thing for three weeks. The force of his erection every three minutes.

Expelling a harsh breath, he asked, "Can I get you something to drink?"

When she smiled and nodded, then told him what she was drinking, Jamal moved away from her toward the bar. He may not take her home. But he could hang with her. Get to know her a little. Allow her to act as a substitute for the woman he really wanted to spend time with. His client. His money–maker, ass–shaker, heart–temptress, object of masturbation.

Fly–Girl. Kat Mason.

Chapter 12

Adjusting her shades, Kat fought back the tingle of apprehension dancing along her spine. She took a deep breath, lifted a warm ceramic mug, and cradled it in her palms as she relaxed in the morning sun. But faking confidence didn't help much. It only intensified how ragged her emotions were. How foolish it'd been to tell lover–boy where to find her.

Old Kat wanted nothing more than to flee. To return to the safety of home. Wild Kat refused to be pushed around, though admittedly, all of her was filled with anxiety.

Never having had much success in bouts of love, she came to the conclusion that her anonymous affair could only end one way. *Badly*.

But oh, the joy of being pleasured by a man who knew how to handle his business. Letting out a long–winded sigh, Kat bit her bottom lip to keep from smiling. Just the memory of his dark chocolate skin and brooding eyes made her feel wet against her panties. She'd never been so sated in her life. She'd never been so horny.

A hot current of awareness swept across her skin. She knew *he* was there. Every one of her cat senses knew it. So did her nipples. They tightened shamelessly.

Forcing a sip of the coffee past the tightness of her throat, she closed her eyes and willed her hands not to tremble. Nighttime exchanges were one thing. She should never have expected to manage a day–date interlude. Not that she planned much more than talking. Yeah, right. She'd take it when she could get it.

Turning slightly, Kat glanced up as Sex Appeal moved up beside her. Yum, he looked edible in the sunshine. Kat licked her lips like a kitten offered cream.

He must have taken her lip–wetting as an invitation. He bent and kissed her gently. Then retreated, damn him. Resisting the urge to sink her claws into his t–shirt and drag him back, Kat accepted the bouquet of white Casa Blanca lilies and Baby's Breath as he handed them to her.

Her heart tightened.

Full of unchecked male confidence, he sat opposite her, his muscular limbs sprawling over the small outdoor patio furniture of the river café. Their eyes met and held. Sparks ignited a flame in her gut. He looked good. Damned good. Reluctantly, she slid her gaze away from the sharp lines of his handsome face, to the soft arrangement of flowers.

"They're my favorite," Kat whispered, inhaling the subtle honeyed scent, then focusing on bad–boy and the devilish smirk turning his delicious lips.

He nodded with a hint of arrogance.

He studied her intently. Brows dipped forward, eyes dark and purposeful. She felt naked beneath his appraisal.

Feeling a bit out of place in her black capris and plain cotton shirt, a wave of heat rippled across her cheeks. Makeup free, hair pulled away from her face, it was much different than the sass of playing the bar–hopping diva. Would he like it, she worried. He'd only met sex–pot, not home–girl from next door.

"You look beautiful, Sweetness," he commented as if he'd read her thoughts.

Feeling a sense of relief, Kat smiled. "Thank you, Mr. Gorgeous."

He arched an eyebrow. "Mr. Gorgeous?"

She mouthed the word "You."

He chuckled, the dimple in his smooth cheek deepening.

"I wasn't sure you'd come." Kat paused, allowing her heart to slow. Desire didn't wane. "I'm glad you did."

"I was here last Sunday, too."

Kat bit her lip to keep her smile from getting too wide. "It was my off Sunday."

"Figured that out," he replied, shrugging those toned shoulders of his. "I waited for a while."

"Why?"

He grew serious. Leaning forward, he rested his forearms against the table–top. "I wanted to see you again." His tone was soothing and intoxicating. The last thing she wanted to hear at night. First thing in the morning.

His warm hand closed over hers, his thumb smoothing caressing circles on her palm. "Listen, baby, we need to talk."

Kat shook her head.

He nodded. "There are some things I have to tell you. Things you need to know." The comforting stroke of his fingers against her skin didn't ease the fear welling in her belly.

He was going to ask again. He wanted to know her name and wasn't satisfied with pretending. She didn't want to know who he was other than wham–bam, rock–her–world lover. Didn't want to be faced with the reality of life but to remain in the fantasy she'd created.

She dropped her gaze to their interlocked hands, willing away the desperate gloss in her eyes. The thump thump of her raging heartbeat drowned out the sounds of the breeze ruffling the river, of birds singing in the summer sky.

She shook her head again, took a deep breath, and lifted her eyes to his. "Please don't. I need this. *I need you.* But there are things I can't share. Nothing I want to know." Her voice was soft, but shook slightly.

"Nothing?"

"Nothing except when you'll be with me again."

Jamal's cock responded by thickening. Her fresh–faced beauty left him feeling like he'd been kicked in the gut. The soft pleading desire in her tone left him hard and aching.

He framed her face with his other hand, her smooth brown skin soft beneath his fingertips.

Alluring. *Seductive*.

"I want you, too," he managed to say, past the rising lust seeping through his blood. This was Kat, his client, his friend. He already knew he respected her. Cared for her. She was also the woman he wanted to fuck.

She turned her mouth and pressed a tender kiss into the palm of his hand. His dick bucked. Her warm whimpered sigh worked its way through his body.

"But there's something I need to tell you, or you'll resent me—"

"Please. I need this." She moved forward on her seat, worry etched around her stunning amber eyes. "Despite how we met, what's happened between us, it's not really who I am."

Hell, he knew she wasn't easy. That she didn't make a habit of screwing strangers. He knew her. Well. "I know, but—"

She cut him off again. "I'll be as honest with you as I can. I'm not married. Uninvolved. No children. I need you. I *want* you. But I can't tell you my name or what I do." She kissed his palm again, lingering a bit longer this time. "Please understand."

Jamal did understand. He didn't want to. Didn't want to accept the wall of privacy she'd created in order to protect the life of the erotica author who dwelled there. He didn't want to, but hell, he respected it. He had to. Or risk not seeing her again. Not being with her again. Not coming inside her again.

Oh, yeah, ruff, he was a dog for sure, because not getting more of her tight pussy wasn't an option. She wanted rules. If it meant he'd be able to keep fucking her, he'd live by them.

"All right, Sweetness." He could live with this. For now. Deep down, Jamal knew that one day the truth would come out. He'd face the consequences then. He only feared the truth would come sooner rather than later. Probably for the best, anyhow. The longer the sex–affair went on—Jamal knowing he was doing his client while she remained clueless—the more danger. For both of them.

Moral issues aside, he just couldn't bring himself to end it. He didn't want to.

She smiled, that beguiling smile that made his body ache. "I find I'm always saying thank you, but thank you, Mr. Gorgeous." She licked her lips, then said with a purr, "You won't be sorry."

Yeah, he would. He knew there would be trouble. His cock didn't care.

"So we'll see each other. Be together. Just no names, cool?"

Jamal took a deep breath, studying the woman he'd spent the last three years fantasizing over. Dreaming of touching. She sat before him so much more womanly, so much more sensual than he'd ever imagined. He couldn't get enough of her. All those nights of thinking of her as a faceless super–star were over. Her image was clear now and she was simply stunning.

He nodded, relaxing in his seat.

"So then, Bad–Boy, what should we do first?" Her tone returning to flirtatious. Sexual.

Jamal grinned like a kid in a candy shop. He was going to enjoy this. Lifting the menu from the table, he answered. "Breakfast."

Hell, what was he supposed to say? *Let me bend you over*

the table so I can eat your pussy—cream and berries—for breakfast? It may be what he'd wanted to say. What he would have said had they had privacy enough to ensure he could enjoy the feast of her.

But it wasn't appropriate for a Sunday morning coffee–and–muffin café. Not in public. Not in broad daylight.

Not when Kat was looking so much more like a woman than a sex–object.

Keeping his gaze trained on the words of the menu, although not seeing a single item, Jamal fought a raging battle with his blood. There simply was no way to keep his dick from getting hard. But then most of his thoughts were coming from the wrong head.

He could hardly think. Could hardly do anything except wonder how quickly they could order and eat. And get the hell out of there. He didn't want to sit in the morning sunshine. Didn't want to feel the heat of the sun on his back, but wanted Kat on hers. Beneath him. Giving him all the heat of between her thighs.

Ruff. The dog in him needed to chase a little pussy.

"Mr. Gorgeous?"

It took him a moment to realize she was talking to him. He glanced up, surprised to see the look of concern etched on her beautiful face. "Yeah, Sweetness?"

"You're not having second thoughts, are you?"

Jamal laughed out loud. Like hell he was. "No, baby, I'm not."

She scooted forward on her chair again, leaning forward over the table. "You looked angry."

"I was concentrating."

"On what?"

Jamal dropped the menu to his lap. Probably a good idea to cover up the length of his erection pulsing in his pants. Leaning forward, he met her halfway across the table. He framed her face in his palms, tenderly stroking over her bottom lip with his thumb. Slanting his head slightly, he whispered in her ear. "On just how I'm going to fuck you as soon as I get you alone."

He was rewarded. She sucked in a sharp breath. Allowing his gaze to slide down the light brown skin covering her neck, her collarbone, her ripe breasts, he was rewarded with the delicious vision of tits crested in dark, tightened nipples.

She closed her eyes, long dark lashes leaving shadows on her cheeks. Unconsciously, she ran her tongue along her lips, wetting her mouth and leaving it oh–so–ready for his kiss. If she'd allow it.

As if she read his mind, she pulled back slightly, her vivid eyes open and brilliant. "Should we leave now?"

Again Jamal laughed. "No, Sweetness. Eat."

"But . . ." Her gaze dropped from his to the edge of the table that shielded his lap.

He knew the look. What she wanted.

"Eat. You're going to need your strength."

She sat back, flashing him the sex–pot smile. The seductive smile that pulsed the blood in his cock hard. Her voice dropped. "Promises, promises." She was the siren again, luring him to doom.

"Oh, you think I'm playin', girl? You better eat," he said with a wink, silently telling her how good he planned on working her.

She grabbed her menu, opening it before her. "I'm suddenly *starving*."

Fuck. He was in deep trouble. Not only did he already know he liked filling her up with his dick, but now he knew he liked being with her. Liked her sense of humor. Liked the way her eyes shimmered with concern, then brightened so easily with desire when he touched her.

Oh, there would be danger if he went down this road, but he was going. Kat was worth it.

Chapter 13

Kat waited just outside the café while Mr. Gorgeous settled the bill. Closing her eyes, she breathed in the freshness rolling off the water. The slight saltiness of the sea, mingled with the late–summer annuals.

Opening her eyes, Kat moved down the sidewalk to a small wooden bench visible from the front of the River Café. Where she could see Bad–Boy clearly when he exited. Where he could see her.

People bustled in and out of the small restaurant, some staying to eat. Others leaving with paper cups of steaming coffee. The line at the register had been long, but she'd chosen to wait outside rather than with her lover. Just in case he used his credit cards or the attendant used his name while he paid.

Instead, she'd kissed his cheek. Thanked him for buying breakfast, then boldly whispered in his ear what she planned to do in exchange for his generosity. Dessert after their coffee cake. Kat smiled like she knew a good secret she wasn't going to share.

Easing back on the bench, she turned her face to absorb the warm sunshine. When deadlines were tight sometimes she felt like she didn't see the sun for days. Didn't get outside. She missed it.

Taking a deep breath, Kat found it hard to believe just how relaxed she felt. How at ease. Unusual for her. She didn't like sitting in public. People made her nervous, always afraid someone would know who she was. That prickling feeling you get when someone is watching you. But there never was. After more than three years working as a word–prostitute she was surprised she hadn't gotten over the need to always look over her shoulder to see if someone was looking her way.

But not today. Not now. He was the reason. It was Mr. Gorgeous. The tender way he gazed in her eyes. The care he used listening to her. The proud confidence in his voice. His gentle manner. His charm. Oh, the way he looked at her like he'd like to eat her with a spoon. Yum.

Hell, was there a thing about him she didn't adore? Not–a–one she could think of. Except that they weren't fucking yet. Hey, she'd eaten her breakfast to get her strength up, despite the nervous excitement fluttering in her gut. She'd downed the meal because of the memory of his promise.

Oh, baby and what a promise it was. Sigh.

"I love your smile."

Kat startled as a man stepped into her sunlight. A shadow fell across her face. But it was *his* voice. She was surprised, not frightened. So intent on her lust, she hadn't even noticed his approach.

Smiling, she looked up at him in awe again that this luscious hunk–of–a–man would give her a second look let alone want to spend time with her. "Thanks," she whispered. "And for breakfast."

"Thanks for inviting me."

Scooting on the bench, she patted the seat next to her. "Want to sit with me?"

"I thought maybe we'd take a walk, Sweetness. Sound alright?"

Kat nodded.

He reached for her. His large fingers enclosed around hers, and with slight pressure, he helped her to her feet.

Inches from his chest, she could smell the spicy masculine scent of skin. Soak up his exuding heat. Hotter than the sun. It caressed her body. Tempted to lean into his solid embrace right there on the sidewalk, instead Kat stepped away.

But he held her hand.

It was a gesture that was so simple, yet it stole her breath away.

Walking along the boarded beachfront, his fingers laced with hers. Almost instinctually. But simple or not, it made her feel valued. Important. She struggled to swallow down the lump clogging her throat. No–name lover was giving her more than any ex–boyfriend ever had. Not like there were many of them.

Still . . .

Sliding her gaze in his direction, Kat looked for the right thing to say. She was captivated by his profile. By a lush mouth that had kissed her body but never her lips. She shivered. Repressed a moan that sounded like a sigh. But they walked on in comfortable silence.

People wove around them, couples with strollers. Twenty–somethings on rollerblades. Teens and children laughing and playing. It made Kat long for things she had no right to desire. At least not with him. Not Mr. Gorgeous. Any man she was with would need to know what she did first. So did Lover Boy but she was afraid the knowledge would chase him away. She wasn't ready to be alone again. Wasn't ready to return to research toys for release.

She wanted the hot–blooded man covered in luscious brown skin and muscle on the other end of her ten–inch joy–stick.

She moaned softly.

"What are you thinking about?"

Kat glanced over at him wondering if answering with *your dick* would be acceptable. "You."

"Oh, yeah? What about me?"

She shook her head, sliding her gaze away from his.

"Hey." His hand tightened around hers. He tugged her to his side, then smoothed his thumb across her palm in calming circles. "Tell me, baby," he said, leaning so he could say the words against her ear.

His warm breath slithered across her skin. Her nipples puckered. Her panties dampened. "I was thinking about your promise."

"My promise?"

She lowered her voice. "How you're going to . . . Where?" *Fuck her*?

Jamal laughed out loud. Oh, yeah, he was going to do that. No doubt. But there it was, the sexy combination of seductress and innocence. Couldn't wait to be boned, but didn't want to ask for it. He'd make her ask. She'd be asking—begging—for it by the time he was through.

Glancing around, he searched for a bench along the beach. One shaded with some trees.

"Come here, Sweetness." He turned them down a narrower path, away from the main walk. It was a wheelchair ramp, but led around the side of the busy boardwalk. The path parted again. He led her down the less–traveled trail.

"Where are we going?"

"Here." They rounded a cluster of tall Agapanthus, the white blooms swaying gently in the breeze rolling off the sea. Several tall willow trees draped over a wooden bench. Sunshine speckled the sandy ground.

"We're going to," her voice dropped, "do it on a bench?" She glanced around. Her brow furrowed when she continued, "Bad–Boy, people could come up on us. Families."

"Trust me."

He stepped forward, but was halted by the hedge of her hesitation. "Baby, we're not getting naked." He kissed the silken skin beneath her ear. "You're not fucking. Not today."

She attempted to draw back. To speak.

"Shh," he said, putting two fingers over her protest. "I'm going to take care of you."

Her white teeth chewed her bottom lip. Damn, it's what he wanted to do. Get that full lip of hers into his mouth. Lave it with the attention of his tongue and teeth.

"But—"

"Let me show you."

She nodded.

Jamal damn near pounded his chest and roared in victory. Despite the drumming of pulse in his dick, making it hard for him to think, except for of one thing, he led her to the bench and sat down.

"Sweetness, like this." He guided her down beside him, turning her into his side. His arm draped behind her, about her waist. He angled toward her, her back toward him. Putting his hand on her knee, he felt her tremble.

He smoothed his palm up her inner thigh, the material of her capris not slowing the up-glide of his stroking. When her breathing changed, he lifted her leg, pulling it back and settling it over his thighs. Okay, hell, the pants were in the way. He silently cursed. Fuck, he wanted to dip his fingers into her pussy.

But this wasn't about him.

This was about pleasing Kat. About showing her that he was worth the risk she was taking to be with him. She'd mentioned her needs. He was going to make her need him. Badly.

"Yeah, baby, like this," he said against her ear, taking the globe between his teeth. Dipping his tongue. Running it along the shell-curve, down her soft skin to where her pulse soared.

"Oh."

"Close your eyes. Imagine you're naked. Imagine the twinkle of sun you see on the water is the brilliance of the moon. Stars."

She nodded, her body heaving as a deep breath seeped from between her lips.

"I'm here with you, baby, and I'm going to make you feel so good. Do you want that? You want me to make you cum?"

She nodded.

"Say it."

She sobbed a needy sound. "I want you."

"To touch you?" He danced his hand up her inner thigh to where heat damped her panties. Capris. He flicked his thumb against her.

"Yes."

"Like this? To touch you like this?" He rubbed a circle over her pussy. Over her clit. Smoothed his tongue across her throat. Lapped like a dog against her heartbeat. "You want me to rub you like this? To pleasure your clit?" he said when her body shuddered before him.

"Yessss."

Jamal grinned against her skin. "Tell me."

Her word was breathy. "What?"

"Tell me you like it."

She made a sound in her throat, but didn't speak. He rubbed harder against her pants, pressing the material into her, wet now, soaking his fingertips. He moved his other hand to her breasts, taking the full globe in his palm. Then rolling the puckered brown nipple between his thumb and forefinger.

"Tell me," he growled, his hard–on making demands.

"I like it. I like . . . it . . . when you . . . touch . . . me." Her words were broken. Her body writhing against his, her hips rotating against his hands.

Oh, yeah, she liked it. Fuck. This was one stupid idea. What was he, into self–torture? Why the hell had he thought this was a good idea? Sure, his client would get off, but he'd go home blue.

Hell no. Brilliance hadn't been around when he'd decided on this idea.

Sucking air between his teeth, he was hit in the gut with the sharp scent of arousal. Of wet pussy. His balls drew–up tight against his body. His cock bucked hard in his pants.

Dipping his head, he closed his mouth over her nipple. The shirt be damned. He drew the hard candy into his mouth and sucked. Sucked in a rhythm he matched with the trusting of his hand to where she wanted him. Where he wanted to be inside her.

"Oh my God!" Her body tensed. Hard. Then shattered against him, trembling violently. "Aaahh," she moaned, but turned her face into the curve of his neck and cried out her climax. Tremors continued to shake her. She clung to him, her jagged breathing and soft whimpered moans were just about his undoing. About came in his pants like a man who hadn't fucked in years.

Hadn't been with a woman two weeks ago like he had. Jamal glanced at Kat, embracing him with her eyes closed and her mouth half opened. This was no ordinary woman. She'd been his fantasy for years. He'd longed for her. Dreamed of her. Now that he had her, he doubted he'd ever get enough of hitting it. Of sinking into her. Fucking her.

Hell, he wanted her now. The bench, daylight, the fact they weren't entirely alone acted as his restraint. He didn't claim to have any where this kitty was concerned. But this affair couldn't last. He knew it. If he thought differently, he was barking up the wrong tree.

She'd hate him when she figured out he knew who she was and didn't say anything.

"Mr. Gorgeous?"

"Yeah, baby?"

"I like what you did to me," she whispered in the sweetest voice he'd ever heard.

He kissed her temple. "I'm glad."

"Thank you."

"Don't mention it."

She sat up, looking him in the eye. "I mean, thank you for doing this for me. For allowing me these pleasures without pressuring. You're exactly what I needed."

Jamal's chest swelled. Why did it burst his pride to hear it? His dick responded the same way. Filled up all hard. Throbbing. She was just what he needed, too.

He nodded. "When's the next time I can see you?"

She leaned into him, resting her cheek over his heart. Her eyelids fluttered. Drifted closed. "Is next Saturday night soon enough?"

Hell no! his cock protested.

"Yeah. Where will I find you?"

"Where I found you," she whispered, tapping her fingers to his chest.

"The Night Kitty?"

She nodded. Her breathing became even.

Jamal stroked the back of his knuckle against her soft cheek, holding her in his arms. He'd see her again. Be inside of her again. For now, he was content to watch her sleep.

Chapter 14

"**Y**ou need to get a little pussy."

Jamal damn near choked on his swig of Gatorade. Oh, he was getting some, no doubt about it, but Kent didn't need to know.

Swallowing down the half–frozen Lemonade Ice, he swiped his forearm across his dripping–with–sweat face. "Oh, yeah? Why do you say that?"

"Because your game is off, my brotha." Kent flashed that golden–toothed smile. The one that declared his was a playa with a dental bill. "I'm putting you on the Learning Express." He bounced the basketball.

"The Learning Express?"

"Where you getting schooled!" His grin widened.

Jamal took another deep drink, swallowing the frosty refreshment as he contemplated how to respond to the comment, and what the hell it had to do with getting fucked. "And pussy would help, how?"

Kent bounced the ball. The thud echoed off the hardwood floor and hollered through the empty gym. "Don't you know, man? When you're busting your nut often enough, you're not focused on it so much."

Jamal shrugged, trying to follow Kent's line of logic. Not

that there was one. Just smack talking. Blowing smoke. "And if my mind isn't on my nut?"

"Fool." He shot the ball toward the net. It dropped through with a swoosh. Kent caught it again, then passed the ball to Jamal. Hard. "Then you can keep your head in the game."

Grinning, Jamal would have loved to shoot down Kent's theory. But his game *was* off. He wasn't handling the ball the way he normally did. Didn't feel the same drive because his mind *was* elsewhere. But not for the reason Kent suspected.

He was fucking. He'd busted–a–nut recently enough. He'd been getting all–up–in–some pussy.

His client's.

That's why he was distracted. Why he lacked concentration. Not because his cum was so back–logged that it was oozing into his brain, but because he'd been blowing his wad into the only woman he was one thousand percent sure he shouldn't have. His super–star.

And to make matters worse.

He knew it.

She didn't.

Shooting the ball, Jamal tried to see only the net. Not the way her eyes looked a few days back when they'd met at the café and she'd told him just what she wanted from him. His dick.

No relationship.

She was all woman Sunday morning. All girl–next–door, take–home–to–momma woman. Not the sex–pot he'd hooked up with a couple times at The Night Kitty. Fresh–faced and innocent was so different than the sassy chick who had seduced him. Seduced him with mile–long legs and an ass that'd make any man with a heartbeat beg.

But there were also things about the two that merged. Like the hunger in her amber eyes. The quick–burning response to his touch. On the bench, she'd melted in his arms and he hadn't even taken off her clothes.

"Hey, man, why don't you go back to The Night Kitty with me later tonight?"

Kent's invite startled him out of his memories. Just in time, too, to keep his hard–on from getting too thick.

Jamal glanced at his watch. Ten–thirty on a Wednesday. He had to meet with a publisher tomorrow for breakfast. Had clients to consider and portfolios to put together. "No thanks."

"Come on. I've had good luck there. The give–it–up girls are abundant," Kent said, grabbing his crotch. "Get show-ered. By the time we get there the hotties will be all sauced–up and hot–to–trot."

He shook his head.

"You practicing celibacy? Gay?" Kent grabbed his crotch again, thrusting his hips. "Ain't got the goods?"

Wild Kitty–Kat seemed to enjoy how well he was hung.

"Yeah, that's it, man."

"You know what the white chicks say to justify their dudes."

"What's that?"

"Not the size of the boat, but the size of the wave."

Jamal rolled his eyes. Dumb–ass couldn't even get his put–down straight. What kind of woman was he taking home each night? Clearly not one with any brains. "Not the size of the boat, but the motion of the ocean."

"Yeah, whatever."

Jamal laughed. Right. Whatever. Grabbing a small terry–cloth hand towel, he dragged it across his face, drying off the sweat, then back over his smooth–shaven head.

"So you coming or not?"

"Not." He bounced the basketball. "I think I'll stick around here. Shoot a little more. Try to get some lifting in be-fore I head home."

Sticking out his hand, Kent gave Jamal a pound. "Suit yourself, man. You'll be missing out."

"You can tell me all about it."

Kent nodded. Permission or not, Jamal knew that bragging is exactly what Kent would be doing for the rest of the week if he managed to hook–up tonight.

"All right, then man, I'm out. Catch you on the flip–side."

"Enjoy."

"You know it. The ladies love me. Can't wait for brotha man Kent to give them what they've been missing. Serve 'em up some of this." He Vanna White–d his body.

Jamal laughed. Oh, yeah, what a pompous ass. Giving a final tilt of his head, he turned his attention back to the basketball as Kent left the empty gym, the door echoing as it closed.

Bouncing the ball, he ran a lay–up at the net, but it swirled the rim, then bounced out. Jogging around the perimeter of the hardwood, Jamal quickened his step and charged for a dunk. With a powerful thud the ball finally dropped through the net.

Feeling like testing his success, he trotted back and arced a 3–point shot. It smacked the back–board and fell off to the side. Damn! He recovered the ball and moved to within free–throw range. "Shit!" Another miss.

"To hell with this," Jamal said, dropping the ball into the bucket of gym equipment and retrieving his athletic bag from the bench.

Clearly, his mind wasn't into basketball tonight. He knew exactly where it was. On Kat. Wondering what she was doing. Was she typing? Making up a not–so–fictional fiction story about a couple on an ocean–side bench?

Would he be reading his story by this time next week?

Probably.

His brow wrinkled, unsure if that was such a good thing. Hell, her writing was incredible. He relived every stroke. Every touch of her skin with every word he read. Every word making him so damn hard he would about burst.

With his fingers tight around the nylon straps of his bag,

Jamal headed to the main part of the gym where the weights and cardio machines where set up.

When he reached the free weights, he stripped off his soaked shirt and dropped it over his bag, then flung his towel over his shoulder.

He'd pump the iron. A meek substitute to the physical release he'd prefer right about now. Damn dick of his seemed to suck the blood from the rest of his body. At least pushing the weighted bar was a good way to work off the pent-up frustration of Sunday's giving-her-pleasure but going home to handle-his-own-business.

Hell. Jamal gritted his teeth, his need for her always with him. No matter where he was and what he was doing. He closed his eyes and recalled how he'd spent Sunday evening. She'd been so wet that her arousal had poured through her thin pants and dampened his fingers as he'd stroked and rubbed against her. For that, he was rewarded with an evening tormented by the scent of her cunt.

The perfume of her cum.

It'd left him hard.

Aching.

Needing his client, his super-star, his lover in a bad, bad way.

He worked the iron. When his shoulders started to burn and the blood had seeped from his blood to his cock with lingering thoughts of Kat, he grabbed his things and headed toward the locker room. He needed to find escape. Something to keep his mind off his Fly-Girl until he could see her again.

Chapter 15

She was mortified. Kat closed her eyes and took a deep breath. Keeping her back to the glass, she fumbled behind her for the clanging bell that signaled their arrival to the staff. Gripping the cool metal, she hushed the ringing, then slid a glance to the front register area to make sure no one had noticed.

Incense perfumed the air, swirling the spicy smoke into the air—a decidedly exotic flair. It stung her eyes and burned her lungs. Or was that the tears of embarrassment and the breath she held?

A sex shop!

What the hell was she doing here? She narrowed her eyes and glared at Sasha. It was all her fault. Sasha had insisted. Something about a new man she'd met and looking for a little something special for a date—a booty-call probably—she had with him later that night.

"You know, girl, maybe I'll just wait in the car," Kat said, pressing into the paneled glass door and hoping the excuse would fly.

"Like hell you will."

"Just get something, and let's go."

"Damn, Kat, do you have to be such a prude?"

Her soon–to–be *ex*–girlfriend rolled her eyes and turned her attention to a sale rack of lingerie not far from the door.

Heat sped across Kat's cheeks. Did Sasha have to use her name? "I'm not," she choked out. Besides, she was no prude. She had toys. Lots of them.

From the internet!

She didn't go inside sex–supply shops to get the goods. That's what computers were for. Shit, Sasha would have a conniption if she had any idea what sorts of things she had stashed away in the back of her closet. In her top drawer. In the bedside table. In boxes lining the spare closet in the up-stairs hall. In the glove–box of her car. Out in the towel bin by the hot tub.

Fuck!

Her skin burned now. She didn't realize just how much she had until she started thinking about all the places dildos and vibrators were stored throughout her house. They were re-search after all. Being mobile with her laptop, that could mean she'd write anyplace she settled into a rhythm. The couch? Her office? Bed? The lounge chair in the backyard? Whatever.

"Come here, girl, you got to check out this outfit."

Kat shook her head, suppressing the thoughts of the pink, purple, dark–chocolate, and black molded plastics she had at home. Turning her attention to her friend, Kat lifted her chin. Squared her shoulders and walked.

A huge step that increased the thundering her of her heart.

Breathe, woman!

"What you looking at?" Kat asked, moving up beside Sasha.

She was holding these funny g–string underwear for men. They weren't merely undergarments, but had the most ridicu-lous fronts Kat had ever seen.

"What's this for?" Kat lifted the trunk of the elephant g–strings.

"For a dude's dick."

"I know. But do guys actually wear this shit?" How would they fit? Bad Boy would bust these seams out. Elephants may be huge, but you wouldn't know it looking at this itty–bitty strip of cloth.

"I guess."

Not my ten–inch sex–toy with a pulse.

Sasha grabbed another. "Look at this one." She held up what looked like a blue collar button–up and the cock was supposed to fit inside the tie. "This would be hilarious for my boss."

"Sexual harassment, more like."

Sasha laughed. "Not if I've fucked him."

"You're bad, girl."

"Shut–uuup! You only wish you were me," she said, adding a wink.

"I don't need to be you to get satisfaction."

"No you don't, Kat. You're hot. You could really turn a man inside–out if you knew how to work it right."

If she knew how to work it? Kat damn near choked. If the amount of fan mail that came in for Glory Cockin was any indication, Kat knew how to work it real well.

On paper.

And, with Mr. Gorgeous. Yum. Just thinking of him wet her panties.

"These things are retarded. Let's see what else they have here." Holy shit! Did she just say that? Kat could hardly believe the suggestion of staying longer had even come out of her mouth. But hell, she was here now, might as well see what other sorts of little treats they had. Besides, it was kind of interesting to see the items in 3–D before she decided to buy.

For research. *Sure, sister, keep telling yourself that*, Kat thought with a smirk. No need to openly admit that no matter how much soap she'd used, a good number of her toys hinted the scent of her cunt.

Okay, fine, she'd used them. *All.* But she wrote fantasies, and needed to know how good an orgasm could feel when the rubber wiggled this way or that. When it rotated in just the right direction to hit her G–spot. When it slid along her clit with just the right amount of friction.

Kat gulped. Squeezing her thighs together, she fought off the need to go running out of the small shop. She could run home and handle this right quick. She could scour the city and look for her dark–skinned lover boy! Oh, God, she wanted him.

Kat had to change the directions of her thoughts.

She turned toward Sasha who was going through a bin of the glow–in–the–dark rubbers. "How often do you come here?"

"Not often. But tonight is special."

"Got a booty–call?"

"If you want to call it that."

"What do you call it then?"

Sasha shrugged. "I don't know. I'm going to fuck this dude for the first time. I want to give it to him a little special, you know."

Kat was silent.

"Oh, never mind. You don't know. You really do need to get a man."

Ignoring the comment, Kat said, "So you just met?"

"Actually no. I've been out with him a few times. Tonight he's going to get lucky."

Impressed, Kat stared at her friend. Usually Sasha sexed a guy the first night if she liked him. Called herself a liberated woman who could find the right dick to please herself rather than using her fingers.

"So why'd you make him wait? That's not like you."

"Fuck you, bitch." Sasha laughed as she swayed her hip to the side. "You calling me a slut, sweetie? Am I going to have to kick your ass tonight?"

"I don't know, ho, I guess if the rubber fits," she giggled, lifting a handful of the packaged latex and tossing 'em playfully at Sasha.

"Ooh, are shy kitty's claws showing? You surprise me, Kat. Didn't know you had a wild side."

Kat's reply was a shrug. *If she only knew.*

"I guess I'm making him wait because I like him."

"I thought you don't make them wait *when* you really like them."

"No. I mean, I like this guy. He's an asshole. Bad. Playa bad. But, I dig him."

Kat turned her attention away from her friend. Instead, she took a moment to examine a row of edible body paints in every possible color. Flavor. She didn't understand women who were attracted to men who would use and abuse them. She was a little shocked that someone like Sasha would be suckered that way. Sasha who personified confidence and femininity. And founder of the women's get–it–when–you–want–it revolution.

"So why you seeing him again if he's a playa?" she finally asked. Why would a woman deliberately let themselves be played?

"He won't be playing me, if that's what you're thinking."

"Yeah. How do you make sure you're not the bitch on his play–of–the–day schedule?"

"Because I'm giving the brotha a chance, that's why. If he steps–up to another chick, you best believe he'll be getting his ass kicked to the curb."

Kat was silent for a moment, afraid to think about Bad Boy's history. She didn't know it. "Why risk it if he has a doggie–dog history? How do you know he won't fuck up while you're giving him the chance?"

"You can never know for sure, sistah. Unless you're with your man 24/7 there is no way to know if he's all he says he is. Unless you trust him. Sure, this dude is used to bouncing.

But that's why I made him wait to get a piece of this." Sasha slid her hand down her waist, then back over her ample ass.

"So you made him wait and work for it."

"Exactly. Got him all hot—and hard—on a few dates. I intend to bring him down a notch. See if I can just tame this dawg. Tonight I'm giving it to him so fucking good he won't be able to walk, let alone look for different pussy. But, if he does mess up a good thing, there won't be second chances. Period."

Kat laughed, surprising herself with how genuinely silly she thought the whole idea. Biting her bottom lip, she brought her giggles under control. "Maybe you'll need these," she suggested a whip and fur–lined handcuffs. She had a pair just like them, someplace on the floor of her closet near her flip–flops.

"Not tonight." Sasha reached for a nightie. Shimmering gold and sequins. "I was thinking of something more like this. Matches his teeth."

"His teeth? Oh, girl, one of them? You're going to fuck a dude who thinks he's an old–school pimp?"

Her friend chuckled, then licked her lips. "Brotha man may not know we're in a new millennium, but he ain't short on fine."

Kat grinned. Moving away, Kat glanced around. They weren't the only women in the store. Several others browsed the racks and shelves, some disappearing into the back room that held the real naughty–naughty stuff. These were just ordinary women, she realized. Women with jobs. Possibly husbands. Families. Women who were secure in their sexuality.

And here, Queen of Porn stood afraid to pick up the things she was really interested in. Hell, afraid to tell the man she was fucking that she was interested in checking out creams and lotions. Enhance sex items.

Not that ten–inch love machine needed much enhancement. *Nope, not that dick*, her dampened pussy cried out. But here she was, standing amidst the items meant for fantasy and she'd never really had one.

She grabbed a bottle. *Co–Him–Nut Cream Body Rub*. In smaller letters it read, Add a little taste of yum to your man.

"Get it."

Kat startled. "Huh?"

"I said, get it. Quit staring, and buy something," Sasha said, handing her a small shopping basket. "Buy shit."

"Yeah?"

She glanced at her watch. "Yeah, but make it quick. I've got a date soon."

Great, so now it was Sasha who was rushing, and Kat would have been plenty happy not coming in in the first place. She'd even offered to wait out in her car.

Kat dropped the body rub into her basket. Three flavors. And a box of Magna Condoms. She was seeing Mr. Gorgeous Saturday night and it wouldn't do to run out. Hell no. Not when having them meant she was getting sexed. Well and often. Not often enough. But damn, more often than she'd ever been serviced before.

Smiling, she added edible panties to her little basket. Not sure how she'd work them into one of her encounters, but thinking about it and planning ahead was fun. Since she was seeing him at the bar, she searched through the novelty items looking for something that would be right for the club scene. Something that Bad Boy could get at easily. Some little special treat that would make him remember her.

If it worked well into one of her articles as inspiration, all the better. She may not have fantasies, but she knew how to create them. She had an imagination after all.

Her gaze settled on nipple pasties. There were stars and moons. Fruit–flavored. Ice creams. Kat lifted a pack of strawberry nipple stickies. It was something she could put over her nipples and in a low–cut shirt, it'd be something Lover Boy could get at easily enough.

Though she prostituted sex stories for a living, Kat was surprised she felt so at ease in a place that hooked with sex toys and candy dildos. Grinning, when her gaze skidded across the magazines behind the counter, she stepped up with more confidence than she knew she had when it was time to pay.

And put her items on the counter for purchase even though her name was plastered everywhere.

Glory Cockin.

There wasn't a book or magazine on the display shelf that her name didn't grace. Something warm uncurled through her system. She'd never been in a place where she'd seen her articles openly displayed. The few places she'd been, like gas stations and convenience stores, all had the X–rated magazines where children couldn't reach them. Or see them.

But here, in Wicked's, her work was on exhibit.

She felt her cheeks go red.

"You're a grown–ass woman. You still get embarrassed about getting your freak on?"

With one last look at the stories she'd spent hours slaving over, Kat shifted her attention. "Oh get over yourself, would you, slut? I'm buying the shit, aren't I?"

"About time, too. I'm ready." She looked at her watch. "Do you want me to walk you to your car? I don't have much time, but I'll call you tomorrow."

"Nah. You go ahead. I'm going to get a latte. I've got a column due at the paper in a couple of days." And a fantasy to create.

"'K, girl. I'll call you." Sasha shifted her bag of purchases out of the way and gave Kat a tight hug. Without looking back, she skipped out the door.

Kat waited until she wasn't coming back. Then, before she

lost her nerve, she asked the cashier for a couple of her magazines. She had them at home, but she'd never purchased her own. Not in three whole years. Grinning like a mouse who'd snuck cheese off a snap–trap, she tucked them into her bag with her other goodies and headed out of the store.

The September air nipped at her bare skin, making her wish she'd remembered to bring something to put over her sundress at the end of the day. Dinner with Sasha had been fine, but now, as the fog rolled off the ocean, a chill whispered across her body.

Picking up her pace, Kat walked quickly down the block toward where she'd parked her car.

Out of the corner of her eye, she caught a yummy image. An image that halted her where she stood. Sucking a breath between her teeth, she turned toward the huge plate–glass street front window into the gym.

A flash of dark skin caught her eye. Naked, sweat dripping skin. Yum. Her body reacted immediately to the vision she saw, with an iron–bar resting across his wide shirtless shoulders, his legs flexed as he squatted holding the weights.

Turning, she rested her forehead against the cool glass, flames licking against her cheeks.

Mr. Gorgeous.

Oh, God, there was no other way to describe him. He was a sculpted masterpiece. She flicked her gaze across the vast weight room, realizing he was alone. And damn near naked besides the jersey black Nike shorts hanging from his hips.

Unable to tear her attention away from his luscious body, Kat watched as he lowered the bar and secured the machine. He grabbed a towel from his bag, and swiped it across his face.

Her nipples pulled into tight balls. Heat seeped between her thighs.

To her disappointment, he grabbed his bag from the floor

and turned away from her. Then walked toward the men's locker room and out of sight.

She stood there staring. Her mouth watering and her body on fire. Fuck. She needed him. How long would it be before he came out?

Chapter 16

She couldn't stand there watching the men's room door all night. Couldn't stand outside the gym hoping to see him come out.

She had to join him.

God, what was wrong with her? The more she screwed Ten–Inch Lover, the less she saw of the shy girl she truly was. He made her forget things. Forget that Wallflower Kat didn't fuck strangers. Only Sassy Kat did. And more and more it was the freak in her that was coming out. *Hiss.*

She glanced at her bangle–watch. It was past eleven and the place was deserted. Besides Ten–Inches–of–Yummy, a man in his early twenties sat at the front desk. He was well distracted with earphones tucked against his head and his gaze trained on a handheld game.

Opening the door to the gym, Kat walked past the attendant at the desk. He didn't even look up, his head bobbing to whatever rhythm he was hearing from inside those tiny speakers.

Kat smirked. Great customer service—though she was thankful to be able to slip past unnoticed. Moving quietly between the free–weights and cardio machines, she made her way to the locker room she'd seen Bad Boy disappear into ten minutes before.

"Mr. Gorgeous?" she whispered, sticking her head inside the door. The room smelled of sweat, faintly of gym socks, masculine, a lingering scent of pine cleaner, and like Ivory soap. Stepping inside, she spotted a single duffle bag on a long bench beneath a row of lockers. But no man.

"Lover?" she called, walking to the line of showers. Silence. Each shower stall was empty and the curtains pulled back. Secured against the wall. Confused, she turned to leave. Mr. Gorgeous must have left, she reasoned. Somehow he must have gotten past her from when she watched from the street through the plate–glass windows. And forgotten his bag.

She took a step toward it, pausing when she realized his wallet may be in there. And his identity. She didn't want to know. Turning to leave, Kat noticed a red light above a wooden door. It glowed like a lighthouse beacon to weary sea travelers.

A steam room? She should have guessed.

She knew she had to have him. Unable to think of anything else, Kat put her bag of goodies down by Lover Boy's bag. Then stripped off her sundress. Slipped off her sandals. Dropped her bra and panties to the floor.

Remembering her bag of goodies from Wicked's, she retrieved a condom, holding it in one tight fist.

Smiling and naked, Kat moved to the door and eased it open just far enough that she could slip inside. Undetected. She'd give Pleasure Man a little surprise. A wall of damp heat cascaded around her. It engulfed her body in long swirling fingers. Steam billowed up from the floor like low–lying fog when the sun–warmed earth was met by frigid winter air.

As her eyes adjusted to the light of a single pale yellow bulb in one corner of the tiny room, she made out the center of the heat. A stove covered in rocks, sizzling as a hose trickled water over each of the burning stones. The rocks hissed and spewed a frothy mixture of moisture. Gray tendrils of vapor. Both sides of the tiny room were covered in redwood and long wooden benches, sanded and smooth from time.

Bad Boy sat to her left, his head resting back against the wall. With his eyes closed, shadows of his thick long lashes swept over his masculine cheekbones. A white towel was wrapped around his waist and secured with a tucking of one corner. His hands lay limp to his sides but his fingers tapped in beat with some silent music, alerting her that he was relaxed but not asleep. Like a hunting predator about to pounce.

His chest, naked and glistening, flexed and released in the same sensual rhythm.

Kat padded to the bench across from him and sat down on the edge, careful to not disturb him. Hungry for him, she watched as his body pulsed with energy despite his seemingly relaxed state—like a beast stalking prey.

Her gaze swept over him. His clean–shaven head glistened with sweat. His oh–so–fine face and square jaw. His wide proud nose. Full, lush LL Cool J lips. Down to where his pulse throbbed in a vein on his neck. Allowing her eyes to drift lower, she looked at his chiseled chest to where his flat brown nipples enhanced his perfectly muscular pecs.

She took in the rich brown of his skin, warm and beckoning like a cup of cocoa after being in the snow. Shadowed by a scattering of curly dark hair, his belly button balanced at the top of the towel. The trail of black hair plunged beneath. With longing and a hint of jealousy, Kat's gaze followed the path into the shadow of his crotch.

She gulped. Her intent gaze locked on the swell of a half erection at the apex of his thighs.

A needy gasp slipped past her lips. Her gaze flew back to his face to see if her slight hungry moan had alerted him of her presence. Apparently not. He remained as he had been. Tapping his fingers and lounging in the humid heat. His image clouded only by the spray of mist that swirled around and between them.

Her nipples puckered. Her skin burned where she gripped the condom packet in her hand. Setting the foil square on the bench beside her, Kat longed to yank the towel away. Drape the latex over his dick and climb aboard.

Mr. Gorgeous moaned. Was he thinking where she was?

She leaned across the narrow space between them and touched his knee with a feathering of her fingers.

His eyes flew open as he jerked to a sitting position. "Sweetness! What are you doing in here?" he asked, his voice thick and raspy.

"I saw you."

"In here?"

"Working out. When you came in here, I followed." Her fingers brushed along the hem of terry–cloth above his knees, deliberately touching his skin as she played with the material. "I like steam rooms," she purred.

He smiled; a slow, sexy–lopsided grin that turned up one corner of his mouth and put a spark in the depths of his dark eyes. "Do you now? I see. So, I guess we'll have to share."

"I'm not so good at sharing," she teased. "What if I want the steam room all to myself?"

"Then, I'd say you have a problem. I'm not going any-where." To prove his point he leaned back and resumed his tapping. His lids drifted closed but Kat could tell that his body was ready to react given the opportunity. She chanced a glance at his crotch where the towel tented around a growing erection.

Agonizing. She was already so hot. Wet and aching.

"I guess you'll just have to put up with me then."

The narrow slits of Bad Boy's eyes opened just enough so that he could watch her. A muscle ticked in his jaw as he sat there, feigning indifference. The tent, erect in the center of his lap, jolted as if it'd been hit by a gust of wind. Damned hard dick was making her horny.

Kat smiled as she leaned back against the warm wooden wall. Keeping her gaze fixed on his face to gauge his reaction, she brought her hands to her breasts, covering them fully. Her damp skin had never felt more sensitive.

His throbbing cock made it clear he wanted her.

Hell, she wanted him, too.

Slowly, her fingers opened, smoothing her palms beneath the heavy globes of her tits. Her dusky–colored nipples puckered. Her clit damn near begged for his touch.

"You'll just have to ignore me, lover, 'cause this heat is making me so feel good."

He made a gruff rumble in his chest.

Lifting her hand, Kat slid her fingers into her mouth. Mimicking the undulations of sex, she slid her fingers in and out. Her tongue swirled until they were nice and wet. Soaking. Like her pussy.

Kat moved her saliva covered fingers to her pert nipple. She tweaked. Rolled the flesh between her thumb and forefinger. "Oh, mm . . ." she whispered, her breathing becoming heavy, her lungs struggling against the humid air.

The tick in Bad Boy's jaw sped up. His breathing quickened.

"You don't mind do you, baby, if I get myself off?" she purred, asking a question that demanded no answer. Blatant sexuality in her seductive tone.

His eyes opened fully, but he remained relaxed against the wall watching her. "Suit yourself, Sweetness. Have a little fun."

Kat felt like laughing. She knew he wanted to join in her little game. His dick was a damned flagpole. Stiff. So aroused, he was like a soldier ready for command. She could hear the husky, desire–laden, sharp, jagged breaths of need.

"I'm glad you don't mind." Kat lifted the globe of her breast. Lowered her head. Her mouth made contact with her sensitive skin.

She shivered. She swirled her tongue over the rigid crest. Laved a rainfall of moisture. Left her skin glossy where her mouth had been. Liquid fire seeped from cunt. That throbbing ache started up, deep inside of her. The one only ten inches could ease.

Hell! She was a tease, a damn temptress eager and willing to bring him to his knees. Jamal shifted, trying to remain in control over the last of his resistance. The truth was, where his client was concerned he hadn't an ounce of restraint. He was dying to grab her around the waist and delve into her pussy with one full thrust.

But watching her was a pleasure he didn't want to miss. He leaned back, enjoying the sensual show Kat was putting on. Her pink tongue licked a path from the rise of her breast to the tip. Creamy brown flesh tipped with a patch of dark puckered skin. The glide of her tongue lifted as she reached her hardened nipple. He would have taken the bud of flesh into his mouth and sucked. His throat went dry. He swallowed.

"Come here, baby," he said gruffly.

Though she didn't lift her head, her dark eyes met his, a playful gleam shining from them. She shook her head. Her tongue made contact with her nipple. A moan escaped her damp, parted lips.

"Just watch me," she replied. She released her breasts and leaned back against the wall, her head falling to one side as she spread her legs and drew her knees apart.

She smoothed her hands down her side. Past the swells of each breast. Caressing her own body, she slid down her ribs to her waist. Teasing and playful. Mingling with the scents of warm wood and sweat, a hint of feminine sex sought his senses. He about came.

Her trim body seemed relaxed as her fingers dipped into her belly button. Petted the triangular patch of silken short black hair above her cunt.

He growled.

She swirled in the damp hair, then dipped a finger into her juicy sex. Back out. Her body trembled.

She twirled in the wetness. Arousal glistening on her inner thighs. Her lips were soaked. Drenched. She plunged two fingers in.

The sass in her was seeping out.

"Oh," she whimpered, a throaty sound filled with pent up need. Pleasure. "Imagine . . . this is you."

"I don't want to imagine. I want to sink into you. Hard. Fast. I want to fuck. Come here, baby." Jamal released the towel from his waist allowing his cock to be free from constraint. It sprung forward, straining toward Kat, begging for him to grab her up and enter her.

Her head turned in his direction, her eyes glossed as she lowered her gaze to his dick. A slight smile spread over her damp lips. "Do I turn you on?"

"Hell, yeah."

"Do you want to touch me?" she asked, delving into her vagina with two of her fingers, her thumb finding her clit and circling it. Her body trembled; a quivering that sped down her inner thighs.

"Oh, hell, yeah. I want to touch you," Jamal replied, leaning forward on the bench. He'd had enough of her teasing. Needed to sink into her before he lost control. Before he came.

Kat slid her sex–dampened fingers from her vagina and wagged them in the air at him. "No, no, no. Sit back down."

Jamal leaned back, grabbing his cock at the base, and stroked upward in the same quick rhythm as her fingers slid into her labia. His flesh bucked beneath his palm. Hard flesh covered in velvet skin. He caressed his head. Found a ball of liquid at the tip, a natural lubricant. He used his pre–cum to glide his hand over his erection, all the way down to his heavily drawn balls. He cupped the tight sacs in his hand.

Biting back a groan, Jamal kept his keen gaze fixed on the apex of Kat, where her sex glistened in the pale light. He stroked up, a swift glide over flesh until he found the rim of his head. Swollen tight beneath his skin, desire pumped through the bluish vein that traversed his length.

The throb of lust zapped logical thought from his mind. Kat, *his client*, sat across from him, her legs spread, her vagina dripping wet, primed and ready for him to enter her.

"Mr. Gorgeous?" Kat purred like a cat being rubbed behind its ears. She slowed her pace. Her eyes were transfixed on the dark rigid shaft he held and stroked in the palm of his hand. "You're magnificent," she cooed, allowing her fingers to slide from her sex. She eased her ass forward, to the edge of the bench.

Too caught up now in his quest for self–fulfilled climax, he didn't pause as he worked the width of his shaft between his fingers. His body flexed. Each muscle trembled as he fought the surge of pleasure building like a summer thunderstorm.

"Perhaps sharing isn't such a bad idea," she said, grabbing something from the bench behind her. He saw a flash of light as the single bulb reflected against the foil packet of a condom. She tore open the package and pulled the circular piece of latex from the wrapper.

"You'd better hurry," he demanded through broken pants.

Kat squatted before him, the condom suspended between two of her fingers. She touched his cock with the hand she'd used to pleasure herself. Her skin slick. Damp. Sticky, from her sex. Her moisture mixed with his, the best musky–scented aphrodisiac he'd ever had.

Kat tightened her hand around him, stilling his upward thrust of his hips, the instinctual reaction to the downward slide of her hand. She gripped him and angled his unyielding ten–inch dick toward her, prepared to drape him in latex then engulf him within her wet heat.

At the first touch of the cool latex to the tip of his heated head, his cock jumped. Started to cum. "Hold on, Sweetness . . . Oh . . . God." Jamal's muscles bucked. His back arched. Hips thrusting forward, he came swiftly. Violently. Frothy white cream jetted from him, spraying his climax onto her forearm. The milky feel–so–good was a stark contrast on her caramel skin.

Nothing but the sizzle of water on hot stones and Jamal's jagged pants could be heard. The air was thick now, heavily perfumed with desire. Slowly, Jamal became aware of what had happened. He had found release. Orgasmed in mind–blowing fashion just when Kat had been about to swath him in latex. Before he'd even given her a wild ride.

He exhaled a jagged breath. "I'm sorry—" he began.

She cut him off by bursting into giggles. So sweet. So feminine and alluring. With her head bent forward by his lap, he couldn't see the sparkle in her eyes, but he could hear it in her laughter.

"Don't be," she laughed. "This is what happens. My plan backfires."

"Give me a minute," he replied, feeling the swell of lust stir his groin again.

"Really?" Her fingers found his shaft, semi–aroused.

"Yeah, give me a minute and I'll be ready for that condom."

"Okay," she said but didn't wait a minute. Hell, she didn't even wait a second. The little vixen. She began working him. Damn it felt good.

Kat couldn't wait. She'd tried to tease him into submission, but her game had backfired. Now, she was hot and wet. A trail of moisture slithered down her inner thighs. Tension snapped like a mid–drought twig in her blood. Mr. Gorgeous had found release. His cum burned her skin where it'd landed with a mocking that heightened her resolve to have him—now!

She caressed him. Stroked him. Dropped the blood from his brain. The beat of his heart surged in the palm of her hand, the same rapid cadence as her own. When his dick thickened, Kat knew she could wait no more. She eased the condom down his considerable length then rose to straddle his lap.

"Where'd you get that?" Good Lookin' asked, his warm hands settled on her hips. He pulled her forward flush against his muscular body. His woody pulsed between them. Throbbed against her clit.

"Wicked's."

He nodded. Ground his length against her, but not entering yet.

"Bad Boy . . . please . . ." she begged between broken sighs of delight. "Don't tease . . ."

"Don't tease, Sweetness? I learned this game from you." He tilted his ass bringing the contact again. Dick to clit.

Kat whimpered, sliding her hand between their bodies as she eased up and tried to guide him into her. "No more games. I want you inside me now. Please baby—I am sorry I toyed with you."

"You're right, no more games." He smoothed over her shoulders. Feathered fingertips passed the pulse point on her neck. Framed her cheeks in his hands. With slow, yet deliberate intent, he drew her face closer to his, the rich chocolate of his eyes gleaming with passion.

"No more games." Their breaths mingled, danced in the narrow hall between their lips. Would he kiss her? Despite never having fully mated mouths before? His kiss was there, a heartbeat away from settling fully upon her, before claiming her. Though it terrified her, Kat had no intention of putting a stop to his claim. A lump formed in her throat, her heart pinched. She knew she was in trouble—and she wanted it.

Damn, she'd begged for it.

The light clicked off. Silence and the pitch black swallowed them up. Lover Boy beneath her sighed—an almost aggravated sound. "I set the timer for half an hour," he mumbled.

"Time's up?" Kat couldn't help the slight sob. Her body was on fire. In the emptiness of dark, she trembled. Unreleased desire pumped through her blood. Breathing uneven, she sagged against his chest. Strong arms circled her, tugged her closer.

A sliver of light sped across the dark. "Anyone in here?" a man shouted from the slightly parted doorway. "We're about to close up."

Lover Boy pressed his finger to her lips. "Shhh," he whispered in her ear. "Let me get dressed and I'll be out of here in a minute," he replied.

"Alright. I'm going to go shut out the rest of the lights." The attendant left the door slightly open, then exited the locker room.

"I am sorry." He kissed her cheek. Pressed his lips to the tender skin beneath her ear. "Do you want to find some other place—"

Yes, her body begged.

Kat shook her head. The moment was gone. The lust tempered with a shaft of locker room light. Wild Kat scampered away, leaving only timid–kitty to clean up the mess.

She waited until she heard the outer door clang closed before she scurried from her lover's lap. Then went naked out the door to her pile of clothing lying on the bench. Thank God the attendant hadn't noticed the women's clothing.

Quickly shimmying into her sundress, Kat shoved her bra and panties into the bag from Wicked's.

With a midnight blue towel wound about his waist, Mr. Gorgeous strolled up beside her, his walk cocky yet not arrogant. He dropped the foil packet and unused condom into the trash. "You okay, Sweetness?"

"Yeah." Heat danced across her cheeks. No, she wasn't okay. Faced with a plentitude of dildos at home, nothing could satiate her need. Except him. She had to get out of there before she begged him to do her.

Do me baby! The attendant be damned.

Her knees shook. Scooping up her bag, Kat moved toward the door.

"Ka—"

Kat swung back to face him, her breathing stopped. Her heart thundered.

"Can I still see you Saturday night?" he finished.

Her breath whooshed out. Her body trembled with relief. For a moment she'd thought he called her name. Smiling, Kat moved back to him. Leaning into his chest, she touched his mouth with her fingertips, then whispered, "You'd *better* be there."

He nudged her fingers out of the way and dropped his mouth to her. Not wild or deep, but he kissed her fully on the lips. His eyes twinkled when he pulled away. "Saturday. The Night Kitty."

She turned. Bad Boy swatted her ass. "I'll buy you a drink."

Kat smiled, nodded, then went out the door. With her teasing fingers and no damned man to make her cum. She headed home.

Alone.

Chapter 17

She'd dressed for the occasion. Strawberry pasties and all. Taking a deep breath, Kat opened the door and stepped inside, the sights and scents of The Night Kitty assaulting her just as they had the very first night. But tonight she wasn't the same woman she once was. Wild Kat had gotten into her soul. Sure, Meek Kitty lived within her, too, but she had less control now. She came out when insecurity pressed through her blood. But that was less and less.

Claws were out, sassy making a definite appearance. Tonight her knees didn't knock. Tonight she didn't need to guess if she'd find a man.

Tonight she had one waiting.

The endorphins primed the air, heavy and alluring. Sex called out through the deep thumping bass of the floor–to–ceiling speakers. *Fuck me just like this*, the rhythm beckoned with an almost forced sway of her hips.

Feeling the aphrodisiac of the place, Kat moved farther inside, hugging the wall as her eyes adjusted the low bar lighting and the flashing strobes streaking across the dance floor. There was something sexy about a fast pace of an intermittent strobe light.

When her pupils had dilated, she crept through the crowd.

Moving to the bar, she slid into the only vacant seat, then waited for a brief moment until the bartender worked down the bar in her direction.

It was the same young, good looking brotha who'd served her up a couple of shots the first time—weeks ago—she'd been there.

"Can I get you something?"

"A Hpnotiq."

He grinned, then slanted his head toward her. "Good, popular choice. Matches the color of your dress."

Kat glanced down at the Marilyn Monroe–style dress she'd selected for the evening. For one reason. The way the fabric crossed over her tits. She bit her bottom lip, resisting the urge to spin on the chair to see if Oh–So–Fine had shown up yet. "Thanks," she whispered, her mind on her man and not on the drink.

"You alone?"

"For the moment."

The young buck laughed. Putting up his hands and with a smile that reached his eyes, he said, "Hey, I'm not hitting on you, if that's what you think."

Had this been the first night, Kat would have thought that was too damned bad. He was a looker even with a few years to go before he reached his manly prime.

"It's alright, really. I'm meeting someone."

"He have a name?"

Not that she knew of. "Of course. Don't we all?"

He laughed again. "I just meant, are you here to meet someone or are you looking to?"

Kat's nipples tightened. Oh, she'd met him. But the memory of sitting here getting juiced up so she'd be able to look wasn't so distant. She'd wanted—and gotten—a man worth the shower and changing from her writing garb. Just the right bit of inspiration she'd initially desired. A fine piece of chocolate. A lover that made her feel hot. Sexy. For the first time in her life.

She took a sip of the drink the bartender placed in front of her. Licking her lips clean, she gazed down at the rich blue liquid. "I know who I'm meeting," she whispered. Liar! She didn't know him at all. Not any more than how well he fucked.

She sighed. That wasn't exactly true either. They were almost dating, she realized thinking back to all the times she'd seen him since the time they'd banged in the alley. They talked. Shared things about each other's lives.

Hell, with the exceptions of her name and career, Lover Boy knew more about her than anyone.

Except Jamal.

Jamal was her best friend. The best friend she'd ever had. The one who knew her secrets—but not how she'd been getting inspired the last month—and didn't judge her for them or what she did for a living.

"Hey, why so sad?"

Kat slushed off the sudden onset melancholy. She shook her head. "Just lost in thought for a moment."

He refilled her drink. "You thinking about whether your man will show or not?"

"No." *He would.*

"Good. Because he's here." He leaned across the bar. Tapping her shoulder, he subtly pointed to the other side of the dance floor where a few bar height tables and stools had been set up.

Kat spun her seat to look behind her. Following the indicated direction, her gaze settled on the man of her dreams. Glancing over her shoulder, she wanted to ask the bartender how he'd known, but he was gone when she looked back. Already moved farther down the bar to serve others drinks.

Didn't matter. It was difficult to tear her gaze from the

man across from her. He hadn't seen her yet, so she took the moment to observe and allowed her languid gaze to stroll over him. The lights shimmered off his cleanly–shaven head. His yum LL Cool J lips lingered in a cocky grin and his dark eyes seemed fixed on the door. Like he was waiting for someone.

Her.

Tightness settled around her heart. Taking a deep breath, she looked at her man. Her man? When had she started thinking of him as hers? She had no claim other than he had a nice fat dick she liked to fuck and he seemed happy to oblige.

Lust seeped from her flesh, wetting the well-manicured hair trimmed into a straight line over her pussy. Didn't take much to want him in there.

She sighed. As if he'd heard her, Mr. Gorgeous's gaze swung in her direction. Stayed. His smile widened. His body tensed and even across the haze of the bumping grinding dance floor, she didn't miss the dark flaring lust flashing in his intense eyes. Or how his nostrils flared.

He wanted her as badly.

She licked her lips. A muscle on his jaw ticked. He scooted back his stool, and said something to the women sitting at the table.

It was the first time she realized he wasn't alone.

Tears burned the back of her eyes. Breathing quickly, she refused them life. She'd not cry over a man who wasn't hers. Who hadn't encircled her finger with his ring. And had a man put a ring on her finger, she'd better never have reason to shed a tear over him.

Besides, they'd made no agreement they couldn't see others. And she had no idea who they were. Friends? Just a couple of women sharing a table in a packed club?

Holding her breath, Kat watched as they talked for a moment. A tall white woman. Thin with long blond hair. A second woman. Her black hair was cropped short. Very short and curled away from her face. She was shorter, but had a nice brown complexion.

Bad Boy touched the black woman on her shoulder, then leaned in for a hug.

Jealousy makes a fool of wise men, her momma once told her. She repeated it twice, breathing slowly as the woman kissed Lover Boy's cheek. He smiled, then turned toward the white woman and leaned toward her.

From her angle, Kat couldn't tell if he was kissing her cheek or whispering in her ear. A half–second later, the woman's blue–eyed gaze shifted in her direction. And, she smiled. Genuinely. There was nothing mocking or insightful. Just a welcoming smile that Kat felt herself returning.

Then Oh-So-Fine was walking toward her, his gait casual and confident. His gaze not breaking from hers as he made his way through the crowd.

He was there, standing before her. She could feel his heat. His unbelievable magnetism. Saying nothing, he removed the drink from her hand and placed it on the bar behind her. His strong hands settled on her thighs and he eased them apart. Filling the triangle with his body. Her legs curled behind his, pulling him closer.

So close that she could feel the length of his hard cock press against her panties. Delicious. Biting back a moan, Kat fought the urge to arch her back and complete the contact. He did it for her. Shifted closer. Through his pants, rubbed his dick against her clit. The stroke of getting laid. Kat felt like purring.

Jamal wanted to kiss her. Deep and wet and hot. Wanted to slide his tongue into her body, past her teeth into the sultry depths. Wanted to spend hours learning the way she tasted. Hear her moans whisper sweetly against his skin.

And hell, judging by the way she licked those luscious lips and gazed so lustily on his, he had no doubt she wouldn't stop him. But she'd set some rules and no kissing was one of them. He was suffering taking what little of her mouth she'd give when what he wanted to do was worship her with his.

Leaning forward, he framed her face in his hands, sliding his fingers along her jaw, back to her thick pressed hair. "I'm glad you're here," he said softly in her ear.

Her warm palm settled on his chest, and the little sex–kitten flicked her nail against his nipple through his shirt.

"Me, too." Her words caressed his neck. As did her tongue. The vixen tease. His gut twisted with need. The dick of his had a mind of its own. Jumped hard toward that tight little pussy, right where he could feel her damp heat through the material of his jeans.

He stepped back. Either that or slide a hand up beneath the loose flow of her skirt, find her core and get something inside her. Quick. Would have been nice if it'd been his cock, but hell, she was sitting at the bar. And while he'd stuck a few digits in this honey before, there was something different about the back of the dance floor. At least a little privacy.

"Dance with me?" *Or fuck*, his dick grumbled, liking the idea of getting in that cunt better than dancing.

She slid from the stool before him, her body pressed against his. Her fingers twined with his, silently giving assent.

They moved together like fluid through river rock. Several times, Jamal felt her being pulled away from him in the shifting crowd, but her fingers tightened around his. Stroking his thumb across the silken skin on her palm, when what he really wanted to do was to take her out of here. To find a place where he could bury himself inside her. A place where he could ease the desire straining in his jeans and free his body of the sexual tension.

His body's reaction to her nearness. Any time he thought about her.

His soul just wanted to hold her. To put her in the circle of his embrace and to keep her in his arms. Pressed against his chest. Going nowhere. But home with him. Oh, what he wouldn't give to take his Fly–Girl home to his bed and make love to her properly. Leisurely. Bit by bit. Little by little, but thoroughly. Like she deserved.

The rocking beat of the Black Eyed Peas blasted through the speakers, but instead of dropping into a dance fitting the rhythm, Kat moved against him and began to dance slowly. He shifted with her. The unhurried sway of her hips, the way she crept her fingers up his back, the way her eyes begged, had him guessing she was thinking the same thing.

Fuck me.

Make love to me.

Oh, God. He wanted to. Jamal struggled to breathe. Struggled with the swirling build of emotional need. The binding connection. Hell, he had a contract with this woman. He represented her literary career, but he knew that once she knew the truth, that would be coming to an end. When she learned that he'd known who she was since their second encounter, she'd never forgive him. Fuck, if he were to be honest with himself, he'd admit he knew with certainty since he'd read her first set up submissions. Since they'd screwed in the back alley.

No, she'd never forgive him.

How could she?

But damnit to all hell, he wanted nothing more than to tell her. To tell who he was. Who she'd been getting fucked by, putting an end to the charade. To give them a chance at a real relationship. To whisper each other's names while they were taking pleasure from each other's bodies. While they were loving.

"You want to get out of here?" Kat asked, her fingers curling around his cock, squeezing gently through the denim. Stroking him.

"Huh?"

"We can go if you're not into this."

Leaving sounded like a great idea. But would put an end to

their time, too quick. He wanted to touch her. To savor her. To spend time with her. The best way to do that was to dance. To use it as foreplay. To keep her from going, whispering their next date in his ear, then leaving him. And him going home alone. To a cold shower.

"No, baby. Dance with me."

She smiled at him, that sexy smile that burned arousal through his blood. If he'd been drinking, he'd guess he'd had too much. She made him feel intoxicated with the simple touch of her hand. By the glimmer of desire shimmering in her amber eyes.

He cleared his throat, dropping his face into the curve of her neck, inhaling the feminine sweetness of her skin. "Baby, dance with me." He lifted her into his arms, moving them now in the rhythm of the beat. The rhythm of how he'd be doing her if he were up in her right then. Not the fast pace of Kelis singing Milkshake.

Kat ground her hips into his, enthralled by the huskiness of his voice. So filled with need. She felt the answering pull deep in her pussy.

And in her heart.

Drawing closer, Kat pressed her mouth to his chest, not caring about the thin layer of cotton that kept his body from being gloriously naked for her lips to devour. She could feel the rumble of his groan, then he arched her back, and attacked her neck with his tongue.

Kat sighed as she curved her spine over Lover Boy's strong forearm, his fingers splaying across her back. Give over to him, no problem. Her head lulled back as the rough texture of his tongue smoothed a trail over her pulse. Up to the curve of her ear. His teeth nipped, then he sucked. Her knees went weak.

"Mr. Gorgeous?" she moaned, wondering how tall, dark, and handsome could make her forget they were in the middle of the dance floor. Around them couples danced and grooved. Hips thrusting. Asses gyrating.

"Yeah, baby?"

"You going to nibble my neck all night?" She grinned at her boldness. She hadn't spined–up in Wicked's for nothing. She wanted him to see all the little treats she had in store for him.

"Where do you want me?"

"A little lower."

He chuckled, but his head came up, his eyes shining with arousal. "Lower?"

"Yeah, Joy–Stick, lower."

He grinned, his brows furrowing together. "You forgetting where we are?" He swung them and moved to the beat as a little reminder. She didn't need it. She knew they were on the dance floor.

Kat felt like laughing. She'd love him to lick that perfectly talented tongue of his across her clit, but hello, The Night Kitty wasn't the right place. Someday. Someplace . . .

Leaning forward, she kissed him square on the mouth, her lips lingering. She tweaked his bottom lip between her teeth as she sipped from his mouth, drinking in the pleasure of his kiss. He growled against her, slanted and tried to deepen it. Oh, God, how she longed for that sort of intimacy. With a regretful sigh, she pulled away.

Recovering, Kat allowed the tigress free. "Ooh, Bad Boy, I said lower. Not that low"—she winked—"but I'll take you up on that another time."

Jamal laughed. Beautiful. Intelligent. Bold. Sexy as all hell and about to make him cum in his pants. Could he have asked for more in a woman?

He shook his head. Didn't think so.

"Lower, huh?" He pulled her close, so her tits pressed against his chest, taking delight in the surprised gasp that hissed from her lips. "With pleasure, Sweetness."

Tight pussy or not, Sassy Kat wouldn't control him. Okay, fuck. She did. Easily. She wanted lower, he'd damned sure oblige. The floor was packed. No one noticed as he slid his hand beneath the fabric crossed over her luscious titties. Seductress wasn't wearing a bra. *Thank you!*

His thumb found her nipple, pulled to a peak, begging his attention. He flicked it and was rewarded with a hiss and claws clutching at his back. Smiling, he rolled her nipple between his fingers, drawing it more firmly into a peak. She moaned and arched, filling his hand with her breast.

Mouth watering, Jamal used the back of his hand to brush the material of the dress away and dropped his head into her cleavage, covering her firm peak with his lips.

Strawberry?

Why, the hottie had baited and switched. Not that he was complaining. Hell no. He got strawberry nipple instead of just her sugary skin. "Strawberry?"

"Wicked's."

"Mmm . . . strawberry." He went back to his dessert. Suckling her into his mouth, bathing her with his tongue. Feasting. Yum.

"They're my favorite," she said in a hushed voice.

He chuckled against her. "Me, too. Now."

Kat smiled. Her lids drifted closed, the lull of desire seducing her into confidence. The treatment he was lavishing on her couldn't have been any better. Unless she was naked. And they were alone. Middle of the dance floor wasn't nearly as private as she wanted it.

Opening her eyes, Kat angled her head, looking for the exit they'd used the first time. A hardcore fuck may be on the menu tonight. Bricks and strawberries.

But her gaze collided with something that tugged her from the urgent need to hit the alley for ten inches of sex therapy.

Sasha. Sasha getting her freak on. With a man.

She narrowed her eyes, trying to make out his features, wondering if it was the playa in for a little surprise a few

nights ago. "Bad Boy?" she tapped his shoulder, torn between forcing him to remove his mouth from her flesh and
curiosity. "See that woman over there"—she paused to dis-
cretely point—"wearing red?"

She was a little disappointed when his head came up, leaving her nipple cold. Wet. And let her dress fall back into
place. Damn. It'd felt so good.

"Huh?"

"There."

He stiffened and didn't answer for a few seconds. "Naa,"
he added with a shrug.

Kat bit her lip. It was the first time since she'd met Bad Boy
that she didn't think he was being completely honest with
her. She went still in his arms, holding onto him as the feeling
of sinking took over. Closing her eyes, she rested her forehead against his chiseled pecs and tried to breathe.

He held her tightly, but said nothing.

She gulped, trying to calm the rapid cadence of her heart
rate. What had just happened? She'd recognized Sasha.
Hadn't thought about anonymity when she pointed her out.
Squeezing her lids together, Kat realized just how stupid that
was. Had Sasha seen her too, remaining unnamed would be
out of the question.

So, had Mr. Gorgeous known one or both of them?
Sasha? The boy–toy? That must have been it. He'd been
silent. His indecision had almost been palatable. He hadn't
wanted to lie, but been forced by the nature of their relationship.

She hugged him tightly. Though she'd love to finish the
evening. With him. With his dick between her legs. She knew
she had to get out of there if she wanted to have the chance
again. She was creamy just thinking about it.

Lifting on tip–toes, Kat smoothed her palm over his
clean–shaven head, drawing him downward. "Joy–Stick, Sat-

urday. Noon. At the Eastern Bench in Shade Tree Plaza," she whispered into his ear. She could feel him smile against her cheek.

He kissed her neck. Her jaw. The corner of her mouth. The sensitive skin below her ear. "I'll be there."

She kissed him quick on the mouth. A mere peck, but made promises. With a smile and a sassy sway of the hip, she turned and walked away, deliberately disappearing into the bouncing, dancing crowd. She intentionally avoided Sasha, went out the door and Wild Kat vanished into the night.

Chapter 18

Kat sat at her kitchen table, sorting the bills from the fan mail from business documents from the relationship column advice requests, placing them into four separate baskets. Not for the first time, she thought she needed a personal assistant to handle opening the huge amount of adoring letters she received on a monthly basis. But something stopped her. Adding a name to the two who knew what she did for a living.

Letting out a huge sigh, and rolling her neck on her aching shoulders, she dropped another handful into her to-be-read basket. Not only did she attempt to read them all, but also answer. At least the ones that weren't duplicates. Or sticky. The sticky letters got tossed in the trash.

Pulling off the latex gloves, Kat dropped them in the garbage can on top of several nasty letters. She figured out early on, men did things on the pages they sent. Things she'd rather not touch, she thought with a smirk.

She'd have bought stock in the rubber glove company years ago if she'd known she was going to be at this for any length of time. Like more than a month or two. Somehow that had turned into more than three years. Three years of writing sex for money.

Closing her eyes, Kat lounged in her chair, her memories

swirling back to the night before at The Night Kitty and her near miss with her Wild Kat identity. After almost being found out, she'd come home pretty wound up, damned horny and hungry from the way Mr. Gorgeous had worked her nipples in his mouth. She'd been tempted to turn to plastic and batteries but had opted for a cold shower instead.

Then she'd lain naked in bed and conjured up images of the perfect lover. But it wasn't Bad Boy who came to mind. It was Jamal. In the quiet stillness of the night, she tried to reason her response, but the need for him had lingered. She had even thought about getting out of bed to see if he were online. That was, after all, how they communicated. That and occasional phone calls.

So why then did her body ache for a friend? For a man she'd never met? And why did trying to picture ten–hard–inches make her think of her agent?

Dawn was beginning to break the eastern sky by the time sleep slowly slipped over her. But before it consumed her, she decided she thought of Jamal because it was his friendship, companionship, his personality that she longed for.

Combine that with a glorious dick like Mr. Gorgeous and she'd have the perfect man.

The perfect husband.

Kat startled, surprised at the direction of her thoughts. Must have been the lack of sleep. Too many hours writing. In fantasy. Shaking her head, she got to her feet, moving the baskets aside. Going to the fridge, she poured a glass of iced tea and gulped down the sweet, cool liquid. Caffeine. Exactly what she needed.

Feeling a little refreshed, she went back to the table and sat down, pulling the business basket in front her. Sorting through, she found a thick envelope, the one with the newest contracts that Jamal had emailed he was sending her. She pulled out the papers and scanned.

Gasping, Kat buried her face in her hands. No. This couldn't be happening. Not now, not ever. Peeking between two fingers, she glared at the contract. Jamal could *not* have let this happen. He'd been her agent for a long time and knew how she felt about public appearances. She refused to do them. Author, Kat Mason was a recluse. A wallflower. She didn't mingle and she didn't advertise what she did for a living. She wasn't proud of it.

Now, those bold black letters gawked at her with a purposeful taunting. *Come out and play.* The mocking fear dwelled around her heart and twisted nervously in the pit of her belly.

Attend or possibly lose the contract. Those were her choices. Bad options. It couldn't be avoided. No escape for house cat or tigress.

A promotional party being thrown by her publisher to celebrate Glory's Stories, her erotica series. And she was expected to be present. Hell, she was the guest–of–fucking–honor.

A Night of Naughty the event was being called. In reality it was a Halloween ball, complete with customary costumes. A costume? A disguise, at least, could make it possible to get through such an evening. Not even wild Kat with savage claws and confidence oozing was into this. Meek Kat was definitely having her say.

With trembling hands, Kat reached for the phone and dialed. It rang twice before being answered.

"Momma, it's me." Her mom would understand. She'd gotten this gig from her after all. Momma would still be working if arthritis hadn't forced her into retirement. She was damn proud of selling sex for money this way. She was proud of Kat, too.

"Uh oh, what's the matter, baby?" her mom's tender voice rippled warmth across the line.

"You can tell?"

"Can't I always? Tell me, what is it?"

Kat took a deep breath to keep her voice from shaking. "A public appearance, Momma. *What's Your Fantasy* is hosting a big bash and I have to attend. It's part of the promotion and written into the contract."

"Then don't sign it. You've got talent, baby, you can do whatever you want with it."

"It's for Glory's Stories." This was her main series. The articles had launched her to the top of the charts and kept her there week in, week out. This was her bread and butter.

Silence crackled painfully across the airwaves. She heard her momma sigh. "What's Jamal say about this? He's your agent, and should be able to get you out of it."

"He thinks I should go. He'll be there, too." So after more than three years she'd finally come face–to–face with the man who'd been representing her interests. The man who'd inspired many nights with her dildo and fully charged batteries. That is, until she met Mr. Gorgeous. She had no need for plastic anymore. She got the real deal whenever she wanted it.

Besides her writing time, Kat had spent less and less time on her computer chatting with Jamal as she'd once done, and more time getting–it–on with her pleasure toy lover. But she missed the ease of saying what she wanted to, when she wanted.

"Well, then baby, go." Her momma's voice tugged her out of her musings.

"You'll be in costume, after all. Have fun with it," Momma continued. Her Momma laughed softly, then added, "Find a date."

"You want to come, Momma?"

"A man, baby. You need a man."

Kat choked back a laugh. She had one of those. Sort of. She had a fuck–friend. A once or twice a week, meet–and–get–freaky–man. She didn't, however, have one she could ask to stand beside during her moment of humiliation. Not without tall, dark, Bad Boy finding out who she was and what she did to pay her mortgage and car note.

Though it'd been difficult, she'd managed to keep her writing life on the down–low for the last three blissful months. Three months of dating, or at least sexing the finest chocolate she'd ever sampled. Melt in her mouth good. Lover Boy was scrumptious, yet they had a deeper connection. They talked. Between hot–heavy fucks. He seemed to understand her. And she only kept one secret. Her name.

There were no whispered words of love. Only acceptance. They were real with one another during their moments. No fake orgasms, no rushed interludes. No fragile egos. Just down and dirty, mind–blowing climaxes.

Feeling a dampness slick between her thighs and a pucker-ing of her nipples, Kat shook her head to clear her thoughts as she glanced at her watch. Two hours until she met up with ten–inches of good–loving. For now, she needed to focus on the event and going dateless. On ways to please Mr. Gorgeous. Tonight.

For the Halloween ball, meeting Jamal would have to do. Hell, part of her looked forward to it. To put a face with the images she'd dreamed about. Her fantasies.

But over the last three months, Kat had received more than good dick. She'd found a way to begin building her confi-dence. To hold her chin high and step away from the wall. Out of corners. To stop hiding and to start accepting herself. After all, when she was with a man who looked and loved like Oh–So–Yummy people noticed. They noticed her, too, and she was getting okay with it.

"I've been seeing a man, Momma." She grinned, surprised she'd done it.

Momma laughed. "Really? Anyone I know? Not a fan, baby, promise me you're not seeing a fan."

She shrugged. She didn't know. *Guess he could be*, she thought with a secret smile. Lucky him. "No, not a fan." *It's not a lie if you don't know, is it?*

"Good, Kat. So how long have you been seeing him? When can I meet him?"

"You can't meet him."

"Why not, baby?"

Because I haven't met him yet. "I'm just not ready for that, yet. Maybe later. If things look like they'll work out." They wouldn't though. Kat already knew that. This was a short–term love affair. Once Lover Boy found out who she was she feared he'd be disappointed. So far, she'd given him a party–girl. Who she really was sat at the table Saturday mornings doing bills. Cooked greens and gumbo when the weather got cold. Ate peanuts from the shell with her daddy at football games. No, Mr. Gorgeous wasn't getting the full story.

He'd go when the truth was out. He'd find the woman right for him. Not her, but she wouldn't cry. "When I'm ready, okay, Momma."

"Sure, you bring him round when you're ready. So, how long have you been seeing him?"

Kat didn't think before answering. "Three months."

Her mother laughed, then mumbled on her end of the phone. "And you're not ready? I hope you're getting inspired."

If she only knew. "Not answering."

Her momma laughed again. "So ask him to be your date."

Couldn't happen. Not without being found out. She couldn't risk her therapy on the same night she was putting her reputation and name on the line.

"Okay, Momma. I've got to go." After a quick goodbye, Kat hit the off button and dropped the phone onto the table beside her. She was terrified to be outed this way, to be known in the public as a superstar in the porn industry. She may not be on screen, but she talked the talk. Same as a hooker walks the walk.

She was known, at least her pseudonym Glory Cockin was known, for getting a man off. No different on the printed page than on the silver screen.

Reaching for her glass, Kat finished off the tea. Fishing for her favorite pen, she signed the contract in all the places

Jamal had left yellow tabs indicating where to put her John Hancock. Though apprehension lingered still, it was time. Time for Kat Mason to accept the glory. Or the blame.

Not allowing herself time to rethink, she shoved it in the FedEx flat mailer and sealed the top. Either that or tear the papers to shreds with her tigress claws and sharp teeth.

Having spent too much time in contemplation and on the phone, the bills and letters would have to wait. She was meeting Mr. Gorgeous at noon and still had to shower and blow dry her hair.

Kat went upstairs but went to her computer instead. She wanted to send Jamal an email first. Telling him the contract would be on its way. And, finally, after three years, she'd see him in two weeks.

Chapter 19

Inwardly smirking at the cleverness of what she'd arranged, Kat leaned her hip against the wooden park bench, sipping her frozen latte in the waning afternoon sun. Over the last three months it'd become a cat and mouse game of sorts. During the gasping–for–air moments following Lover Man's orgasm, she'd whisper where and when next time. Like a good puppy, trained well at obedient school, he was always there with a bone and ready to fuck.

"Sweetness," he said coming up from behind her, fitting his muscular body against her. Ten hard inches pressed against her ass, making her creamy. Her knees weak.

Kat giggled, turning in his arms. "Guess what," she whispered, pressing a quick kiss to his edible lips, to a mouth made for titty sucking.

A black brow arched. "Hmm?"

She smoothed her hand over his shaven head, trailing her fingertips down the pulse of his temple and dipping into his dimple. Lower, she traced his jaw. His lips. A tiny scar on his chin she just now noticed. Lifting on her tip–toes, she pressed her mouth to the faded skin and wondered how he'd gotten it. So many things about him she didn't know. So many things she longed to find out.

She kissed him quick on the lips again. "Something fun."

Dark chocolate eyes melted. "Yeah?"

"I need you to help me pick a costume." She may not be able to invite him without risking self–exposure, but that didn't mean she couldn't get his advice on the right façade to create for the evening. Wild Kat had something in mind already. He'd enjoy it.

A grin spread across his face. Smooth, dark skin, eyes the shade of rich coffee. A dimple sharpened. "Oh yeah, you can trick–or–treat your fine ass right into my bed." He kissed the sensitive skin below her ear, his words warm against her skin. "I'll need you out of costume, not in one."

Kat laughed. Sounded like a good plan to her. Definitely a pussy tease. Meow, she'd strip for him. Climb into his bed. Ride him hard and leave his world a bit tilted. "Really, Bad Boy, I have to go to a party."

Jamal shut his eyes and nearly groaned. So, she'd decided to go. He'd known his author was going to freak when she saw the clause stipulating the promotional party. He could have fought to have it removed. But hadn't. Time for his sassy Kat to learn the truth about their sex–game.

There'd be consequences. He'd deal with them, but anything had to be better than all this lying. Memories flashed of the scene in the bar the night before. Omission of truth was not the same as openly lying. Last night he'd looked at Kent and denied knowing him. From Kat's reaction, he knew she knew and he had to believe she understood why. But hell, that didn't make it easier to look in her eyes and not tell her the truth.

He'd wanted so badly to share things with her, but it would have revealed his identity and he was trying to respect her wishes. No names. No pasts. Today. Tomorrow. A good time only. He understood her rules. He played her game.

"Come with me," she said, wiggling out of his embrace, her hand instinctively falling to his.

Fingers intertwined, he fell into step behind her. His gaze on the sensual sway of her hips. The hypnotizing movement of her alluring body. Not easy to walk with a hard–on. He checked his lust and shifted his stride.

With the click of her sandals across the pavement, she led him toward a strip mall, to an upscale costume shop advertising their Halloween specials in the window.

Inside smelled of sweet fruit and wax. Candles burned in small lanterns behind the front counter. "Monster Mash" wailed in the background.

"Come with me," she said, curling her finger, beckoning him to follow. Cock smelled pussy. He'd go wherever she led him.

They moved through rows of costumes—clowns and ghosts and witches—toward the back of the store. They went through a door that led to the back storage room. Off to the left doors labeled restrooms. An employee table and water cooler kicked it on the other side of the storeroom. Kat led them silently through another door, into a dressing room.

"Stay right here." She brushed her fingertips over his lips, then draped them down his chin. "You won't be sorry," she said as she turned him by the shoulders so he was facing away from her. And the mirror.

Jamal did as she bid him. All the blood filling his erection left him damn senseless. Not that he cared. He studied the wall as he listened to the rustling of clothing. If she was getting naked, he'd tattoo *fool* on his forehead for obeying and not turning to appreciate the view.

"Did you set this up?" he asked, realizing there were already costumes in the dressing room that she was trying on.

"Earlier." The lock clicked.

Oh, yeah, she was playing with him. His hard dick jumped in his pants. He bit back a groan. A few moments passed. He could feel her movements behind him and fought like hell to keep from turning around and catching a hint of her yummy caramel skin. Just a glimpse of her smooth brown skin was all he asked for.

Pussy–whooped stood in the way, his nose against the wall.

A hand slid over his ass, squeezed, then slithered up his back, roved to his shoulder. "So what do you think," she purred.

Jamal turned, his erection bucking hard at the sight of her. She was suitably dressed in a skin–tight tiger outfit, the black and gold stripes of the spandex highlighting every lush curve. Her nipples beaded beneath the thin material.

She rubbed a paw down her body. "Meow."

And the zoo went wild.

Can't keep a beast caged for long. Jamal was on her, crushing her body against his, her tits against his chest and he pressed her hard to the wall. He slid a hand down her nice round ass, lifting a juicy thigh and pulling it over his hip as he ground his throbbing cock into her heat.

She moved with him, her mewing and moans fuel to the fire of his control. Damned cat–suit blocked the pussy. He needed in. He thrust his body to her, rotating his hips, finding a rhythm to the groove, the pace he was setting. Fucking the shit out of her through their damned clothing.

"How do . . . I get . . . this off you?"

With a husky moan, she arched her back, lulling her head to the side. Her amber eyes setting off the vibrant tawny shade striped around her body. Her gaze settled on his. Desire so forceful he felt kicked in the gut. The truth burned with his breath in the back of his throat.

Crazed, he brought his mouth down hard against her offered breasts, finding her nipple and rolling it between his lips through the spandex. A cry ripped from her, but she muffled it somehow, turning it low and raspy.

"Get this . . . off!" he ordered, but the rolling of her hips against his rocked–up dick distracted him.

Moving with her ripe body, he used the mirrored wall and

lifted her other leg around his back. He thrust upward, her damp heat spilling across skin. Rolling his hips, he ground into her, the simulation of fucking so intense he almost came.

Wiggling her ass, she worked a leg free, then put a hand on his chest and shoved him back. "Not so fast, Bad Boy." She was panting. Her lush skin shimmering with need.

Jamal sucked in a wheezing breath, reaching for her, but she side stepped in the tiny space of the dressing room. With her hand on his chest, she backed him up until he was pressed with his back against the wall.

He didn't argue. Hell, he assisted.

She dropped to her knees before him. Her fingers worked free his button fly. Pop. Pop. Pop. His jeans sagged open. Holy shit! One wrong stroke and he'd cum prematurely. He closed his eyes and struggled to breathe as she eased his throbbing cock from behind his boxer–briefs, tucking the elastic beneath his sac.

"You're not complaining, are you?" she teased, her pink tongue coming out to flick against his head.

Oh, yeah, do it again. "Hell, no." She did. Her tongue moved across his tender flesh, sucked at the ridge, licked down the vein, back up again. Her soft fingers closed around him, beading pre–cum on the head. She swirled her tongue, lapping it up, her warm breath dancing across his skin.

Then her hot, greedy mouth closed around him and inhaled him deep.

Trembling, Jamal opened his eyes and gazed down at the woman kneeling before him. Her gaze flicked to his, brightening with a smile. He'd never seen Fly Girl look as sexy as she did with his dick encased in her lips, his head jutting down her throat.

She went to work.

In. Deep. Out. She set a pace, deep and fast. Then slow, long strokes that made him want to beg for mercy. He sagged against the wall. What had he done to deserve this?

Sliding a steadying hand away from the wall, he touched her shoulder, then rested his palm on the back of her head, caressing her soft pressed curls.

"Deeper." He worked with her, thrusting his hips to meet her eager mouth. Request granted. Her searing tongue licking every hard aching inch.

Sliding his gaze across the small room, he caught their image in the mirror. Sweat broke out on his brow, beads rolling down his temple and neck. Breathing tightened in his chest. There she was, Kat, before him, giving him the best damned blowjob he'd ever had—the most erotic vision he'd ever seen.

He was in love with her.

Gulping the raw emotion, Jamal focused on the ball of cum working its way from his nuts. The clamoring need to finish took command. The distant voices in the costume shop faded away. The music disappeared in the rhythm of her slurps and sucks. The speed of his pulse. The tell–tale buck of his cock.

Oh, yeah, she knew what she was doing. She knew he was going to cum. And hard. She was working him, not letting the climax back off. No matter how he tried to stall it.

She tightened her fingers around his erection. Added a little suction. Jamal shook. His body reacting to her command. He held his roar in check. They were in public. A dressing room in a costume shop. A feline worked his cock. She knew just how to handle him.

One last quick caress. Hot, sticky cum shot from his dick down her throat. She accepted it. Holding him deep within her sultry lips as he pulsed pearly liquid.

He didn't move, could hardly breathe. Her demanding strokes to his flesh now turned delicate. Tender. She massaged his nuts, knowing the wad he blew down her throat had left him dazed. Wrung out. Gently she eased his dick from her mouth, kissing his head as he slipped past her lips. Followed by an open-mouth kiss to his naked thigh.

With a wicked confident smile, Kat stood before him licking her swollen lips. Her warm eyes glowed with satisfaction.

Oh, yeah, he was done for. Head over heels. In love.

Jamal grabbed her shoulders and pulled her firmly against him, wrapping her in his embrace. Closing his eyes, he nuzzled his face to the slope of her neck, breathing in the softness of her feminine scent. The mingled fragrance of unsatiated need clung to her body. She'd unselfishly pleasured him while remaining famished. Poor little pussy needed him.

He kissed her skin and listened as she whimpered. Oh, baby, he loved her. Hell, he'd been half in love with Kat for the last three years—before he knew who he was fucking. The last three months had only told him for certain what deep inside he already knew. His super–star was made for him. And him alone.

But how to convince her of that? He couldn't even tell her his name. He closed his eyes and trailed his tongue along the racing pulse beneath her sugary skin. He kissed her neck. Her ear, nipping tenderly with his teeth.

Her seeking finger started working seductive magic over his back and shoulders. Her body moved against his, undulating and sensual. Her pants short and needy.

They damned well better get out of that dressing room or he'd be knocking–paws hard in a few more minutes.

He eased her away from him, his erection tight again and protesting. Eyeing her sleek tiger–clad body, he wondered if he'd ever get enough of her sweet pussy. Enough of her.

"I guess you're getting this costume," Jamal said, arching a brow and rubbing his forefinger against a bead of his iridescent liquid that had landed on a black stripe across her chest.

Kat's smile stole his breath. "I guess so. Now, Mr. Gorgeous, pull up your pants, then turn around so I can get dressed."

No way. He was going to see her naked. He'd missed it once. He wouldn't miss it again.

"Like hell I will." He reached for his pants, freeing his nuts from the elastic of his drawers and shrugged the material over his hips. Casually working the button fly, he leaned against the wall, his gaze glued on the costume–clad woman who'd sucked him dry today but had stolen his heart long ago.

Kat glared at Oh–So–Fine as she did up his pants, the confident tilt of his chin warning he wouldn't be melded. Reaching behind him, she swatted his ass. "Turn around, Bad Boy."

His eyes twinkled. "Get dressed, girl. You keep standing there and I'm going to fuck you."

Yes, please. She bit her bottom lip to keep from smiling. That was the best threat he could come up with? Maybe she'd just get undressed. Slowly. He wouldn't turn around, then she could make him pay.

"Suit yourself." Reaching behind her, she freed the zipper, then shimmied as she worked it half–way down her back. Enough to ease the fluid material off her body. Naked beneath, she knew she may just get a good screwing after all.

As she pushed the material down her legs, she watched the apex of his thighs and saw the material rise. So ten–inch melt–in–her–mouth had a little more loving in him, did he?

Her cunt went all creamy.

Reaching for his hand, she lifted it to her mouth. She kissed his palm. "Since you didn't listen, you'll have to be at my service." She licked down the length, then sucked his forefinger into her mouth.

"Do your best, baby."

Kat felt like laughing witnessing the direction of his blood flow. Right to his glorious dick. But she knew that getting all that yumminess inside her meant she wouldn't be able to be quiet enough to keep them from getting discovered.

But she needed him. Needed the release. Hell, it'd been a stressful morning, learning about her impending doom. And after the little treat she'd given him, she deserved to cum. Yeah, and she intended to get it good. Now.

She licked his finger again, getting it good and wet even though she was wet enough already. Liquid seeped from her lips, arousal streaming through her blood.

Dropping his hand, she guided him to her, pressing the pads of his fingertips against her clit. A gasp of air escaped. "This won't . . . take long." Climax was already building.

He chuckled, the sound music to Kat's senses. "Take your time, baby. Make yourself feel good." He dipped his tongue into her ear, then whispered. "That's it, baby, fuck my fingers."

But damn it to hell, he didn't help her. He kept his hand relaxed and Kat was forced to rub against him to push his thumb against her clit. To slide his fingers into her throbbing sopping wet pussy.

He did her one favor. He curled his fingers toward him, oh, God, found her G–spot. And all that need shattered in a hot rush of orgasm. Her muscles clamped down, released, then trembled violently.

Catching her breath, Kat giggled as she sagged against Mr. Gorgeous's chest. "Told you."

He laughed with her. Easing his hand from her body, she felt revered as he held her in his embrace while her breathing returned to normal. He tenderly stroked her back, down the curve of her ass, then retreated as if he were memorizing the slopes of her body.

Minutes passed and he continued to hold her until nearby voices penetrated the sanctuary of the small dressing room. Heat flamed across Kat's cheeks. No doubt that the scent of sex fragranced the air.

Lover Boy kissed her cheek, then spoke softly. "Get dressed, baby. I'll take you to lunch. Take the tigress with you." He slanted his head toward the discarded tiger costume on the floor.

Kat let out a deep sigh, then turned from his arms as she slipped back into her panties, bra, and sundress. "I wish you could be there with me," she murmured as she slipped on her sandals, reaching for the costume.

Silence. She knew he couldn't go. She knew he knew it, too. She shouldn't have said anything about it, but sometimes when she was with him he made it so easy to forget their biggest secret.

Taking the costume from her, Bad Boy gripped her hand, twining their fingers. "Pizza or burgers?"

Kat sighed and followed him out the door.

Chapter 20

He'd become a regular when he used to avoid this place, thinking he didn't have the time to fuss with a bar. Yeah, at night this place pumped with twentysomethings looking for one thing. To get lucky. Hell, he'd been here, too, and was over thirty. And he had, he thought with a grin, thinking about how a chance meeting with his fantasy–lover had led to him falling in love.

But during the day, The Night Kitty was pretty laid back. A nice place to have a drink in the afternoon. To sit in the dark corner with his laptop and remain undisturbed as he read through numerous slush submissions.

Hell, he'd been there enough times now he knew the bartender by name, his favorite ball team. The man still tried to argue that Williams was better than James, even after the weed thing. Lloyd had even called a few times with ticket invites to a couple of games.

Oh, yeah, it was a cool place to hang.

Jamal finished his burger, twisting the to–go wrapping paper into a ball. McD's and Kitty, the perfect lunch time cuisine. He gulped his bar served cola. As good as the beer was on tap here, he didn't start drinking this time of day. Too damned early. Resting his forearms on the long wooden bar in front of him, he lowered his head, his lids sliding closed.

Tonight was too important.

He had a date with Kat and wanted clarity. He wanted to be able to remember everything about her. The scent of her skin. The texture. The way her eyes became sultry when he was up in her. Wanted to recall the way her breath danced across his skin when she came.

Hell, tonight he wanted to burn one last memory into his brain. Into his heart.

To know how her mouth tasted.

Just thinking about those luscious lips caused blood to drop to his cock and he groaned.

"You alright, man?" Lloyd asked.

Jamal nodded, willing away the erection. Like hell, the lust in his soul answered. Opening his eyes, he slid a glance at Lloyd as he filled up another frosty glass for Kent.

Miserable sap sat one seat down, drowning his playa–got–played life in Grey Goose and juice. The top–shelf vodka sat next to him, with a half–empty pitcher of cranberry cock-tail. The fool finally got what he'd been giving each time he fucked a chick and pretended he cared. Then moved on to the next poor honey who was stupid enough to fall for that shit. And there were plenty.

Rebecca sat on the other side of Kent, her blonde hair twisted into a bun on the back of her head, her blue eyes fixed on Kent, but Jamal didn't miss how they glowed with annoyance.

"Them bitches don't know how good they got it when they're with me," Kent mumbled, lifting the glass to his lips. "She didn't appreciate a good brotha."

Becca rolled her eyes, her gaze catching Jamal's. He grinned. They both knew what was up. Kent had fallen. Got hooked on some good pussy and she had dogged him. Probably found out how many hotties he was sexing and kicked his ass to the curb. Just what he deserved. Maybe just what he needed to have the lesson served.

You got to be honest with your girl. Faithful. Treat 'em with respect. Please 'em. Not just high–maintenance chicks, but also the home–girl you could take home to Momma.

Kent hadn't figured it out yet, but Jamal had. And despite how tender he'd been with his client, he'd violated the most important rule. Trust.

Kent brushed his elbow against Jamal's. "Dawg, don't let them bitches get their claws in you. They ain't about nothing but what you can give 'em. They—"

Becca cut in. "Kent, you know that's not true."

He shook his head. Downed his drink, slamming the empty glass upside down on the bar. "The hell it isn't. I stop opening the wallet, the honey stops opening her thighs."

"That's what you think it's about?" Jamal couldn't believe how stupid Kent sounded. A ho opens for cash, but a woman opens for affection. Like his own little wild kitty–Kat. She didn't expect gifts or paid dinners. She didn't need bling to make him want it. To give it to him good. She just needed him to treat her right.

Jamal felt sick. And he needed her. Period.

"Lloyd, can I get an iced glass?" Kent asked, then turned his attention back to them. "That's what Sasha wanted. Wanted me to shower her with gifts. This brotha—" he pounded on his chest "—ain't going down like that."

"You know, Kent, shut the fuck–up. Sasha didn't end it with you because you didn't offer up bank routing numbers. She broke it off because you're a cheating ass." Damnit to hell, but Jamal had heard enough of this tired sucker.

"I didn't cheat."

Becca choked on her lemon water. "Since when is getting your dick sucked by another woman *not* cheating?"

"Hey, we'd never made a commitment."

"You said, she said she loved you."

"While we were fucking."

Rebecca gasped and turned away.

Jamal let out a disgusted breath. "Yeah, whatever." He flicked his hand in a dismissive manner, then glanced at his watch. This was one too long lunch hour. Couldn't wait to get back to work where he wouldn't have to listen to a heartbroken ass mope and complain. Act like he was the victim.

He stood. "You 'bout ready, Becca?" She slid from her stool. Tossing a few bills on the counter to cover his cola and leaving Lloyd a tip, he headed toward the exit.

"Wait. What am I supposed to do to get her back?" Kent hollered, his words slurring from too much Goose.

Pausing, Jamal glanced over his shoulder at Kent slumping in his seat. "Be a man."

That's exactly what he planned on doing tomorrow night when his client learned the truth about how they'd been fucking. When Kat learned how he'd been making love to her over and over.

He held the door for Becca and headed outside, pausing to allow his eyes to adjust to the midday light. The bar was just a few blocks from their office building, they'd walked over, stopping for burgers on the way.

Now they headed back toward the office, walking down the sidewalk in silence. But Jamal knew it was coming. The *I told you so*'s. Becca had warned him not to mix business with pleasure. Had told him what he already knew—how much he risked by sexing Kat Mason, erotica author extraordinaire, fantasy–fuck of many, his Fly–Girl. The woman who owned his heart.

But by then he'd already sampled and it was too late to save himself. Too late to go back down the road he'd already traveled. The die was cast. They'd become lovers. Nameless. Lovers.

"She's beautiful," Becca said softly when they reached the end of the block.

He smiled. "Yeah, she is." Oh, baby, was she ever.

"She seems nice, too."

He nodded.

"Did she trip when she saw you with me and Tonya?"

Apprehension had shimmered in amber eyes, but he understood what that was about. She was his closest friend and he'd long since learned how little experience she'd had in relationships and her fear of being hurt. He swallowed, trying to chase the dryness of his throat. He was going to hurt her.

"Nah, she didn't fuss about it. Didn't mention it at all." Didn't think she'd even remembered once he'd distracted her with his mouth. And she'd surprised him with strawberry titties.

Becca put her hand on his shoulder. "So, what are you going to do?"

They crossed the street.

"Don't start with how you told me."

"I wasn't going to. I'm just wondering, JJ, because this isn't just about sex, is it?"

He shook his head. "I'm in love with her."

She laughed quietly. "Thought so." They walked on, in silence. The faded autumn sun seeped through the low murky clouds, the air taking on a cooler bite as the weeks shifted further from summer. "And she still doesn't know who you are?"

"Not yet."

"You plan on telling her?"

"She'll find out at A Night of Naughty." He was so not into twenty–fucking–questions. He'd been mulling over these same questions for weeks. They were killing him. But Rebecca had been a good friend so he answered anyway.

They'd reached the block their office building was located on. She paused a few yards away, putting her hand on his forearm, her tone dripping with concern. "Do you think she'll forgive you? Will you be able to fix things?"

God, he hoped so.

He took a deep breath and glanced at the storm laden sky, the sun fighting a losing battle. "I'm going to try." He kept looking at the sky, not wanting Rebecca to see the fear in his eyes.

She squeezed his arm, but then moved away. A few seconds later he heard the door slide open, then closed.

Shrugging his shoulders, Jamal rolled his head, then ran his palm over his shaven head to grip the bunched muscles in his neck. Tonight he was going to love Kat the best way he knew how.

Tomorrow he'd face losing her.

With a heavy heart, he headed inside, then toward his office. For now, he could lose himself in his job. He sunk into his leather chair and flicked on his computer. He had a few emails he could purge from his box with delete. Things he had no intention of ever reading. A few others he'd print off and read 'em over when he got the chance.

It wouldn't be long now before he saw her. Tonight he'd make the most of the time they had together. Damned dick of his would probably be throbbed hard for the rest of the afternoon. Down boy. But at least if he was thinking of fucking her, he wouldn't be tormented with thoughts of after.

Shaking his head, Jamal attempted to focus on work.

Tormented, Jamal shut down his computer, tossed a few files in the outgoing bin and gathered his thoughts. In twenty minutes he was meeting Kat for dinner—possibly their last. The following evening A Night of Naughty *would* put an end to their anonymous affair. His secret would be revealed. It could—and probably would—end everything between them. He was out of options.

He couldn't go on this way. He wanted more. Or nothing. It was the nothing part that freaked him the fuck out. Had he known beforehand who he'd taken against the brick wall so many months ago, he'd never have continued it. One sample of her juices and he was hooked. An addict.

But it was coming to an end.

Forget unethical. This was about his heart. It's not like he didn't know this was going to happen. They were friends. She shared her secrets, worries, and her dreams with him. She trusted him. For three years she'd been a major part of his life. He'd loved her then. Not that he'd admitted it. Or even realized it. But it'd been there, lingering just beneath the surface of desire. Of the fantasies she'd created for him. The ones of her he'd created for himself.

Fucking her had sealed his fate. He loved her and wanted a future. But first she had to know the truth. First he had to risk it all to hope at a future.

Shaking his head, Jamal moved away from his desk and gathered his jacket and briefcase. Hopefully the office would be empty at this time of day and he wouldn't have to deal with the ass, Kent. Not again. Once was enough in a day. He didn't need that shit tonight.

Tonight was about pleasuring Kat. Working her so good that no matter what happened at the Halloween Ball, he'd be burned into her memory permanently. He'd give her a sexing she'd never forget. Even if she refused to see him again. His chest ached.

Even if loving her tonight was a way to say goodbye.

The sky was a strange mix of golden sunshine on the horizon and pink tinged clouds. The crisp October air crept over his skin as he walked across the parking lot to his Escalade.

Slipping inside, he drove the few miles to the restaurant where they were meeting for dinner. Blood rushed to his dick just thinking about the surprise he had in store for her. Hell, he was going to get as much pleasure from this as she was. And she was. No doubt. It was the rest of his life without her that he worried about.

Chapter 21

"What did you do?" Kat asked, moving away from her lover's side as she surveyed their surroundings. He'd been rather quiet over dinner and during their walk along the riverbanks. Brooding even. She'd wondered about it, but never expected this. A hotel room. A suite. A small living area. And just beyond double doors, a king–sized bed.

Behind her she heard Mr. Gorgeous fumble with the keys and the second lock click into place, assuring their undisturbed privacy. This is what she had in mind all those nights ago when she'd first met and seduced Bad Boy, though the brick wall fling had turned out just fine.

She smiled, trailing her fingertips over the bed, feeling the silken comforter, the firmness of the mattress. An answering ache built between her thighs. Arousal slick against her panties. She kept her back toward him, hoping he'd take the gesture as an invitation. A come–to–me–please.

She waited in silence for a moment, then glanced back over her shoulder. Oh–So–Fine stood a few feet from the door, his arms hanging by his side, his deep, steady gaze fixed on her.

"You got us a room."

"I wanted you slow."

Oh, yeah, baby, she liked the sound of that. Kat turned toward him fully, need growing at a rapid clip. "You could've taken me home."

"Could I?" He lifted a dark brow.

"Your bed sounds good to me," Kat whispered. She swished her hip to the side, her gaze dropping to the straight line of his full lips. Her nipples tightened.

He moved toward her, his stride purposeful, his swagger confident. He touched her chin and tilted her face toward his. The brooding stranger was back—dangerous—his ebony eyes intent on hers, his mouth drawn like words lingered at the tip of his tongue.

He brushed his knuckles over the hardened tips of her breasts, then curved his long fingers around the swell, claiming the weight in his palm. "Really?" He leaned closer, his other hand sliding to the nape of her neck, drawing her face within a breath of his. He smoothed his lips across her mouth. "And risk discovering who I am?"

Kat blinked her eyes slowly, the line badly blurred between Shy Kat, who would have feared knowing his identity, and the untamed tigress who was almost desperate to really know him. All about him. Not just the parts he shared about his life that protected his anonymity. To not only know his name, but his family. His friends. What he wanted in the future. Everything. Not just his condom size. Not just the style of his pleasuring.

Somehow, since she'd been being sexed by Mr. Gorgeous, she'd learned a new confidence and the wild–chick persona she'd tried on for show was becoming more of who she actually was. She liked it. She felt bold and attractive. Able to take the steps to get her own needs met, with a real–live man. No vibrating dildo any longer.

Kat lifted on her tip–toes and closed the distance between their mouths. Sure, they'd been kissing, but it was the melding of lips, not the blending of souls. She wanted deeper. She closed her eyes. She needed deeper.

Swallowing down the pang of sorrow, she opened her eyes and looked at him. This no–name relationship couldn't go on forever, but she was damned well going to enjoy it while it lasted.

"Make love to me," she whispered against his yielding mouth. *Love me*, her heart begged. Emotions weren't supposed to be part of this game. This was about mutual physical satisfaction. Yeah right, sistah, keep telling yourself that. Maybe you can make yourself believe it.

"I intend to." He touched his tongue to her mouth, sliding it along the crease of her lips. He tasted vaguely of the chocolate they'd shared after dinner. Dessert had been yummy. The taste of him was better.

Kat opened her mouth, yearning to kiss him fully. Needing to be and feel connected to him, despite the fact that she'd held off full tongue kisses as a way to protect her heart. Too late. She was going to really experience her all–too–real, make her freaky lover. For the first time.

He smiled at her eagerness. "Slowly."

"To hell with slowly. I want you, Mr. Gorgeous."

He chuckled, then took a step away from her. "Not tonight, Sweetness."

"But—"

"Sshhh." He touched his finger to her mouth, silencing her objection.

Kat wanted to protest, but the words lodged in her chest. Her pulse sped up. The pads of his fingers trailed along her jaw, then down the slope of her neck. With deliberate languor, he smoothed across the tender skin below her ear, to the point where the rhythm of her pulse soared. To her collarbone. To her shoulder.

With a simple nudge, he turned her so her back was facing him.

A take control sort of man. She liked that. Kat closed her eyes, allowing the texture of his magical hands to caress her. He moved to the zipper of her black silk dress. Her breath caught. The jagged teeth gave way easily.

Jamal held his breath as he stalled the descent of the zipper, admiring the way the black cloth enhanced the heavenly luster of her brown skin. She was dressed elegantly. It didn't matter. She'd soon be naked.

He wanted her naked. Beneath him. Wet. Ready. He wanted her crying out her pleasure by *calling his name*.

Gulping down his need to drive into her, Jamal gathered his wits and plunged the zipper so the dress hung open to the generous swell of her ass. A glimmer of a black lace thong teased his resistance. His cock reacted with a rush of hardening blood.

"This is my night." He pushed the material from her shoulders so the cloth pooled around her feet. "I'm going to take you slowly. Bit by bit." He traced the thin strips of black lace that supported her ripe breasts, the same lace that slipped between the cheeks of her ass—that hugged the pussy he couldn't get enough of. Or wait to get into.

Leaning forward, he pressed his mouth to her skin. The essence of her was there in her fragrance.

Sweet, feminine. *Alluring*.

"You don't want a hard fuck, do you, Sweetness?"

She nodded. Quickly. Jamal held back his laughter.

"No. You want to be touched. Kissed. Loved. You want me to worship you." She shuddered before him. He heard the low escaping moan. He relished her response. With one hand he continued his caresses, feeling the smoothness of her skin. The soft curves of her womanly body.

With his free hand he stripped off his clothing. To hell with slowness when it came to getting as close to her as he could. But this wasn't about his pleasure. This was about Kat Mason. His super–star. His lover.

The love of his life.

This was about their last time before she knew the truth. Before she hated him for it.

Not his dick. Not his begging orgasm. Not his need to fuck her like crazy.

He closed the distance between them, bringing her back into full contact with his chest. She trembled, sucked a breath between her teeth. Attempted to turn in his arms. But he held her there, before him, fighting his own overpowering lust.

He was going to go slow if it killed him. Judging by the amount of blood throbbing in his cock, it just might.

He breathed her in deeply, memorizing the way she felt in his arms. Trying to calm the wild cadence of his pulse. The longing for forever with this woman. This woman who meant everything to him.

When he could take it no longer, he bent, reaching behind her knees and swooped her into his arms. She gasped in surprise, then looped her hand over his shoulder and held onto him.

He moved the several steps to the bed and laid her in the center of the king–sized bed, atop the smooth comforter. He went with her, the mass of him forcing her back so her hair sprayed across the cloth, her shoulders rested on the material.

"You're beautiful, baby." He dropped his gaze from hers, roaming over her body. Appreciating every inch of her glorious skin, the milky chocolate tone making him damned hungry. "Beautiful."

His heart tightened when a sigh of pleasure passed her luscious lips. But she said nothing. Her body responded with the answer he needed. Those dark crests of her breasts drew up tightly. Her legs relaxed, her knees falling apart.

He bent his head and flicked his tongue across a begging nipple through the black lace of her bra. Then he released the front snap, pushing it off her shoulders. "I'm going to give you what you need." He closed his mouth around the peak, swirling his tongue, then lifted. "Let me love you. I know what your body's begging for."

"You . . ." Her voice was breathless.

He glanced up and saw her lids were closed, her long lashes leaving shadows across her cheeks. Her lips quivered.

Reaching for him, she touched his forehead with her fingers. Ran her palm back over his skin. "I love your head."

"I know you do, baby." He chuckled when she applied pressure, her demand evident. He nipped at her breasts, then closed over it. Swirling, he sucked it into his mouth, laving it with attention.

Her back arched off the bed. Sweat broke on his brow, the fierce need to just drive into her overwhelming. Slow down, man, he warned. He moved from her breast, kissing downward. Ran his tongue across her ribs. Lower. Lapped at the shallow indent of her belly button.

His Kat deserved to be worshiped. He intended to do so. Jamal watched her face as he moved lower, dropping tender kisses on her hip. Down. Tucking his thumbs beneath the hem of her lace panties, he tugged them down off her hips, down juicy thighs, and tossed them aside.

Then his mouth was back on her. Sliding his tongue across short black hair, cropped perfectly.

Her mouth opened into an O. Her chest rose and fell quickly as silent shallow pants escaped.

Her skin was satin beneath his lips. Tasted of honey. The sweetness intensified as he slipped his tongue between her lips. She gasped. A hand settled on his shoulder. Her legs parted, welcoming him.

He moved deeper, pressing his tongue against her clit. Oh. God. She. Tasted. Delicious. He growled. Her body trembled.

Jamal was going slowly insane. He wanted to love this

woman. He wanted to make love to her but most impor-
tantly, he wanted her to remember.

He slid his hand down the back of her leg to her upper
thigh. He lifted it over his shoulder, spreading her labia.
Sucking at the arousal dripping from such yummy pussy.

"Bad Boy!" she cried out, trusting her hips upward so his
tongue slid deeper inside her.

Oh, yeah, she was liking it. He thrust in. Out. Replaced his
tongue with two fingers. She was sopping wet. His mouth
moved greedily to her clit. Fluttered his tongue across it.
Quickly.

She writhed. Cried out. He sucked the nub into his mouth.
She came.

Sweet. So sweet. Juicy. Creamy.

Jamal's cock bucked. Damn near emptied his wad against
the bed. He licked her cum from her lips. Her inner thigh.
Around his fingers, her body continued to shiver with release.

Her voice was broke. The tone almost like a sob. "Thank
you, Mr. Gorgeous."

He gritted his teeth together for a moment. He held his
breath. What would he do when she wasn't around to call
him that name? His chest ached.

Sliding her leg from his shoulder, he moved up her body.
Every muscle tense. Desire overpowering restraint. Sprawling
next to her, he gathered her into his embrace, kissed her eyelids, then rested his forehead against hers. He wanted her to
recover before he drove her wild again.

She wiggled against him. Damn. Kat knew how to make a
man hard. Blood thickened his cock until it was throbbing.
With her forearms pressed against his chest, she framed his
face with her hands.

Smoothed her fingertips across his lips. Jamal held his
breath. Then she shifted. Rose slightly.

And kissed him.

Kissed him.

Not a tender peck of prior exchanges. Her mouth opened. Her tongue touched his lips, inviting. Tantalizing. She whimpered. And led him in. His tongue touched hers. She moaned softly into his mouth.

Aw, hell, he was losing his fucking mind. This is what he wanted. This is where he longed for a lifetime to be. She was kissing him. And, oh, god, how could he ever kiss again and not know that only his Kat could do this to him?

This is what he wanted.

This was intimacy.

He closed his eyes and gave over full power to instinct. He could kiss her for hours. Eternity. Mate their tongues. Suck from her supple lips. Live off her soft breaths and pleasure moans.

They'd met and fucked. As strangers. Now. Finally. They loved as lovers.

Jamal felt the shift. Knew he'd never be the same. Accepted it. And kissed Kat with everything he had.

So this is how love tasted. Kat welcomed the stroke of Lover Boy's tongue, the pressure of his oh–so–yummy lips. Firm, yet yielding. Why had she waited so long for this? Why had she been so afraid?

Because now her heart was undeniably involved. Now she had something to lose when this silly game of meet and release came to an end. Her soul. It'd be the price she paid for traveling along this foolish path of pretending she could sex without attachment. Fuck without caring. Love without loving.

All a lie. An ugly lie. Just like the falsehood of who she was that she kept so cleverly hidden. Behind a wild–Kat who liked his dick so much she'd do anything to get it in her.

She sighed. Including forgetting who she truly was. A wallflower who'd been pretending.

Gulping down emotion, Kat moved her mouth on his. Stroked her hands across his shoulders. Down his back.

Touched him. Needed to feel the burn of his sweaty skin rock against her. She shifted her hips. Felt his cock throb against her clit.

Putting aside the rest, that's what she wanted to focus on. Him. Pleasure. The right here. The right now. How they could make each other feel.

Rolling onto her back, he shifted between her thighs, dragging one leg over his hip. She ran her heel up the back of his leg. Thrust her hips upward. The motion welcoming.

He entered her. Hard. Ten thick inches ground downward.

Kat cried out into his mouth, their lips never breaking. Breathing labored.

Out. In. Out. Stroke after stroke building in intensity. In power. In lust and need and desire. Climax was coming already, her body already primed. Her clit swollen and sensitive. With his grind of his wondrous dick, his pubic hair set fires across her skin. And the build tightened.

Orgasm drawing near.

Beneath her roving hands, Kat could feel his muscles bunching. His tension growing.

The rhythm of his pumps wild now.

Pulling up her other knee, Kat wrapped it around his back. And was gone. She yelled, but the sound was lost into Lover Boy's mouth. Tremors took over her body, tightening, then free . . .

Inside her, he thrust his dick one last time, then pulled from her body as his body shook. A deep groan emptying onto her tongue as she felt his dick buck against her clit between them and the hot gush of his nut on her belly.

The wildness of the kiss slowed peacefully. Ended as he dragged his mouth away, collapsing atop of her, his weight supported on bulging muscles of his arms. His face fit into the curve of her neck.

He ran his tongue across her pulse point. "I'm sorry, Sweetness," he whispered.

Kat choked. "For what?"

"That wasn't as slow as I wanted to go."

"It was perfect."

He rolled to his side and gathered her against him. Kat pushed back a curl. It clung to her damp skin. Tilting back, she looked him over. From his dark chocolate body, shimmering with sweat, to his closed eyes. A chest that rose and fell quickly. To lips that kissed her tenderly.

This was her man.

She curled into his body, draping his arm around her. Her man for tonight.

"I'm love ... you real ... slow ... " he took a deep breath, his voice thick with sleep. "Next time."

She smiled. Her man was going to do her again tonight. She kissed the skin over his heart. Closed her eyes, smiling.

She looked forward to it.

Chapter 22

Kat opened her eyes, forgetting for a moment she wasn't in her own bed. But in a hotel. Naked. With a man. He slept soundly behind her, her back snug against his chest. His breathing even. Morning wood wedged between her butt cheeks.

Pale sunlight filtered in through the drawn curtains, washing the room in a golden hue. Specs of dust danced in the shards of yellow.

Taking a deep breath, Kat closed her eyes and snuggled back into the warmth of Bad Boy's body. Oh, what incredible heat he created. The faded scent of vanilla air freshener lingered in the room. And the pungent odor of sex. With a purr, she squeezed her thighs together, still slick from making love.

Making love? Kat tried to ignore the pang of worry that tightened her heart. That stole her breath. Tried, desperately, to shake off the feelings clawing their way from her soul. How could she admit the man who had no name, no identity—other than one she'd made up—was the man she loved?

The deep–down, earth–moving love that makes a woman complete. Soul mate love. Like when a puss finds the right Tommy. This agreement was supposed to cover their needs.

Desires. To be a good time only, as long as it lasted. Certainly not a lifetime.

Squeezing her lids closed, she wondered how could she be happy in the present, when there was no future? Only the moment.

Only this moment.

She had to focus on now. Not missing him yet. There'd be a time for that.

Drawing a deep breath, Kat eased her eyes open and glanced at the clock. Mid–morning. Closer to lunch than breakfast. Her stomach grumbled. Peeking over her shoulder, Kat looked at Lover Boy, the yummy color of his dark brown sugar skin glistened in contrast to the pale blue hotel comforter. Naked, the material draped low on his hip, and she had to resist wanting to lick the chiseled muscles, hidden by faint shadows. Delicious. She wet her lips.

Kat's stomach growled, demanding food. Nourishment after getting down for the better part of the night. Turning her attention to the bedside table, she noticed a hotel service booklet, and a room service menu.

She wiggled away from him, trying to reach the phone.

"Mmm–mmm," Mr. Gorgeous grumbled. His arm tightened around her waist. His hips tilted, digging his rigid cock into her side. Just like that, she was wet. Her nipples puckered. She wanted to climb on. Ride him. Hard.

Pressing her thighs together, she whispered, "Bad Boy." Despite his protective arm and hard–on, his body was slack from sleep.

She tried again. "Bad Boy?" When he didn't reply, she moved toward the phone.

He tightened his arm around her and pulled her closer. Flush against him. And that oh–so–tempting pulsing cock. Despite being slightly distracted by wanting to fuck, her hunger persisted.

She curled her fingers into his, bringing his fist to her

mouth, she kissed him. "I'm going to get us some food," she whispered, thinking *you catch more flies with honey* . . .

"Later."

Apparently Mr. Oh–So–Fine was comfortable where he was. Didn't need food. She did. Anything short of tying him up, *she was stuck*, she realized. Kat's lids popped open, her intent gaze searching the end of the bed for the pair of cotton terry bath robes the hotel provided.

Just where they'd tossed them aside, after a brief post–shower use, last night, she spotted them draping just within reach. Two terry robes.

Two terry belts to tie around his wrists.

Grinning wickedly, Kat worked one belt from the loose waist–loops. The second.

"Oh, yeah, baby," she said, then tossed a glance over her shoulder to make sure Ten–Inch Joy Stick was still asleep.

Grabbing one belt, she wound it around the hand draping over her middle, his hand resting near her tits. Once the knot was tight she carefully pulled his arm up and secured the loose ends to the wrought iron bed frame. One hand tied. *One to go*, she mused, holding back her excited purring.

Easing slightly away from him, Kat turned toward the man sleeping behind her. When he began to move, she dropped her head to his chest and snuggled into him. She was rewarded with Mr. Gorgeous' cooperation. He rolled onto his back and tossed his free arm above his head.

Perfect position to be tied.

Balling the second terry cord in her hand, she cuddled into his warm body, kissing his jaw line to keep him distracted. To keep him from knowing he was about to be at her mercy. Her sex slave.

Running her tongue over one nipple, then the other, she took delight in the way they beaded against her. She used the motion to move to his other side.

"Morning," she whispered, brushing her lips to the soft

skin below his ear. Tracing the curve with her tongue. Biting the fleshy globe between her teeth.

With his eyes still closed, he smiled. "You're beautiful in the morning, Sweetness," he mumbled as he stretched.

"You can't even see me," she replied, nipping harder at his ear. Teach him to fib. She pressed a light kiss to his lowered eyelids watching the shadows of his lashes on his dark skin.

The dimple in his cheek deepened. "I don't need to. I know," he said. He arched his back and rubbed his hard–on against her inner thigh. "He knows. He needs you."

Pussy needs him, too. Meow!

He bent his arm around her. Ran his palm over her butt. Caressed her back. Shoulders.

Kat took a deep breath and bit back her smile, thinking about what she was going to do with his hand. Better do it quick. Before he was awake enough to realize his other hand was already secured in her knot.

Wallflower Kat hesitated briefly. *To hell with good–girl innocence.* Wild Kat was in control here. Time to take full advantage of his willing body while she had the chance. She was a woman with needs. *And, she knew exactly what she wanted.*

Lover–Boy. Hard. Inside her. Meow, yeah, that's what she hunted. She knew how to make it happen.

Reaching behind her, she grabbed his hand and tugged it forward. Kissing a trail down his biceps and to his fingers, she kept him occupied while she fastened the robe belt around his wrist.

"Haven't I tired you out?" he asked, his teasing voice gruff from sleep.

Kat stalled. Hell, no. Not yet. But he would. Smiling, she didn't reply. She wanted him tenable on the bed so she could pleasure him while at the same time appeasing her appetite.

She flicked her tongue out to taste his skin, finding him salty from sweat. Familiar. Like her man.

She ignored the pang in her heart. *Not her man.* Just the man she was using instead of the dildo and batteries.

Once the knot was tight around his wrist, she nibbled up his arm, learning each carved muscle with her lips as she guided his hand above his head. To the iron bed frame.

He only grumbled slightly. "Forget my arm. Kiss my lips."

Kat laughed as the last bond was secured.

"Okay," she answered. "I'll give you a kiss. Your wish is my command." She turned back to him, pleased with her handiwork, and kissed him fully on the mouth. Slipped her tongue along the lush rim of his lips. She lapped from him, building her own desire like a drug–addict after one hit.

"Or better yet, *my* wish is *my* command," she said after ending the kiss. Sitting up, she tossed the pale blue blankets back. Flipping the warmth from his body, she left him completely nude, his dark muscular body a beautiful contrast to the light bedding.

And his glorious cock jetting toward to the ceiling, throbbing and ready for more sex.

With the blast of cool morning air, Mr. Gorgeous attempted to sit up but was restrained. His eyes flew open and his arms yanked at the terry cloth cording holding him to the bed. His muscles flexed and strained.

"What the hell, Sweetness? What'd you do?" His midnight gaze found hers. Settled heavily upon her.

A bolt of pure electricity shot through her body. He was surprised all right. But turned–on. There was no mistaking the pulse of his dick or the glistening pearly bead of pre–cum on his plum–shaped head.

His eyes were alert, his jaw tight, his nostrils flared, like a stallion ready to claim its mate.

"Do you want me to untie you?" she asked, dropping her voice an octave.

"What are you going to do with me?" His full lips curving into a reluctant smile. Beneath the dark chocolate of his skin, his muscles rippled and worked. His abs carved into a six–pack. His pecs flexed and twitched. Though she could see the tension in his body, she also saw consent. He leaned his head back against the pillow. The glowing look in his eyes was almost like an 'I dare you'.

"Nothing. I'm not going to do anything to you. I'm just going to have breakfast."

Scooting on her knees to the end of the bed, Kat bent and pressed her open mouth to the inside of his thigh. The thorough kiss left moisture gathering between her legs.

A rough guttural groan escaped his mouth. He tried to reach for her again. The cotton ties strained under his force, yet held. His attempt at escape failed so he used his legs to try to capture her.

Kat was too quick for him. She leapt from the bed laughing. Grabbing the phone from the bedside table, she tossed a kiss over her shoulder and moved from away from the bed.

"Wait, baby. Are you just going to leave me here? I'm hungry, too," he said.

"I bet you are." She smiled as she spoke, then deliberately ran her own hands across her chest. She tweaked her extended nipples with her thumbs, grinning when his cock jumped in response. She licked her bottom lip and moaned.

"If you're good, Bad Boy, I may just bring you something good to eat."

Tossing one of the discarded robes over her forearm, Kat didn't wait for his reply. She glided from the bedroom, butt–ass naked. Grinning like a cat that'd found a mouse in a trap, she walked to the main room of their hotel suite.

Sliding her arms into the warmed fluffy cotton, she pounded out the pound seven, the number to get her room–service.

Jamal wrenched at the cotton ties wrapped around each wrist. *She'd better not leave me here*, he thought, pulling and tugging to no avail. *She'd better get her ass back in here.* "Get your ass back in here," he barked.

Hell, she'd tricked him all right. Kept him all hot, bothered, and distracted with soft, yet deceptive, kisses. Growling, Jamal glanced down at his drawn–up sac and hard–on pulsing, eager for her return. She'd managed to use her brains to outsmart him, when his brawn could have easily flipped their situation and it'd be his client pinned to the bed.

Fuck! He was tied to the bed and she'd just walked out the door. Could she have figured out who he was? Was she so pissed she planned on leaving him there? Exposing him as the sort of agent who screws their clients. Literally!

His dick didn't give a shit. Blood raged in his cock, the head jetting toward the ceiling, damn aroused by the lingering scent of her cunt and the memory of how damned hard they'd fucked.

How well they'd made love.

Love? Could the love of his life have just walked out the door? Jamal glanced around the room. Naa, her dress was on the floor. She'd be back. Ruff. With him tied to the bed, ready for the pleasure of her abuse.

Chapter 23

Jamal closed his eyes and waited for her to return, feeling a little helpless. He'd best check his ego at the door, for his Fly–Girl seductress had caught him in her web. He strained at his bindings. And he wasn't getting out. At least he trusted Kat not to torture him. Not before offering up some of her sweet, tight pussy.

Hell, masculine pride be damned, this was a fantasy come to life and his dick damn well knew it. Poor thing couldn't stay hard forever, or could it? Around this honey, he seemed to have a perpetual boner.

Mocking himself, Jamal rolled his eyes in his head, then focused on the ceiling. What an idiot he was. Deep down a need to be honest with Kat burned in his gut. Guilt like a hang–man's noose, tightening around him. But once the truth was out, these wham–bam, mind–blowing flashes of passion would be over.

His body didn't want to give her up. His heart couldn't take it. But tonight, at the Halloween party, the truth would be out. The best fuck of his life would be saying goodbye. That's why last night, he'd loved her so thoroughly.

This morning, she turned the table.

A knock at the hotel room door drew his attention. Muffled

voices. Kat's and someone else's. Then the thud of the door closing, leaving him in silence. Making him wonder again, if she'd left him tied that way. Like a bad dog, tethered for the public's safety.

Perhaps she had left him. He could hardly blame her. But not even that could temper how he felt about her. What he was soon going to live without. Though he may never bury himself in her again, he'd never forget the look of pure rapture on her face when she came. Never forget the breathy moans. They way she cried his name. Mr. Gorgeous.

Jamal's cock jumped. A raspy groan rumbled from his chest.

"I hope you're thinking about me," she said from the doorway.

He'd been so deep in his thoughts about sexing her he hadn't even heard her return. He lifted his head, the ties at his wrist keeping him from rising from the bed. "You finally came back? I thought you'd left me."

"Why would I do that? Didn't I tell you I was hungry?"

Jamal laughed. He was damn hungry, too, but he sure didn't need food. Only Sex–Pot. "Did you get something to eat?"

She lifted a tray so that he could see it. "I sure did," she cooed. He hadn't noticed it at first. He hadn't noticed much except the way her dusky nipples puckered or how her heavy breasts begged to be licked.

"I've been a good boy, Sweetness. Stayed right where you left me. Did you bring something for me to eat, too?" he asked.

"Maybe." She walked forward and settled the tray on the edge of the bed beside his right thigh. Sliding down next to him, she placed her hand on his leg. Feathered her fingertips provocatively.

It could only be better if she worked her way up a bit. To his drawn–up balls. To his aching dick. As far as Jamal knew, there were no erogenous zones on his knee. But, damn! He wanted her. She was twisting him bad with need.

He gulped for breaths. "Maybe, huh?" he asked. He needed to keep her talking. Either that or he'd embarrass himself and cum from the merest hint of her touch. And, he just might.

"Yeah, maybe."

He watched as Kat plucked something from the tray. A red ripe strawberry. She bent forward, holding the berry between her perfectly manicured fingernails, and touched the cold fruit to his chest. An avalanche of wild fire rippled across his skin. She swirled it in a circular motion, closing in upon his flat nipple. Squeezing, the berry left a trail of red, sticky juice.

Sweetness leaned into him, closing her lips over the crushed berry. Over his beaded nipple. Making him squirm, she used her mouth to finish the fruit and nectar. Used her tongue to torture him.

Sucking air between his teeth, Jamal bucked his hips off the pale blue comforter. She nipped, catching his nipple slightly with her teeth. Wild, sassy Kat. But she eased the quick sting with her warm tongue. Her soft moans and purrs of pleasure were damn near his undoing. Oh, God, he was about to cum.

He forced himself to hold on. To concentrate on the texture of her tongue—warm, slightly rough, completely captivating. On her scent—feminine and floral, like roses and her pussy. Like their sex.

She scraped her nails through the strawberry juice. Dipped those teasing fingers into the hollow of his belly button. Swirled them in the dusting of hair that crept from his belly button to his balls.

"What are you doing to me?" Jamal growled, his throat closing as restrained desire choked him.

"I'm having breakfast. Can't you tell?" she responded, mumbling her words as she lifted, just barely, from her teasing nips to his small, stiff nipple.

Driving him insane.

Kat sat up and reached for the tray. She grabbed a second

strawberry but wasn't gentle with it. She crushed it in her fist. Juice and chunks of berry flesh dripped across his chest and abdomen. She wiped her hand on the fleshy part of his inner leg.

Grabbing up a small tub of yogurt—vanilla–cherry—Kat turned to him, a wickedly playful smile curving the lush line of her lips. "Shall we share?"

Mr. Gorgeous made a gruff sound in the back of his throat. Clicking the inside of her cheek with her tongue, she tipped the small plastic tub to the side. Smooth, creamy yogurt spilled over the crushed strawberries. The abs he'd worked on for months in the gym now served as a breakfast dish.

Kat used her tongue as the spoon. Lapped at him like a kitty with a bowl of fresh cream. Yum.

Jamal kept his gaze trained on the chick working him like a champion. She was making all these sweet little sexy sounds, slurping yogurt off his body like the kitty hadn't eaten in weeks. Hell, it'd been less than an hour since he'd been all up in her and he felt like he hadn't hit it in years. Damned cock of his wanted to fuck.

Now.

The air around them was perfumed with the freshness of strawberries and cream. With the smell of her aroused pussy. The combination reminding him—again—of the paradox. She was a sensual tigress. A siren, tempting and alluring in every way. But with home–girl innocence.

He gulped down the need squeezing his throat closed. That talented mouth of hers didn't quit. She swept long strokes of her tongue across him. Swirling in the cream. Lapping it up. Purring and mewing these soft little moans that made him damn near explode.

"You taste yummy, Bad Boy." He leaned forward, nibbling a piece of berry near his collar bone with an I'm–gonna–tease–you–till–you–cum attitude. Leaning forward, her pert nipples grazed his skin. Those luscious tits hovering too temptingly close. His mouth watered. He wanted a taste.

"Damn, girl." He tested his bindings, but the terry cloth held. Shit!

Turning his wrist, Jamal tried to loosen the knots. To ease the loops over his hands. Anything to get free. To roll her on to her back and give her the same agonizingly slow seductive treatment. But, she'd managed knots with a perfect combination of not–too–tight, but no–fucking–way–to–get–free.

Pulling back, Kat straddled his waist. Strawberry clung to her lips. Her chin. Cream kissed her dark chocolate nipples. Damn, if it didn't look like cum on her chest. Jamal tossed back his head and laughed. If she wasn't careful, that's exactly what it'd be.

"Enjoying yourself, are you?" Kat asked.

"Yeah, baby. You're not full are you?"

"Do you want to know if I'm all finished?" she taunted playfully, lifting a third strawberry. Her dark eyes twinkled with pleasure.

Jamal held her gaze, focusing on the gleam in her eye that told him he hadn't seen anything yet. He nodded. "You'd better not be finished. I'm not through with you yet."

The rich sound of her feminine laughter wafted in the air. "You're in no position to make threats, now are you?" She scooted down his thighs, lowering the strawberry to the head of his cock and swirling it in the pearl of glossy lubricant at the tip. Then she plopped the berry in her mouth and ate the whole thing, her fingers lifting another berry as she chewed. That one was dipped to his erection and crushed.

A line of red slithered down the hard length of his cock, cold and intoxicating.

"Mmm, strawberries and yogurt. One of my favorite morning treats." She held the berry with two fingers and brought it to her mouth. One by one, she stuck each sticky finger into her mouth and licked it clean in long smooth strokes.

Damn dick of his had a mind all its own. Possibly because all the blood that should have been in his brain had migrated south and pulsed between his legs. His shaft bucked, pleading for the same attention she was giving her fingertips. Like KFC. Finger–licking good.

"You know, Mr. Gorgeous, I can think of only two things that go better with strawberries than yogurt." She smoothed her middle finger across her tongue.

He gulped. Hard. "Oh, yeah? What would that be?" *Please let it be him.*

She didn't answer right away, but turned toward her breakfast tray, laden with goodies and lifted a canister of ready–made, fresh–for–the–licking whipped cream. With a flick of one finger to the plastic spout, she sent a frothy cloud of pre–sweetened cream to his cock.

It swirled around his head, then smoothed down the underside of his dick. To his drawn–tight balls. His entire erection was well encased in the dessert topping. *He'd rather be encased in her pussy*, he thought, fighting back a shiver as the fridge–cooled cream covered him. *At least it'd be warm in there.*

"What's . . . second thing . . . goes well with strawberries?" Jamal managed through gritted teeth. He was having a hard time stringing words together, but figured she'd make sense of him or he'd die a happy death of his straining engorged member while she thought about it.

"You do," she answered, dropping her head to his erection and finally, oh yeah, baby, finally offering a bit of reprieve for his aching hard–on.

"Ahh . . ."

Her hot little mouth closed around him. Her soft lips were pure heaven. She drew him deep inside her. Jamal closed his eyes, rocking his hips to greet her downward thrust. She accepted him deep into her throat. He felt the spiral of fire. Lust–enraged passion built in his balls like a maddened pasta pot about to boil over. A groan bubbled up from someplace deep in his gut as he repressed the need to climax.

Save it for later, he urged his reaction to follow his orders. Not an easy feat. His lungs burned, each ragged breath becoming shorter. Balling his hands into fists, Jamal focused on the feeling of being inside of her. Not the impending orgasm.

Whipped cream and dick—Mr. Gorgeous' dick, Kat clarified. Nope, nothing better. Such a yummy treat. She eased him from her mouth with a little pop as the swollen tip of him slid past her lips. Making him feel good made her so wet. She could feel how close he was and knew if she didn't slow down the fun would be over before she was finished with her breakfast. Wrapping her fingers around his rocked–up flesh, she eased her hand down to his wide base, then slipped lower so she cupped his balls in her palm.

Kneading the drawn flesh, she used her second hand to get another strawberry from the bowl. Rolling the soft fruit between her fingers, she brought about a rush of juice that she used to bathe his dick. With her tongue she followed the line of red as it rolled from his head down to the base. The extended veins throbbed beneath her touch.

Listening to his husky groans and guttural moaning heightened her own gratification. She liked giving him enjoyment. Liked it a whole lot. A fucking turn–on.

As much as she enjoyed the taste of him while she sucked, there was a building ache deep within her just to get on his stiff ten and ride him hard. Arousal slid down her inner thighs. Her breasts were heavy. She wanted him inside with a raw, unchecked urgency.

"I'm close, Sweetness," he growled.

Kat glanced up. Small beads of sweat shimmered on his

brow and upper lip. Tension vibrated through his defined body. His biceps strained as he instinctively pulled at his bindings.

"I'm close," he snarled again, like he didn't want to cum yet.

Licking away the last of whipped cream from her lips, Kat moved up his body, straddled him. His heavy flesh brushed against her clit. She rocking her hips to further complete the contact. They shivered in delight.

The last treat on her tray of delights was a condom. She quickly divested the wrapper and draped it over his dick.

"Untie me."

She shook her head.

Concentrating on the building climax centered in her cunt, Kat forgot everything but getting him inside her. Mindless with lust, she rose up on her knees, grabbed his jimmy– capped cock and brought it to her pussy lips.

He tilted his hips away. "Untie me," he demanded with a roar. "Untie me now!"

Kat complied. This had started as a playful game. She'd never guessed how bad it'd be for her on the end of the getting-teased stick. She wanted to finish with a good hard fuck.

Like her back was against the bricks.

She leaned forward, reaching the knots of terry cloth. The belts that held Lover Boy to the bed.

On a rush of her exhaled breath, the first knot slipped free from the wrought iron bed frame, the cotton still wound around his wrist. His hand landed on the small of her back and ground into her welcoming wet heat. She moaned. Slanted the other direction, she freed his still secured hand.

When the second knot was loose enough to pull, Jamal yanked free and grasped her around the waist. He lifted her above him, and slammed her down upon him. Impaling her completely on his long, thick dick.

"Ahh! Oh, god," she screamed. Her head lolled to the side. Her back arched. He was deep up in it now. In heaven. In the heated depths of ecstasy.

He lifted her again. Thrust upward. Finding a desperate rhythm of swift forceful drives. The barrage of impetus strokes continued. Her inner thighs burned. He was trembling beneath her.

"Sweetness," he roared. His dick pulsed those relentless convulsions of cum. He slipped one hand forward with his last powerful thrusts, his skilled thumb finding her clit and pressing the little button in a cadence that mimicked the cum jetting into the condom.

Shy wallflower or not, this is just what Kat imagined. Wanted. With one last push, she was shoved from the precipice of orgasm into the freefalling bliss of climax. Every muscle in her body clamped down. Then shattered into tremors of heaven.

She became aware first of the slow throbbing where they were connected. A beat that matched the thump of her heart. His hand smoothed up and down her back. His second hand framed her cheek and his thumb slid leisurely back and forth across her lips. This was tenderness. This is what she'd been missing her entire life. Oh, god, why with a nameless man, she silently questioned, allowing her lids to drift closed.

It was a gesture so gentle—so loving—she hiccupped to keep from sobbing. Was she to believe this was just sex? Just sex that soothed the body's wants and needs? Why then did she feel his affectionate caress all the way to her soul? Why then did it feel so right to be draped across his chest, so close emotionally she was unsure where he stopped and she began?

After a lifetime of searching, it finally seemed as if she were exactly where she belonged. Keeping her eyes closed, Kat vowed to never forget this moment. To never forget how it felt to be held with love and tenderness.

As good as this affair was it couldn't last forever. He didn't know who she was. Wouldn't approve of her prostitution. Selling sex for money, on paper rather than the streets. She needed to end it soon because she just couldn't imagine disappointing him. Couldn't imagine the pain of looking into his intense eyes and knowing he felt badly about what had happened between them. Without this man, she thought, smoothing her hand over his pecs so his heartbeat thumped beneath her palm, long, lonely days would come.

She swallowed the lump in her throat. Mr. Gorgeous grew still beneath her. She could hear and feel the pounding of his heart. After a long quiet moment, his thumb began to glide across her lips again. It was almost as if he'd been waiting for her to say something or that he wanted to, but decided against it.

Without warning, he rolled her onto her back and came up on one elbow beside her. His midnight gaze assessing as he studied her face. Kat felt like blushing. Her cheeks warmed.

Did he wonder, as she did, what the shift in the moment meant? Something was different between them. Her heart ached. Tears burned the back of her eyes. She forced them away before any had fallen.

The poignant moment passed. He smiled a charmingly boyish grin and bent forward to nuzzle into the hollow of her neck. Between light kisses he said, "You didn't share breakfast, and I'm starving." He softly nipped her collarbone.

Kat tried to shift away from him. It was afternoon already and she had a hair appointment in an hour. Her pulse jumped, the shy her clawing free from the confidence. Tonight was the Halloween Gala. The night she'd made her first author appearance. She was scared to death. Wanted to cancel.

She glanced at Mr. Gorgeous. She felt so safe in his arms. She wanted to take him with her. To hold his hand. To have him whisper that everything would be alright. To help her face the public when she'd much rather hide in the corner.

But she couldn't ask him. Even with the costumes, people

would know who she was. Why she was there. The guest of honor. She couldn't take her lover no matter how badly she needed him at her side. Not without him finding out who she was and what she did for a living.

"I need to go," she whispered, when his tongue covered a pert nipple.

"Not yet."

"I have to."

"Tell me when. When will I see you again?"

A tear slid down her cheek. Unnoticed. With her heart racing, she whispered, "The Night Kitty. Next Saturday. At eleven."

He nodded. "I'll go shower."

Kat smiled at him as he rolled from the bed, then walked butt–ass naked toward the bathroom. By the time he got out, she'd be gone.

But they'd have tonight.

Chapter 24

Kat smoothed her hands down her thighs, wiping the dew from her palms as she tried to settle her nerves. Taking a deep breath, she stepped from the shadows and moved toward the reception area set up just outside the Grand Ballroom. Hanging over the double doors, a wide, black satin sash had been tied. *A Night of Naughty* written across it in red.

From within the thin hotel walls, she could hear the music thumping. Snoop Dogg's voice was doing his bow–wow doggie–shizzle thing to the beat of the bass.

Sinking her teeth into her bottom lip, she glanced down at her black and tawny tigress suit and wished she'd chosen something that would disguise her face. Cat ears and whiskers didn't do much to hide her features.

A burst of giggles drew her attention. She took a step. Another. Moving, she approached the table before the entry to her greatest fear. A public appearance.

Behind the table two women who worked for The Marriot Hotel sat waiting with lists of invited names, their heads bent together as they whispered and laughed. Dressed as Playboy Bunnies, the two blondes looked every bit the part, complete with floppy ears.

Most likely had fuzzy tails stuck to their asses, too, Kat decided. Making fun of their costumes didn't do much to get her mind off facing the crowd of fans partying within the ballroom walls.

"Your name, please," one of the blonde bunnies asked.

She took a deep breath. Swallowed the terror and hoped to hell her body wasn't shaking. At least not visibly. "Kat Mason."

"Oh, *you're* Kat Mason? The author? You write Glory's Stories?"

Kat pasted on her best fake smile. There had been times in her career where she'd been greeted by fans. Couples she'd helped through her relationship column. Never, ever had she been faced with a fan who knew what she really focused on writing. Sex.

"Yes, I do."

"Wow," the second bunny said, jumping from her seat. "That's so neat."

So neat? Were these girls even old enough to be working the door of an *adult only* party? Barely legal by looks of them. Kat ignored her cheerleader bounce, offering a small smile. "Is my name on the list?"

She knew it would be. This was her party after all. A celebration of *her* success.

"Oh, um, sorry." She dropped to her seat and grabbed the list. But instead of checking, she kept staring at Kat. "I'm such a fan, Ms. Mason. I've been reading Glory's Stories for years."

Since she was in kindergarten? Kat blinked. "I'm glad you've enjoyed it."

The girl nodded, then checked the list of names. She scratched Kat's off, then went about searching a stack of paper name tags cut into different sexy shapes. Figures.

"So what inspires you?" the other girl asked.

Mr. Gorgeous. Big black cock. Lips like LL Cool J. Sex appeal that makes your panties wet. The man who'd been her fantasy when she'd been reduced to batteries. The man who'd been sexing her good since the night they met. Sort of met. Bad Boy, her lover.

She took a deep breath. "Well—"

"Here's your name tag, Ms. Mason," hippity–hop interrupted, handing her a shape.

A black paper dick.

KAT MASON spelled out in red latex. Oh, god, she was supposed to wear this? She choked. "This." She lifted the form. "Thank you, ladies." She escaped through the double doors with the dick in her hand. As soon as she was out of sight, she crushed the cock in her fist, then dropped it in the trash.

Damn! There was a par–tay going on. Lots of hos and pimps in the house. What else would there be when the party was designed around the sex industry? Got to look like a hooker. Walk the walk. Work the strip, selling sex for money. Hell, she was included even if she had no skin showing. This was her show.

Skirting the edge of the room, Kat took in the decorations, the two DJ tables, the flashing strobes and disco balls shimmering rainbows on the dance floor. Long flowing sheets of black and red satin hung suspended from the ceiling and draped on the floor.

Moving into the room, she kept her back to the wall, searching for anyone she knew. Wishing she'd brought her Momma. Her mother had always fit in with this crowd. Open. Wild. Feared nothing. No one.

But Kat? She was a meek little kitty, hugging the wall, her claws so tightly imbedded that it'd be shredded if she were forced from her safety zone, on the outskirts of the party.

"A drink?"

Kat startled. "What?" She turned quickly, to a white dude

wearing a caveman costume. Basically naked. A little bit of cloth covering up his little bit of package.

"A drink, Ma'am?" He extended his tray of small shot glasses, each filled with a dark liquid.

She grabbed one. Downed it. Damn near sputtered it back in his face it burned so bad. "Thanks," she hissed, fighting to breathe past the sting in her throat.

"Sure thing, Kitty."

"Kitty?" Kat arched a brow at him. She'd tossed the name–dick in the trash, no way this guy could know who she was. Right?

"Your costume." He grinned as he walked away.

Glad to be alone again, Kat moved to a grouping of out of the way chairs and took a seat. The music changed. 'Lean Back' pumped through the air and all the pimps and hos in costume angled their bodies on the dance floor to mimic the lyrics.

Warmth uncurled through her blood, thanks to the shot she'd taken. She tapped her toe to the beat, the volume and rhythm seeping into her body. The huge ballroom was packed with people. What was she doing here? So what, she was the guest of honor. No one knew who she was. No one would miss her.

She could be with Bad Boy instead.

Her lids closed and she breathed deeply. Last night they'd become lovers. Just this morning she'd been in his arms, with his big dick making her feel good. She sighed. Oh what a memory.

Opening her eyes, she stared across the dim ballroom, out at the dancing couples, all of them getting their groove on. More dressed–to–the–nines couples lingered by the bars set around the room. Drinks in hand. Laughing. Talking. Being with their friends.

Kat sat alone.

But she could be with Mr. Gorgeous. Like she had been

that morning. When she'd been bold enough to tie him to the bed. Just that morning, she'd been confident enough to be in charge. She wasn't scaredy Kat. She hadn't lacked self–assurance when she'd ordered up strawberries and cream and made Mr. Gorgeous suffer.

And he'd loved every minute of it.

Kat grinned. And stood. People glanced her direction, but she didn't feel like slinking away. She smiled back. Over the last several months, facing crowds didn't seem so difficult.

Being alone did.

Being without her man. Lifting her chin, she squared her shoulders, took a deep breath and took a step toward the heart of the party. Where the booze was being served. No one looked at her awkward. No one sneered because she wrote about sex. Hell, they bought her shit and enjoyed it. They'd come tonight because of what she did for a living.

Hell, there were tables set up with stacks of her magazines and bowls of condoms in come get some packages. Displays of sex toys, all items she'd used as props in her stories, decorated seating arrangements and were used as embellishment on long tables of finger–foods and sweet desserts. Feeling the apprehension twisting in her gut, she ignored it and allowed Wild Kat to lead her.

She took a deep breath again and moved through the crowd.

"Excuse me, Miss?"

A hand touched her shoulder. Kat turned, her heart racing, doing everything she could to keep the tremble in her hands from showing. "Yes?"

"You're Kat Mason aren't ya?" an older white man said in a Texas drawl.

Kat almost laughed aloud. "Yeah?" A costume?

If it weren't for his twang and accent, she would have thought this man was dressed in a costume of an old west cowboy. But judging by the wear on his boots and the big loopdy–loop mustache she figured he was the real deal. Old school Texan. She glanced at his waist, surprised he wasn't packing a pair of silver pistols.

"I thought so. I've been wantin' to meet ya."

Kat glanced at the tittie pasted to his chest. Marshal Thomas. Marshal Thomas, owner of *What's Your Fantasy*. Her largest publisher.

Damn. Old Kat would have felt the need to slink away. To run and hide. To bury her face in her hands.

"I'm thrilled to meet ya. Can't say how much I've enjoyed reading your work."

Yeah, she bet. She smiled. New Wild Kat didn't want to run. She felt proud. Accepting of what she'd accomplished. "Thank you." She shook his offered hand and didn't even tremble. Okay, maybe a little, but she was controlling it.

Loving *him* had given her strength. Being with *him* had changed who she was as a person. *Him*, chocolate skinned Lover Boy, who may have claimed her body, but damn, he'd also worked over her heart. Pleasured her soul. Opened the door to a whole new perception on how she saw relationships.

Though it wasn't easy, Kat kept on her smile, forced the tremors from her hands, and engaged in a conversation with Cowboy Publisher Dude.

Jamal held his breath as he watched the confident honey he'd seen all those nights before at The Night Kitty sway her hips, smile and speak with her publisher. He'd been watching her since she'd arrived, shooting back the booze and working the outskirts of the room.

But the sassiness returned. The attitude. The appeal. The woman who'd seduced him with her siren call. The sensual way she smiled. The heated way her eyes looked into his with I–want–you–baby passion.

His client.

His superstar.

Kat Mason.

The words buzzed around Jamal like gnats, but he didn't hear any of them or even bother to try to follow the conversations. Becca wasn't too far off, hanging on her man's arm. Even Kent was around, being an ass as usual, but now for a different reason. No matter how he tried, the woman he'd cheated on last time wasn't taking him back. Playa had played his last game.

Stepping forward, Jamal was drawn to Kat like a lion to his in–heat lioness. With his gaze intent upon her, he moved through the crowd, lingering back as she finished her conversation with Marshal Thomas.

He knew tonight was it. Tonight was the night of discovery, he wanted one last taste of her lips. One last time to hold her in his arms. One last chance to show how deeply he felt for her.

How much he loved her.

With his heart drumming, Jamal waited until Kat was alone. She bid her publisher goodbye with a smile, but the moment he turned his back, Jamal saw how the fake grin slide away and the glimpse of insecurity peeked through the seductress who had claimed him.

He approached from the side, touching her forearm just as she turned to walk away. "Hello, Sweetness."

He felt her flinch. Her brilliant amber eyes swung in his direction. First alarmed, they quickly warmed as they settled fully on him. With so much heat, blood poured to his cock, hardening him in an instant.

"Mr. Gorgeous," she whispered, glancing around briefly. "What are you doing here?" She settled a hand on his naked chest, scraping a nail over his nipple.

He knew he was grinning like a school boy looking at a stick of cotton candy. "I managed an invite."

Sneaking her fingers upward so they settled on his bare shoulder. "I'm so glad you're here." Lifting up on her tip–toes, she leaned into him as she dragged his head down to greet her. Not that it took much pressure of her hand in order for him to close the distance.

Her mouth met his lips, and opened. Her tongue slid across his, curling and mating. She whimpered, angling her head so he could kiss her more deeply. And he took full advantage. Despite the fact they stood in the center A Night of Naughty.

Slowly, she eased back. The kisses now were tender, but short. He tried to recapture her mouth, but she stepped away, a smile dancing on her luscious oh–so–kissable lips. Tasty.

"Damn, girl, I could kiss you forever."

She ran her pink tongue across her full bottom lip. "Mmm, you should then."

Oh, hell, yeah, Fly–Girl was back. Big time! She strolled around him, keeping her fingers on his skin. Burning him to the core. Searing his soul. Driving him fucking insane with desire. In front of him again, she shifted on her high–heeled beg–for–mercy stilettos, placing a hand on her hip. With her other hand she teased, dipping a nail into the shallow indent of his belly button, then lower. Smoothed her fingertips against the line of hair that dripped beneath his suede knee–length leggings.

"What are you Bad Boy?"

Jamal grinned, his gaze roving slowly over the skin–tight tigress outfit she was sporting. The same one she'd kneeled in front of him in. The one he'd shot his wad down her throat while she was wearing. Damned wanted to laugh with pleasure.

"A lion–tamer." He slanted his head to the long leather whip secured to his belt. Black leather boots rose over his shins.

Kat's brows knitted together and Jamal could sense that

she didn't really get his costume. Dropping his voice, he said, "I tame wildcats."

Her mouth formed a pouty O. Then she graced him with a melt–chocolate smile. She traced his nipple, skimming up his body until she was so close he could smell the subtle hint of her perfume. The aphrodisiac of her arousal. Knew she was ready for him.

She pressed her body against his, her hand behind his head, she dragged him downward. Her lips skimmed the shell shape of his ear, then she whispered, "You want to tame my pussy, Lover Boy?"

Hell, yeah! She better damn well believe it. His cock bucked hard behind the tan brushed leather.

Like she knew just what she did to him, she stepped away, her gaze dropping to the bulge of his hardened dick. Her hand closed around his length. Stroked. Teased. The crowd faded from notice.

Afraid he may cum right there, Jamal grabbed her hand, smoothing his palm across her palm as he entwined their fingers. "You find a place to go, baby, and I'll do my best to tame you." He kissed her neck, tugged her close to him and lowered his voice. "I don't know, though. Your pussy may bring me to heel before I manage to tame it."

Damn wicked honey, ground her hips against his, then moved away before he could recover. Keeping hold of him she led him through the crowd toward the restrooms. But instead of turning into either men's or women's, she opened a third door and tugged him inside after her.

A supply closet.

Thank God.

White linen table cloths and napkins were folded on the shelves along with rolls of fluffy toilet paper and Halloween decorations for the party. Perfect.

"Meow, Mr. Gorgeous. Do your best," she purred.

His dick rose to the challenge. Grabbing her around the waist, he lifted her, pulling her thick, juicy thighs up over his hips. He pressed her back against the wall of folded table cloths. Ground into her, rotating his hips as his mouth settled hungrily over hers.

He was starving to death.

Jamal slipped his tongue into the sultry depths of her mouth, sweeping. Learning. Exploring every inch of her like he'd done last night to her pussy.

He rocked his hips. Molten heat poured out. He could feel the damp heat seeping through the thin spandex of her suit and onto his leather pants.

Like he was fucking—hard—he thrust against her with his dick against her clit and his tongue thoroughly kissing her.

Skimming his hand over her body, he settled on her breast. Tweaked a nipple with his thumb and forefinger. Heard her soft moans, throaty whimpers. Tasted the sweetness of her breath.

He dry–fucked harder. To hell with clothes. He could feel her wet. Knew she was ready to be entered. With his balls pulled tight, he damned near came. Knew she was about ready to explode.

In a desperate need to burn this memory into her mind before they left this room and the truth was revealed, Jamal slipped a hand between their grinding bodies. Stroked her firmly with his fingers against her clit.

Two gyrating strokes and tremors broke through her body. "Loooovver Boooy!" she cried out against his mouth, her body shaking in his arms.

He held her. Allowed her to enjoy the pleasure of orgasm. He allowed her the climax as he stood before her, his dick so rocked–up he thought his skin might burst.

And he kissed her. The passion of his kiss didn't stop while she recovered from cumming. The intensity in which he thrust his tongue into her mouth didn't let up.

He kissed with obsession, totally in awe of Kat. The woman he held in his arms.

For the life of him, he couldn't stop kissing her.

Not even when the door opened.

Chapter 25

"JJ? Jamal, are you in here?"

The sound of a woman's voice slowly penetrated the fog of lust. The power of orgasm. But Kat ignored it, focusing only on Mr. Gorgeous and the tender way he kissed her.

"Jamal?" the woman repeated from the supply closet doorway.

The man Kat was kissing tore his mouth away, panting. "Yeah?" he said, glancing over his shoulder.

Jamal? Her heart skittered to a halt, then throbbed into a rapid beat. She'd been kissing Jamal? How could that be? Jamal was her agent's name. The man in her arms was Mr. Gorgeous. Wasn't he?

"JJ, they're looking for Ms. Mason."

Chocolate–skinned lover turned back to her, his eyes imploring. Sweat shimmered on his brow. His body tensed before her, but his hands were gentle as one stroked the back of her thigh that encircled his butt. His other hand touched her cheek, brushing his thumb across her sensitive kiss–swollen lips.

"She's with me."

Kat swung her gaze to the same blonde woman she'd seen in the bar with Bad Boy not long ago. Her blue eyes were filled with so much empathy. They held hers for a moment, then the woman blinked and looked away guiltily. "Well, bring her out before they find you like this." And then she disappeared, the door smacking closed behind her.

Kat's heart raced. What the hell was happening? Confusion held back the truth, but God, how could she have been so blind? She knew it even when she didn't want to.

"Jamal?"

He let out a deep sigh. "Yeah, Sweetness."

Oh. My. God! She wiggled, trying to get her feet to the floor. He held her, his massive shoulders unmoving. His muscular body unyielding. "Let me go."

He did, reluctantly. She wobbled on her high–heels, the speed of her pulse making breathing difficult. Her knees shook, and she almost reached for her man. Ha, her man! What a mockery.

"I've got you, baby."

She steadied herself on the shelves of folded cloths. "I'm not your baby." Anger now surfaced. Fresh. Hot. Biting. He'd played her. For how long? How long was she the laughing stock, the butt of his joke? Her hands balled into fists. Her chest heaved as she struggled to slow her breaths.

"You're Jamal James? My agent? My best friend?"

He nodded.

"You're Jamal!" she shouted. Oh, god, how long had he known? Had she said something in an email that would have sent him to The Night Kitty on the same night she had? Had he set her up for this?

"And you know who I am? You know I'm Kat?" She knew her voice was elevating, but she didn't give a shit.

Nodding, he reached for her. "Sweetness, let me explain."

"You *mothafucker*! You *sonofabitch*! Let you explain? What? How you used me?"

Wild Kat had her claws out now, her teeth sharp. He was supposed to be her friend. How could he have done this?

How could he have betrayed everything they had? Everything they shared?

"Please, it's not like that."

This was Jamal. Her lover. Her agent. Her best friend. *The man who'd deceived her*. Tears burned at the back of her eyes, stung her nose. Tightened her throat. Kat swallowed down the lump of sorrow, fighting the freedom of her tears. Afraid how crushing it'd be if he saw that he'd reduced her to weeping.

She took a deep breath. "How long? How long have you known?" She closed her eyes as she waited for his answer. She didn't want to look at his handsome face. Didn't want to remember how good it felt to have him inside her. Didn't want to think about how wondrous it was to be kissed fully and thoroughly by him.

She didn't want to, but damnit, with her lips burning still from his touch, how the hell could she not.

A sob escaped. She tugged in a breath.

"Kat, please." He put his hand on her shoulder, but she shrugged away from him. He attempted to gather her into his arms, but she swatted his hands.

Opening her eyes, she blinked her lids hard, to chase away the salty liquid. To keep it from dripping from her lashes. From rolling down her cheeks.

"I didn't know, Kat. Not at first." He caught a tear as it slid down her cheek on his fingertip. The droplet looked like dew, but held so much pain that Kat had to slant her face away.

"When? How long have you known who I was and said nothing? How long do you hit it and keep the secret? Was the pussy worth it, Jamal? Was fucking worth putting an end to us?"

"It doesn't have to be the end."

"Oh, but it is!"

"Look, Sweetness, it's not how you think—"

Kat stepped forward, getting right in his face, no matter how he outsized and strengthed her. Despite the rippling heat moving from his body, still instinctually affecting her. "What could you possibly say that would explain?"

"That I—"

Kat put her hand in his face. "Save it! That was a rhetorical question, asshole! There's *nothing* you can say to undo how you've betrayed me."

Jamal groaned. "Kat," he whispered, "Please."

Closing her eyes against his gorgeous image, she steadied her breath and willed the tears away. No more would fall over this man. A man who'd used her wasn't worth it. Breathing in deeply several times, anger grew so that the air was stained with his masculine scent. She opened her eyes, lifted her chin and pulled back her shoulders. Tried desperately to salvage the shreds of her dignity.

She narrowed her glare. "I never wanted this, Jamal," she spit out. "I never wanted to write sex. Never wanted a career in the porn industry. I'm not doing it anymore. I want to write romance complete with happily–ever–afters." She took a deep breath. "I'm not being used anymore."

Turning as steadily as she could on four–inch spiky heels, Kat walked out the door. The ballroom was dark aside from the strobing lights and flashing disco balls.

And crowded. She shoved her way past dancing couples, gyrating to the beat, swaying with the masses.

Jamal pursued. She could feel his presence stalking behind her. "Kat, wait!"

She kept walking, pretending she hadn't heard. Refused to acknowledge his calling of her name despite the fact she felt him moving closer. Closing the distance between them.

His hand settled on her shoulder. "Sweetness, wait."

"Leave me alone!"

She ducked between two large men, each with a hooker on

their arm. Damn costumes looked so genuine Kat almost looked twice because they looked legit. Street girls, and she would have thought they were if she didn't recognize one of them as a fellow author. Through the blur of tears, she could tell they were watching her, but she no longer cared. What she cared about was getting the hell out of there.

Away from Jamal.

Jamal grabbed her hand as she attempted to slip through a group of people. "Baby, you've got to listen."

Kat spun on him, trying to shake his hand from her wrist, but it held. "Let go."

"Stop, please, let me explain."

"Let go!"

"Is he bothering you, Ms.?" one of the big pimps asked.

"Yes."

"No, I'm her agent," Jamal said, never breaking his gaze from hers. He caressed the sensitive skin on her inner wrist, his rich eyes begging for her to listen.

Kat took a deep breath. Slanting her eyes around the room she noticed a crowd had begun to gather like traffic around a car accident. People were morbid, always circling when they smelled blood. Damned vultures. Groups pressed closer, all eager to hear the gory details of the latest gossip.

These were the times that old Kat dreaded. These stares and looks were what she feared most. Public. All eyes on her. The center of attention.

But that was the old Kat. The old Kat was reclusive. The old Kat that was a wallflower. Scared. But lifting her chin and glancing around at all the interested faces, Kat realized for the first time that she'd never been scared of them.

She'd been scared of herself.

What did she want most? Love and a family. Security. She feared herself because she worried she didn't deserve it. That she wasn't good enough. That's why her relationships soured.

Didn't last. Why she wrote relationship columns so she could live vicariously through the couples she helped, because deep down she was scared to death she'd never be part of one.

The pain of realization was magnified by loving and trusting a man who wasn't worth the emotions. Love? Oh, god, no wonder this hurt so badly. She buried the sentiment. She'd have to examine it later.

Now she had to end it. All of it.

She drew back, tugging her hand away and repressing the burning of tears. "No Jamal. You're not my agent. You're not my lover." She swallowed. Hardening her heart she looked into his pleading eyes. "You're not even my friend."

"Kat," he whispered.

She shook her head.

Turning her attention to the people who surrounded them, she pulled back her shoulders and cleared her throat. Calm settled over her, relieved by finally doing what she believed was right for her life. Right to be on the path of her own happiness.

She hoped.

"I'm Kat Mason. You probably know me as Glory Cockin." A murmur spread through them, as they whispered to the person next to them, all curious eyes fixed on her. She knew they were shocked since over the years she'd kept an invisible profile. She lifted her hand and swept her arm slowly across the room, indicating the tables where her magazines were stacked. "Those are my final issues. There will be no more Glory's Stories."

The din in the room grew, rising above the hum of the music. She almost grinned when she saw some people snatch collector editions, now, from the tables. Almost.

She turned her glare back on Jamal. Defeat was etched across his handsome features. Pain so intense it mirrored her own reflected from his dark eyes, but she used it for strength.

"No more. Ever."

Looking one last time at Mr. Gorgeous, Kat tried to fill her heart with the memory. The memory of his lips. The shape of his nose. The passion in his eyes. Muscular shoulders. Skin the shade of smooth dark chocolate.

The best ten inches she'd ever had.

But she was fooling herself if she thought for a second that she could look her fill. And be satisfied. That the memory of him would ever be good enough. She couldn't cuddle up to a memory in the chill of the night. She couldn't fulfill her desire with a dream. And now that she'd sampled the wondrous feel of real rocked–up dick, vibrating plastic and AA batteries would never do again.

While they may relieve the physical need, they would never ease her loneliness.

Kat curled her hands into fists, ignoring the shouts and questions being tossed her way, all the while Bad Boy remained silent.

Dejected.

Good. Let him hurt as bad as she was.

Turning on her heels and keeping her chin high, she walked away. The crowd parting for her as if she were dangerous.

She was in a kick–ass mood, so them getting the hell out of the way was for their own benefit.

The burning in her eyes was unbearable by the time she reached the exit. The first tear slid down her cheek by the time she hit the street.

That night, she was weeping by the time she hit the sheets.

Chapter 26

"You've got to make her understand."

"And how the hell do you expect me to do that?" Jamal asked, not bothering to look up at Kent. Not bothering to spend too much time reflecting on the fact that it was Kent—the playa—who was offering the advice.

"Don't know, man." Kent blew a breath out between his teeth, then lifted the beer bottle to his lips. "You've got to do something. You've been moping for weeks."

"I'm hardly moping."

"Whatever, dude, you ain't the same no more. That Kat chick is the reason."

Jamal gulped down his brew. He knew Kent was right. Wild Kat, Sweetness was the reason. The reason he was different. A different man now. With different needs. Different desires. Oh, he missed the sexual part of their relationship. Hell, he'd spent hours with her stories over the last five weeks.

Hours reading. Wanting. Hardly breathing.

Setting the empty bottle aside, he grabbed a second and used the cold liquid to wash down the bitterness of sorrow. At last, the mild dulling of alcohol. No wonder folks got addicted. It worked wonders to alleviate the pain of heartache.

He cleared his throat. "You have any luck getting Sasha back?"

"Nah."

Jamal eased back on his sofa, turning his attention back to the 49ers game. They were losing again. Damn. But even the distraction of beer and football did little to keep his mind off Kat. Seemed impossible to keep her from his thoughts. He kept returning to the same questions. What was she doing now?

Was she alone?

Was she missing him?

As badly as he was missing her? He may be a fool, but he was smart enough to know this was coming. Hell, he'd known this was coming from the second he was stupid enough to agree to fucking her and remaining nameless. One sided nameless. He'd known who she was. Her submissions had given her away.

"Hey, JJ?"

"Yeah, man?"

"I wouldn't have let that honey suck me off if I'd known Sasha wasn't going to forgive me."

Jamal stared at Kent, not sure where he was trying to lead by sharing that bit of info. "You'd have taken the blowjob if you knew you weren't going to get caught."

"No. That's not what I mean. The honey wanted a suck of the ding–ding–dingaling. I just did it. Didn't think about it. Didn't think about Sasha."

"Her feelings?"

Kent nodded, swirling the dark beer in the bottle. "Didn't know she cared enough to be hurt by it." He took a swig. "Didn't know I did."

Jamal was silent. They watched a couple of plays of football. A long pass to the end–zone that the quarterback over-threw. A few running plays that didn't pick up more than a few yards and not the needed ten to get a first down. The punter kicked the ball away.

He rolled his head on his shoulders, trying to ease the mounting tension. "She won't listen."

Kent laughed sarcastically. "Man, you got to find a way to make her. Say something she wants to hear."

"Nah, dude. That's what you do. You tell the woman what they want to hear. Not the truth. That's what got you into trouble. And I'm not going down like that."

"Then you won't get the chick."

Jamal shrugged. "I'm not going to lie."

The game drew to a close. Kent rose to his feet, stretching his arms over his head, then fished in his pocket for his keys. "I'm going to head to The Night Kitty. If you ain't going to be hooking–up with Kat no more, why not go with me. See if we can find some hit it and quit it girls."

"Go ahead. I'll pass." He didn't go to The Night Kitty anymore. He couldn't. Not without being reminded of Kat and how they'd met. How they'd fucked. And how he'd loved. He hadn't been to the bar since before A Night of Naughty. He just couldn't bring himself to go there, though he and Lloyd had hooked up for a tailgating party in 3Com Park's lot before a home game a couple weeks back.

"It may be just what you need to get your mind off of her."

"Nah, I'm cool. See you tomorrow at the office," Jamal said, giving Kent a pound as he headed out the door.

Once the door was closed he grabbed his own keys and headed to the garage and his Escalade. Kent was right. He had to make Kat listen. Maybe not understand, but at least hear him out. He'd never been to her house before, but he'd spent the last five weeks MapQuesting from her mailing address.

She didn't live too far away. With traffic, maybe thirty minutes at the most. The City was busy on a Sunday afternoon, despite the miserable December. It took him forty–five.

And the entire drive he kept thinking about what he'd do if he found another man at her place. Damned near sucked the wind from his lungs. Made it hard to breathe.

Gripping the steering wheel, Jamal tried to calm the drumming of his pulse behind his temples. He parked on the street in front of her house. Christmas lights hand been strung up across the front of her home and were shimmering against the storm laden sky.

Breathing deeply, he felt unsteady as the wind rocked his big SUV. Rain pelted his windshield.

Fearing he may drive away, he hopped out and jogged up to the door before he could have second thoughts. He jammed his thumb into the bell, ignoring how the wind tugged at his sweatshirt. And waited. He rang the bell again.

"Patience, Sasha." Her voice called from within. The door was yanked open. "Oh!"

"Hello, Kat." Jamal took in the sight of her. Oh, yeah, she was exactly what he needed. Five weeks seemed like five years. His body ached to hold her. Blood rushed to his cock. Down boy, he silently scolded.

"What do you want?" Kat asked, folding her arms across her chest.

She wasn't wearing a bra. Jamal could see that right away. Her nipples puckered beneath her thin t–shirt. Probably from the cold of the outside air, rather than the sight of him. Knowledge that did nothing to hinder his body's reaction. His mouth watered. Ruff. Gray sweatpants hung from her hips. She looked a little thinner than the last time he'd seen her. In a tigress spandex suit.

He shook his head to clear the stirring lust. "I want to talk to you." With him on the outside step, she was standing eye–level with him. A gust of wind whipped several curls from her ponytail. She didn't move. He watched her reactions and found them impossible to read. Damn.

She sighed. "There's nothing left to say, Jamal."

God, he hated the way she said his name. With anger and resentment.

How he wanted to hear it was breathless and passionate. "You're wrong. There's a lot left to say."

"No." She attempted to close the door.

He put his hand on the solid wood to stop it and fought back a grin when she didn't press it very hard. She wanted to listen or the door would have been slammed.

"There's a lot to say, Kat. Please, I need you to hear me." She shook her head.

Jamal stepped forward. He took a chance, brushing his fingertips across her cheek. Her skin was warm. So soft. He heard her suck in a breath, but she didn't pull away. Didn't slap the shit out of him. Always a good thing.

"You don't have to talk. But there are a few things I need to say."

She shook her head again.

Stroking his fingers over her lips, he reveled in the balminess of her breath on his skin. Cursed the hard–on begging for attention in his pants. Damn loss of blood in his upper head was making it hard to think.

"Please, hear me out. I did what you wanted me to. I respected your wishes."

"By deceiving me?"

"Sweetness, I didn't know the first time. In the back alley. I had no idea who you were. After I read your submissions, I suspected, but I still didn't know."

She scoffed.

"Really. Maybe I just didn't want to believe it. I dismissed it as my client knowing how to tap into a man's fantasy. And you'd tapped into mine. A coincidence—that's all, I told myself."

"And I'm supposed to believe that?" She side stepped so his hand fell from her.

"It's the *truth*."

"But you knew the second time. In your truck."

"No."

He looked at her and saw that she didn't believe him. This wasn't the time for half–truths. Tell–all. Now. "Not at first. Not until I saw your panties."

Her lips formed an O. "The condom–pocket panties."

"Those are the ones. You'd told me about picking them up, baby, so when I saw you wearing them—" He broke off, running his hand over his shaved head, swiping away the gathering sweat. "Hell, I was so rocked–up, Sweetness, I just wanted to get in you. I wasn't thinking about anything else. Just pleasuring you."

"More like getting–off."

He nodded. "That, too." He stepped in her direction, touching her shoulder. Allowing his hand to slide down to her hands folded across her chest. He smoothed his thumb over her brown skin. Tried to take her hand in his, but she dropped her hands to her sides, then put them behind her back.

Bad idea. Her titties pressed forward into the t–shirt. And cold autumn air. He could see the perfect circular shadings where her nipples beaded against the thin material. He swallowed. Hard.

She cleared her throat and Jamal lifted his eyes. Knew he'd been caught staring.

"What do you want Mr . . . Jamal? Why did you come here?"

"I wanted to see you."

"Why?"

Jamal slanted his eyes away, passion flaring out of his control. He wanted to grab hold of Kat. Cover her luscious mouth with his. Kiss away the question. Express with his body what he so badly wanted to say.

He reached for her again, but she stepped back, grabbing the edge of the wooden door and narrowing the space between them.

"Kat, I did what you asked me to. I tried to tell you who I was. Don't you remember?"

"No. Not a word. You knew my name and sure were careful to not call it out while we were fucking."

"Making love."

"Don't patronize me. Making love takes emotion. Don't get it twisted, Brother–man, what we had going on was purely physical." Her voice was cold. Her stare angry. Her frosted over amber gaze slid to his semi–hard dick and lingered. "I like what you got going on."

"Kat, it was more than physical."

She lifted her eyes to his, lowering her lids. "What it is, is over." She went to close the door.

He put his hand on the door. "Baby, please. I need you."

Her lips trembled. Not a lot, but enough that Jamal caught the movement. Even the hard–edge of her fierce look softened, just slightly.

"It's not enough . . ." She shook her head, pushing the door further. Closing out the storm that rolled off the ocean. Closing him out.

"Kat, I gave you what you asked for. I'm sorry this hurt you. I played by your rules. You wanted anonymous. Not me. This was your idea, baby, don't you remember? Your rules. No names."

She shook her head, the shimmer in her gaze brightening.

"I need you."

Kat dropped her hand from the door, her shoulders slumped. "It's not enough," she whispered.

Jamal couldn't breathe past the building regret. Kat wasn't merely sex. She was his friend and because of his cock—and her damned–good pussy—their relationship was coming to an end. He pounded his hand over his heart, in tempo with his words. "Sweetness, I need you."

A tear fell. Dropped from her thick lower lashes. Slid silently down her caramel cheek. Rolled over her lush lips.

She swiped it away with the back of her hand before it fell from her chin. "It's not enough . . ."

Her words were so softly spoken, he could hardly hear them over the blustering air. With one last look Kat closed the door.

Jamal stood on her stoop. Stunned. That's not how he'd expected it to go. Hell, she hadn't even invited him in, but left him out on the cold step, subjected to the chill of the storm and the frostiness of her angry glare.

Rolling his head on his shoulders, he worked the twisted muscles bunched into balls of tension.

He stood there. He stood there hoping that the door would open. That Kat would come back out. Say that she forgave him. That she understood this wasn't his fault. Invite him into her house. Invite him into her bed.

Invite him into her heart.

He heaved out the sorrow after minutes ticked by and it became apparent the door wasn't opening. Kat wasn't coming out.

His sweatshirt soaked with rain now, he walked slowly back to his Escalade and slipped into the seat. He shoulda been up front with her as soon as he'd suspected what happened. Coulda told his super-star client that he suspected they'd fucked. Woulda made a different choice if he'd known he was going to fall head-over-heels, stupid in love with Kat Mason.

The only woman who'd pussy-whooped him.

The only woman who'd ever claimed his heart.

And she owned it.

He started the ignition and turned up the heater, then tore his wet sweatshirt over his head and tossed in on the passenger floor, leaving only a half-dry shirt beneath.

He didn't want to head home. Didn't want to see all the reminders of Kat, the woman, the friend he was now without.

For a moment he thought about going back to The Night

Kitty. Kent seemed to get over hotties easily enough by finding another. But that wasn't his style and besides, The Night Kitty was their place.

And they were no more.

Completely dejected, he drove away from Kat's house and got on Highway 101, heading south. Leaving behind The City and heading away from pain. For now, he couldn't face the pain of losing her.

He loved her that damned much!

Chapter 27

Kat took a deep breath and held it, trying to listen over the raging storm for Jamal's breathing through her door. She could feel him there. Just standing on the other side of the two–inch thick wood. And it took all her strength not to yank her front entry open and allow him in.

To rush into his arms.

Leaning back, she used the wall for support, her liquid–filled gaze fixed on where moments before she'd been standing talking to Jamal.

Jamal James. Her agent. Her friend.

It was hardly comprehendible. Jamal was Mr. Gorgeous. Her bad boy lover who had a ten–inch that he worked with expertise. Bro knew how to work it, all right. She sighed, her panties dampening.

Jamal was her ex–sex toy. The reason she'd quit writing. The reason she'd finally stood up for herself.

The reason she was damned miserable.

Tears slid down her face when she finally heard his footfalls move away from the door. Sobs broke free when the engine in his SUV hummed to life and then the sound fading as he drove away.

Pulling off her clothes, she dropped them to the floor as

she made her way up the stairs. What she needed was a hot bubble–bath. Something that smelled of flowers. Sweet, feminine. Anything but the masculine fragrance of Jamal's skin. Anything but salty sea air that reminded her of the morning he'd held her in his arms, first bringing her to climax, then allowing her to sleep.

Entering her bedroom, she ignored the shelves with pink–latex dildos. Vibrating black cocks. Clit stimulators. Multiple packs of AA's. She ignored the extra closet stuffed to overflowing with wicked outfits and lingerie that she'd been gathering for years. Things she'd used for inspiration.

Used. Just like she'd used a man as her pleasure–stick, never once giving more than a second's thought to how he'd feel when she tired of him and tossed him away.

Only she hadn't tired of Lover Boy.

Kat swallowed the lump in her throat and shook her head. Not Lover Boy. Jamal James. She hadn't tired of Jamal. She needed him now more than ever. Moving away from the evidence of her former life, she wasn't writing erotica anymore. Hell, she'd hardly written a single word at all. She missed it. But not as much as she missed her secret encounters with a man who had chocolate brown skin, eyes filled with passion.

Lips that belonged on her body. Belonged on her mouth. Belonged kissing her.

Standing naked, Kat studied her reflection in the floor–to–ceiling mirror in her bedroom.

"Who am I?" she asked.

She touched her breasts with both hands, completely cupping her fingers around them. Her nipples puckered in response and pressed against her palm. She imagined Jamal's hands there and the picture felt so much more complete.

"I'm not Glory Cockin." She glanced at the piles of publications her material appeared in. She shook her head. She'd never been proud of writing erotica. But one thing she'd learned loving Jamal was that she wasn't ashamed of it either.

So what she sold sex for money. People enjoyed it. A harmless way to offer mere amounts of pleasure in this oh–so–difficult world.

What she was ashamed of was that she'd used writing sex as an excuse to not follow her heart. To not write the types of stories she longed to write. But that was changing.

Then there were her relationship columns. They helped people, too. No, she'd never had a successful relationship, but maybe that's why she knew what was lacking in so many. Why she was able to offer small amounts of advice that could help others obtain the happiness she'd never felt.

The love.

A sob escaped. Kat attempted to gather in the cries of pain, but they overwhelmed her. Sliding with her back against the wall to the floor, she squeezed her lids closed, images of Jamal burning into her memory.

His words vibrating through her soul.

"My game," she whispered. "My rules."

Her mind twisted her back to the first time at the café. The day they'd—or she had—agreed to carry on the anonymous affair. And whose idea had it been?

Hers.

Who had pushed for it? Begged for it? All her. Jamal was right: this is what she'd asked for. He'd given her just what she wanted from him. And more.

She'd given him her heart.

And a door in his face.

Scurrying to her feet, Kat knew he didn't deserve her re-action. He hadn't betrayed her like she'd accused him. He'd obeyed her desires. Given her a fantasy come true. Ended the wet–dreams of him and given her real ones.

Retracing her steps, she gathered her clothing, trying not to think about the pain in his eyes as he'd told her he needed her. The break in his voice as he'd insisted on it.

Oh, God, just thinking of the hurt she'd caused him tightened her heart. Twisted knots in her belly.

Dressed, she slipped her feet into shoes as she picked up the phone and dialed the number to his house. The answering machine clicked on after a few rings.

"Jamal, it's me." She took a deep breath. "I'm sorry. You were right. You gave me what I asked for." Kat fought down a sob, her throat feeling so tight. "I need you, too," she whispered, then hung up the phone.

She dialed again. His office. But voicemail clicked on there, too. It was late Sunday afternoon. What did she expect? "Jamal, call me when you get this," she whispered. Pausing, she blinked back tears. "Please." She slowly turned off the phone and dropped it onto the table.

She had to see him.

She had to find him. Tonight. Before anger grew between them. If it wasn't too late already.

Grabbing her car keys, Kat headed to the only place she could think about going in order to find him.

The Night Kitty.

It wasn't long before Kat pulled up across the street from the nightclub. She shut her car off. Much like the night she'd first gone there, she leaned her forehead against the cool glass of her window. Breathing deeply, she closed her eyes but knew there was nothing else she could do.

If she went home now, she'd be destined to live her life without Jamal by her side. Without him sexing her at night. Without him, and that was something she didn't think she could do.

Hell, even if she found Jamal here, she wasn't sure he'd want her. She'd turned him away just an hour ago, but the pain she'd seen registered in his eyes was soul–deep. Not easily recovered from. Easily turned to anger. She gulped down apprehension, silently praying it wasn't too late to snag her man.

Opening her eyes, she stared at the brick building on the other side of the street, neon lights reflecting on the rain–washed pavement. Just a hole–in–the–wall sort of joint, it was surprising she even ended up here in the first place.

Opening the door, she slid from her car and shut it firmly behind her. She took a step, her knees trembling. The down-pour had now turned to a drizzle. Tiny droplets clung to her skin. To her lashes. Ignoring the rainfall, she steadied herself. The decision made. The hiss of desire not her only motiva-tion.

She was here again to find a man. But she wasn't wearing heels or skimpy clothes meant to impress. She wore Phat Farm sneakers. Grey sweats. An over sized t–shirt.

The first time she'd strutted up to the door in a false per-sona. Tonight she approached as the real woman.

The first time, she'd plastered on a façade of sassy and confident. Tonight she was everything she wanted to be. No longer wallflower Kat, she knew who she was and where in the world she belonged. Wild Kat. Shy Kat. Seductress. Friend. After her man. She'd grown into all of these and so much more. With Jamal by her side.

Nameless or not, he'd changed her life in a manner on her own she'd never have attempted.

Scoffing, Kat reached for the door. A dull thud of bass seeped through the brick wall and shimmied through her body. Pulse drumming, erotic humming of arousal swept through her blood. Oh, yeah, baby. She was a new woman. A new woman who was after one thing. Not a back alley screw. A lifetime.

The truth was she was a better, stronger woman because she'd fucked him. Because in fucking him, she'd found the liberation to allow herself the freedom to love him.

And she did. She loved him with everything that she was.

With sheer determination and confidence, she opened the door to the bar and stepped inside. The beat of the music was slow tonight. The lyrics soulful. Brooding and moody. On a Sunday evening, the club had a different sort of atmosphere than other nights she'd been here.

The dance floor was crowded, but the rotating of hips and tittie searching hands were subdued. Though not smoke, the air seemed murky, filled with endorphins. Brimming with sexual–headiness.

Moving through the people, she made her way to the bar, narrowing her eyes. Searching faces. Looking for him.

Looking for Jamal James, ten inches of pure pleasure.

The chirping of his phone startled Jamal as he cruised down the freeway. After an hour of driving, finally heading for home. He thought about ignoring it. Then grabbed it.

"Yeah."

"JJ, it's Lloyd."

Jamal rotated his head on his shoulders, attempting to ease the tension. "What up, man?"

There was a moment of silence before Lloyd spoke. "She's here."

Thank you, God! Jamal's pulse jumped. His cock throbbed to life, not taking much blood to fill from his semi–aroused state of always longing Kat. Three long months of it. Hell, three long years. *Down boy.*

He took a deep breath. Let it out slowly. "Don't let her leave." He snapped his phone shut, taking the first exit off the Interstate.

To hell with the Highway Patrol, there was no way he was driving within the speed limit and risk Kat getting away. She'd gone to The Night Kitty for a reason. He needed to be there to hear it. It hurt to breathe. Pain twisting through his gut, tightening around his heart.

It wasn't long before he arrived, the clouds darkened into night. The streetlights illuminating the shimmering rain–soaked streets. Parking, he hurried inside, hoping he wasn't too late. Hoping Kat was still inside. Waiting. For him.

He hopped from the SUV and jetted into the bar. Sweeping his gaze across the bumping–and–grinding couples, he saw her. Standing on the far side of the dance floor, her amber gaze fixed on the door.

On him.

She'd been crying. Liquid glistened on her long, thick eyelashes. Salty paths stained her creamy cheeks. Her clothing was damp. Long, dark ringlets began to frizz around her face.

She'd never looked more beautiful.

Damn near holding his breath, Jamal skirted the perimeter of the club, making his way to her.

Facing her, he balled his hands into fists to keep from dragging her against him. To keep from dropping his head and claiming her lush quivering lips.

"Jamal," she said softly.

Oh, hell, yeah, that was how he wanted to hear his name on her lips.

"I need to ta–"

Jamal gently touched his fingers to her mouth. "Shhh, baby. Dance with me." He stepped closer, assaulted by the sweet feminine scent of her. Blood filled his dick as her warm breath washed against his storm–drenched clothing.

She shook her head. Her tawny eyes filling with liquid. The corner of her lips twitched into a slight smile. "I don't want to dance."

He touched her shoulder. Ran his fingers down her arm. Entwined their fingers. He stepped closer, bringing her hand to his lips. "What do you want?"

"You." There was no hesitation.

Lust made him dizzy. His heart raced. Letting go of her, he put his palm to the small of her back, felt her tremble beneath his touch. "You've got me, baby."

She slid one hand behind him. The other touched his racing pulse on his neck. The feathering stroke of her fingertips was going to be the death of him. He gulped and she lifted on tip–toes and kissed his skin.

"Jamal. You were right. You played by my rules." She closed her eyes and took a deep breath. Tears spilled from her lower lids, evoking such a fierce protectiveness in Jamal. He wanted to rid her of her demons. She opened pools of amber eyes and gazed directly into his. "I used you," she whispered.

"Shhh, Sweetness." He put his fingers to her mouth again, then slid his hand beneath her jaw. Cupping her chin, he tilted her face so she'd look only upon him. "I know our affair was for inspiration. Baby, I don't care about being used. I don't care that you wrote fictional stories of our very real nights."

"But—"

He shook his head to silence her. "I don't mind being your inspiration for the erotic, Kat, so long as you allow me to be the inspiration for the romance, too. Let me show you how I can love you, baby."

She nodded.

He brushed a kiss against her damp, pouty mouth.

"Then love me," she murmured against his lips. "Love me like I love you."

Jamal groaned, slipping his tongue into her sultry depths. He slid his hand from beneath her chin, down to her throat. Curling his fingers around her back, he drew her closer. Close enough to feel pert nipples through the cotton of their shirts. Close enough for her to feel his raging hard–on.

She edged back a step. She tilted her hip, a smile playing on her kiss–me, tease–me lips. The sassy honey was back. Dressed in sweats, she could still bring him to his knees. "Show me."

He laughed. On the dance floor? "Yeah, Sweetness, what have you got in mind?"

Her vivid eyes flashed to the sign hanging by the bar. Exit.

Brick walls and neon signs. Hard fucks that led to happily–ever–afters.

Oh, yeah, his Kitty–Kat knew what she was doing when it came to making him want it. He wanted her bad.

He was a fool to dismiss her idea of a hard–core, back alley fling–thing. But he had something else in mind.

He grabbed her hand and kissed her palm tenderly, then twined their fingers. "Kat, baby, I love you enough to take you home. To make love to you in my bed."

She kissed his mouth. "And I love you enough to still be there in the morning."

Turn the page to find PASSION!
Coming May 2006 from Aphrodisia.

Chapter 1

A poem called "The Highwayman" made me cry. That's why I started to write. In the poem, the Highwayman and the innkeeper's daughter, Bess, die trying to save each other. The thought of them being separated upset me so much, I changed the story.

In my version, the Highwayman would kidnap me and gallop away on his black stallion, taking me to his hideaway. Or maybe he would stay at the inn and lure me to his room. Once, I found him wounded. In order to care for him, I hid him in a secret room at the inn.

I started to write down my stories, so I wouldn't forget them. I recently unearthed several stories about my Highwayman in a box of old papers. For well over a month now, I have fallen asleep, thinking of him, my Highwayman.

Just last night, I stayed awake until after three in the morning, the story I had woven feeling more real than my life. Even though some of the details changed from night to night, the core story remained the same.

I looked up as the door opened. A large man stood there, tall, muscular and powerfully built. His thick beard framed a rigid jaw. He wore a heavy black coat, made of coarse wool. Both it and the cape he had on over it smelled like wet horse hair, being damp from the melted snow. The cape barely hid the hilt of a sword.

He looked directly at me, with an intense, penetrating stare. He seemed so big and so totally unaware of how fiercely intimidating he looked. His swagger and his comfort with his size sent a shiver down my arms. Even though he frightened me, I still felt drawn to him.

I raised the bottle I had in my hand and beckoned to an empty table in a secluded corner. He took the bottle I offered to him in one hand and my arm in the other. He pulled me toward a table, drinking as he walked. I knew the bottle would relieve the chill in his bones from the cold.

I started to undo his cape, but he pushed me away. Untying it himself, it fell to the floor. He removed his sword and then his coat, being careful to position his sword within easy reach.

He sat with his back to the wall, staring both at me and over me. I watched his eyes, sensing his tension as he surveyed the room for possible threats. It was not uncommon for two men to lay claim to the same woman. He positioned himself to watch for anyone who would challenge his right to me. No one did.

We drank together for a time. He pushed the bottle at me and I drank from it as he did. He kept staring at me with those eyes. I could not look away. He asked, "Do you belong to a man?"

I answered him, "No, not until you walked in."

He touched me. I did not pull away. His hands were large and very strong. He put his hands behind my neck and pulled me to him with a squeeze of his hand. I did not know if he intended to love me or to kill me—and I did not care. I felt his fingers on my neck. It made me feel lost in his power. He nuzzled my long, red hair. He sniffed at me, smelling both my skin and my hair.

I could feel how he wanted the pleasure only a woman could give him. Keeping his hand on my neck, he drank

again. I felt his fingers sliding up into my hair and felt the
ends pull as he closed his fist. I did not flinch. He looked at
me as if not understanding why I did not push him away. I
asked, "How long since you've had a woman?"

He answered, "Long enough."

He pulled his knives out of his waistband and threw them
on top of his cape. Then he did the same with his belt. After
taking another long drink from the bottle, he threw his coat
in the corner along the wall.

Grabbing my arm, he yanked me down on top of his coat.
He put both hands on my ankles and shoved my long skirt up
by moving his hands up my legs. Then he knelt to open his
breeches. I started to pull down my loose fitting pantaloons
to ready myself for him. He had just exposed himself when
he saw me reaching under my skirt. He grabbed my hand and
stopped me. He said, "What are you doing?"

"Baring myself for you," I replied angrily. I tried to free
myself from his grip, but could not loosen his hold. He
shoved my hand away and pulled off my pantaloons. Before
dropping them, he crumbled the garment in his hands, to
make sure that I had not hidden a blade in them. Pushing my
legs further apart, he lowered himself on top of me. He entered me with one long stroke and I met him with an upward
push.

I put my arms around his back and ground myself against
him, pushing the length of him as deeply into myself as I
could. I hissed "fuck!" at him, wanting him to move inside of
me. He looked startled and then a sound came from him as if
someone had knifed him in the back.

He pounded me with his body, his thick organ stretching
me almost beyond endurance. Still I met him head on, stroke
for stroke, with the heart of a lion. I slammed against him
with each powerful thrust.

Suddenly, his body went rigid. He nearly pulled out of me,
then drove himself back into me, pinning me to the floor.

Unable to move underneath him, I held him as he spurted inside of me. The growl started in his belly and moved into my ears.

The sound I heard had come from my own voice, as my orgasm shook my body. I hugged my damp pillow to myself. In my mind, I held him as tightly as I could, wanting to pull him inside me, my Highwayman.

The vividness of the fantasy distressed me. It seemed so real, I totally lost myself in it. The morning after, I realized I had been alone too bloody long. It frightened me to think I could lose myself so completely inside my imagination. I needed a serious reality check, or perhaps, I needed to check in with reality.

Both my schedule and my budget allowed me the freedom to get out of my imagination and have some jollies, something fun to shake up my isolated routine. So I decided my lifelong fascination with horses would finally become real. I would take riding lessons.

I knew my friend Gwen dated a fellow who owned a local stable. She claimed he had the best stud service around Shaftesbury, perhaps even in the whole of Dorset. When she told me that, I laughed. Of course, I had to ask if she knew that first hand. She smiled and simply said he's the dog's bollocks. The color in her cheeks told me she probably did know his stud service first hand.

I really needed to do something immediately, to convince myself I still had a grip on reality. I rang up Gwen to find out if I might be able to get riding lessons there. She told me that if I wanted to learn about horses, her friend, Steve, could help me. Horses had been in his family for generations. She said she would speak to Steve, to make sure he did right by me. So, I gave Gwen a little time to ring him before I did.

When I spoke to Steve, I told him I wanted to learn how to ride, but hadn't really been around horses. Growing up in London, I never had the opportunity to learn. I wanted someone who could teach me to ride, and also teach me about horses. I asked him for an instructor who had patience and a lot of "horse sense", one who didn't mind answering silly questions from a novice. Steve told me he had the right teacher for me and that I could sign up for lessons that afternoon.

My stomach had butterflies as I drove to the stable. I met Steve at his house and took care of the paperwork. He agreed to let me pay lesson by lesson, until I knew for sure that I wanted to continue. Then he asked me when I wanted to start. I told him right away, if possible. I had made up my mind to do this, and dash it all, I would do it now!

Steve took me into the stable to meet my new teacher. When I saw him, I almost forgot why I came. As I watched, he lifted a bale of hay and carried it into an empty stall. He took a knife out of his pocket to cut the twine and then spread the hay around the floor. I knew he had to be over six feet tall, with long dark hair pulled back into a ponytail. He had a mustache, which curved in a thin line around his mouth, filling out into a goatee at his chin. When he bent over to cut the twine, I saw the tightest bum and the longest legs in recent memory.

Somewhere behind me, I heard Steve yell in his direction, "Hey, Ivan. Come over here. I have a new student for you." I noted his pronunciation, i-VAHN, with the second syllable accented. I thought his name suited him. Ivan turned around, obviously startled we had come in. He regained his composure easily. His T–shirt, damp with sweat and covered with straw, stuck to him. Some delicious tingles fluttered inside me as he came out of the stall, brushing bits of hay from his chest as he walked.

Pulling off a crusty glove, he shook my hand and said, "So you want to learn how to ride? We'll have to see what we can do about that." My attraction for him was undeniable and I felt myself blush.

* * *

My summer job in a stable takes me as far away from a classroom as I can get. Even though I love teaching, I need a break from academia. When my eyes start to feel like piss holes in the snow grading spring finals, I know I have to come up for air or burn out real damn fast.

My best friend inherited his father's horse farm near Shaftesbury. Every summer, I travel from Northamptonshire, where I live and teach, to stay at the farm and work. All I take is room and board. I grew up working there. Going back feels like going home.

Even though Steve's father hired me as a horse groom, Steve never treated me like hired help. Since neither of us had siblings, we grew up like brothers. His father taught us how to ride together. We got hammered on ale Steve pilfered from his father's stash. And, of course, we shared learning about women.

Steve assumed I would stay on at the farm and help him run it. But I decided to go to University on scholarship instead. Once my parents passed, Steve's family was the only family I had to invite when I graduated. They all came, too. By the time I got my doctorate, only Steve came. His father had died and his mum had moved to London. That left Steve to run the farm alone.

After becoming a professor, I bought myself a house and some property near Thrapston, Kettering. My colleagues thought me daft for buying a house so far from Northampton, but I wanted a place where one day I might have a few horses of my own.

When I realized I actually had a growing bank account without the summer term, I figured what the hell! I asked Steve if I might stay with him again over the summers. I knew he might not take to the idea, since he felt like I did him dirty not staying at the farm after we graduated. But, to my surprise, he welcomed me back.

When I arrived this summer, Steve made it clear he needed

me to teach more. He hadn't yet replaced an instructor who recently left. I reluctantly agreed to take on a few students if the need arose.

When he called me over to meet my first student of the season, I rather expected to see a gangly teenager waiting. Instead, there stood a short, shapely redhead, about my age, looking very apprehensive. Steve introduced her as "Pash", a name I had never heard before. I hadn't enjoyed a female liaison in some time. I smiled to myself, thinking, "This could be an unexpected pleasure."

Steve asked Ivan if he could spare an hour now to get me started with a few basics. Ivan hesitated. Steve took him aside and spoke to him. When they came back, Ivan smiled and said, "Of course I can jump start you today. Let's set about it." That began what may be the most embarrassing hour of my life.

Everything started well enough. He asked me, "Have you ever ridden before?"

"Only once. I rode a pony at Battersea Park Children's Zoo in London. But I have read books and watched documentaries!" Realizing how utterly lame that sounded, I added, "I dare say I don't know too much."

Since he realized I knew absolutely naught about riding, he started from scratch. He took me around the stable, showing me a few horses. Then he opened a stall and led out a horse. "This horse, Nutmeg, has started more than a few riders on their way."

I thought she seemed awfully big for me. He patted her neck. "She's gentle as a lamb. I've put children on her and she's absolutely fine."

As I imagined myself trying to get on this monster, I started to walk around her. She snorted just as I stepped in front of her and it startled me. I jumped off to the side, thinking she was going to charge or something.

I tripped on God knows what and fell, right into a big puddle filled with slimy mud and straw. Both knees sunk in the muck. I did manage to catch myself on my hands before I went completely down. Nevertheless, I made an unmitigated mess of myself.

Ivan helped me up, saying as he lifted me, "I am terribly sorry. Before Steve came in with you, I had been cleaning the horses. I should have warned you to mind the gap." His apology barely hid his amusement.

"I've made a dog's dinner of myself!" He didn't seem to notice that he had mud all over himself from picking me up.

I assured him I had not hurt myself. With his arm still around my waist, Ivan dragged his boot through the puddle. "There is a drain here, but I think it is blocked with hay."

"You are nearly as mucked up as I am. I'm terribly sorry about that." He still held me very tightly against himself. With all the mud, we were practically sliding against each other.

"That's quite all right, I don't mind." He cleared the drain with his foot. "Now, let me clean you off." He picked up the hose and turned on the water. There I stood, muddy straw all over me, with the sexiest man I had ever seen looking me over and offering to hose me down. I just wanted to disappear.

Steve caught me totally unaware when he asked if I could spare the time to start Pash's lessons right away. I wasn't prepared to be teaching a new student at that moment, even if I did find her tempting. I hadn't finished hosing the horses and cleaning their stalls, not to mention I really needed a shower.

On the pretense of asking me some inane question, Steve took me aside and said, "C'mon, guv - Pash rhymes with cash. Don't make me look bad in front of a new student!" So I agreed. I needed to find out straight away what she knew about horses, to figure out where to start. Turns out she rode a pony once upon a time. That summed up her total direct exposure.

I knew I had my work cut out for me, but reminded myself that she could be that gangly teenager coming at me with the same story. Perhaps this totty might be inclined to ride more than a horse!

To see how she responded to the animals, I walked her around the stable. She seemed a little jumpy, but I supposed that would pass soon enough. I picked Nutmeg to get her started. Nutmeg has the disposition of a kitten, quietest damn mare I've ever seen. She is on the large side, being a retired farm horse. Steve keeps her around because she is gentle and even tempered with children.

She is a good old girl. I like to make sure she is seen earning her keep. When I took Nutmeg out of the stall, I noticed the color drain from Pash's face. I tried to reassure her. "Don't worry, my dear, Nutmeg is a sweetheart. She won't give you any grief."

Before I could finish my pep talk, Pash stepped right in front of the horse. Nutmeg must have thought Pash had a treat for her, because she raised her head, blew some air out of her nose and opened her mouth. The next thing I knew, Pash jumped a couple meters off to the side, stumbled on an uneven part of the floor and fell right on the spot where I had just hosed off a horse.

Christ, I looked down and saw the new student Steve wanted to impress kneeling in water thick with mud. That's not all I saw. She had her arse in the air, down on all fours. Bloody hell, she looked like she wanted a good seeing to!

"Please, allow me." Bending over her to help her up, I fought the urge to join her in the mud and have it doggie fashion.

I put my arm around her to help her stand up, brushing her breasts as I did so. To prolong keeping hold of her, I asked, "Are you all right? You didn't hurt yourself did you?"

"I'm quite all right, thank you. I just need a bath."

"Well, that's better than a slap in the face with a wet kipper," I said, trying to make her laugh. She barely managed a feeble smile.

It felt damn good having a woman against me again. I didn't want to let her go. So, I continued holding her while scraping the drain with my boot to clear it. "I should have seen to this clog earlier. It never occurred to me I would have company in here today."

Then, I held her at arm's length to survey the damage. "You are a mucky pup, all right." She had mud, hay and horse hair covering her legs. Somehow, I had to clean her up.

The only thing I could think to do was to hose her off, the way I did the horses. She had on jeans and sneakers, so it wouldn't hurt anything. "Now, let me clean you off." I picked up the hose. "You will be wet, but at least you will be clean."

"I suppose I have to. I can't get in my car like this." Seeing as how she didn't have much choice, she agreed.

"This wont hurt a bit, I promise." Turning the hose to a gentler spray than I used for the horses, I washed her off. Straight away, I got myself a hard on. When she fell, her tight jeans gave her a camel's hoof, clearly outlining her privy parts. I made sure I hosed her thoroughly. "Spread your feet apart so I can clean your legs properly." What better way to get a good long look at her bits!

I finished my lesson soaking wet from the waist down. How absolutely humiliating! After Ivan hosed the mud off of me, he turned the hose on himself to wash off his own legs. I couldn't help noticing he had quite a package, which seemed to have grown since I arrived. When he brushed some hay from my shirt, his hand grazed my breasts. My nipples turned into pebbles.

Once he made sure he had properly cleaned me up, Ivan

wanted me to get right on Nutmeg, saying, "It is best to get comfortable mounting during the first lesson."

My nerve completely left me. "Couldn't we wait for a bit? I've never been around horses before and would like to get used to them first." It's the only excuse I could think of for not mounting as he asked.

Ivan seemed a little perplexed. He took a quick look around the stable before he said, "All right then, let's go over the gear first." I made a half hearted attempt to listen when he explained the parts of a saddle as he put it on Nutmeg's back. "Always from the left side," he said. "Our horses are trained to be handled from the left."

Then he showed me how to bridle a horse. I cringed when he put the bit in Nutmeg's mouth, wondering how the horse could stand that chunk of metal across its tongue. "This is an eggbutt snaffle. It doesn't hurt her at all." I didn't believe it!

After he had Nutmeg ready, he demonstrated the proper way to mount a horse by climbing on her himself. "See how easy it is! There's nothing to it." He looked magnificent sitting on that big horse, like I had always imagined my Highwayman would look.

I could see the outline of his thigh through his wet jeans. My eyes followed his leg up to his crotch. Realizing how utterly unseemly staring at his bulge would appear, I made myself look away. He dismounted and again encouraged me to try it. "Why don't you give it a go? I'll help you up."

I politely declined. "No, thank you. I think I've had enough for one day."

"Well, next time, we'll practice mounting."

I wondered why in heaven's name I wanted to do this in the first place.